"You don't mind having me around?"

Suzannah met Craig's gaze straight on, knowing he was flirting. "No," she said, a smile playing about her lips. "You're not a *complete* nuisance."

"Then you think I'm a useful sort of guy," he said. "But you've barely tapped my resources, you know."

"No?" He was stepping closer. She stood her ground. "What talents have I overlooked?" she asked wryly.

"This," he said softly, pulling her closer. Then his soft and supple mouth was touching hers with feather lightness. As she felt his fingers moving through her hair, drifting across her bare shoulder, it was she who increased the urgency of their kiss, without thinking, swept up in the moment...

Other Second Chance at Love books by
Lee Williams

Lee Williams, *who also writes songs and scores for musicals, lives in New York City's Greenwich Village. Although she enjoys the bright lights of the city, she's most content at home with her husband and cats, cooking up desserts of her own invention.*

Dear Reader:

Signs of spring are popping up all over—what a relief!—and this month's six SECOND CHANCE AT LOVE romances are brimming with all the elements that make radiant love stories. So choose a sunny corner, make yourself comfortable, and enjoy...

We begin with *Ain't Misbehaving* (#256), another heartwarming read from Jeanne Grant. All-man Mitch Cochran is captivated by gregarious Kay Sanders, but he has a problem. A long-term illness, from which he's fully recovered, kept him bedridden during the years when other young males were struttin' their stuff. Now he's somewhat chagrined to find himself a virgin at 28! To our delight, Jeanne Grant tackles this sensitive subject with tenderness, humor, and masterful skill.

Our next romance, *Promise Me Rainbows* (#257), is by Joan Lancaster, a new writer whose wacky, wonderful story is filled with lovable, eccentric characters. A runaway chimp, two giant St. Bernards, and a mysterious "fairy godmother" keep the action lively, while Alec Knowles's hot-blooded pursuit of feisty Nora Flynn ensures that the romance is offbeat and steamy.

In *Rites of Passion* (#258) by Jacqueline Topaz, Corky Corcoran's life of barely controlled suburban chaos becomes even crazier when she falls head over heels for brilliant, sexy anthropologist Kristoffer Schmidt. This romance has one of the funniest scenes of madcap domestic catastrophe I've ever read. Don't worry, I won't give the surprise away, but I will promise that once you've read *Rites of Passion* you'll never again think of anthropology as a dry-as-dust science!

In *One in a Million* (#259) by Lee Williams, heroine Suzannah isn't rich, but she's having a ball playing the part of a wealthy socialite on her aunt's estate—until her Rolls Royce breaks down in Craig Jordan's humble back yard. Suzannah hires Craig as a gardener and has fun playing a grand lady to his deferential servant. But soon deception piles on deception, and Suzannah becomes determined to exact revenge—with hilariously calamitous results!

In *Heart of Gold* (#260), Liz Grady once again creates a hero you can't help falling in love with. Roarke Hastings, handsome and self-assured, enrolls in Tess Maxwell's dance school to tame his two left feet... and learns she's a damsel in distress. But are his offers of knightly assistance an expression of true love, or only of heart-felt kindness? Be assured, Liz Grady has written one powerful romance!

Finally, in *At Long Last Love* (#261) Carole Buck presents a funny, moving story of a friendship that blossoms into love. Allie Douglas and her boss, Chris Cooper, have been buddies for years, but something strange is happening to their comfortable companionship. Will it destroy their camaraderie or lead to a more exciting union? Carole Buck's realistic yet thoroughly entertaining approach to her subject makes *At Long Last Love* a special treat.

So, please do get outside and enjoy the fine weather, but don't miss any of this month's SECOND CHANCE AT LOVE romances. And thanks to all of you for sending the hundreds of questionnaires and letters we continue to receive. We love hearing from you!

Warm wishes,

Ellen Edwards

Ellen Edwards, Senior Editor
SECOND CHANCE AT LOVE
The Berkley Publishing Group
200 Madison Avenue
New York, N.Y. 10016

ONE IN A MILLION

LEE WILLIAMS

A SECOND CHANCE AT LOVE BOOK

ONE IN A MILLION

First edition published April 1985

First printing

Printed in the United States of America

Second Chance at Love books are published by
The Berkley Publishing Group
200 Madison Avenue, New York, NY 10016

Many thanks to
Mr. Bruce,
Nan and Sandy,
Madame Tanda,
and the other Californians
who helped with the delivery
of this one

A Memo From C.J. Young

Walt:

Hang the "Gone Fishing" sign on my inner office door. Your dedicated but dazed-with-overwork boss is out—out of town and out of touch for the next three and a half weeks. No address, no telephone, no nothing!

And no funny stuff from the guys in publicity, okay? Last time I tried to grab a vacation incognito, some joker sent a writer from Personality *out to track me down for some fool article on "Young Millionaires at Leisure"—and we're still in court with a lawsuit because I busted his camera and the jaw behind it. Solitude is what I'm seeking, and the spartan life. Got it?*

Hey, don't blow a gasket, relax. Now that we've shown the Fall collection with all the necessary hoopla (check those Vogue *shots for color on the evening wear, will you? Last year's spread came out too dark) there's nothing of great importance to take care of until the week the new store opens in Los Angeles. Don't worry! I'll surface in time to look the place over and make the necessary appearance at the opening party.* WWD, *Ralph Lauren, and too many others will be coming to check us out, so I may only last for a few minutes, but, yes, I will be there.*

Check with Tracy should a crisis arise. I leave everybody else's problems, which are no doubt coming at you, in your hands. If you're going to get that raise you've been badgering me about, pal, here's your chance to earn it. I'll check in midway to make sure our NYC building's still standing. Hopefully you'll be vertical, too. As for me . . . horizontal on a beach, I believe. In blissful peace and quiet.

Best,
C.J.

CHAPTER ONE

SITTING AT THE wheel of a vintage black and maroon Rolls Royce, her face caressed by the warm breezes of a eucalyptus-scented California night, Suzannah Raines wondered if Cinderella had ever had it this good. In addition to the sumptuously sculpted mass of gleaming metal and plush upholstery that surrounded her, Suzannah had in her possession the keys to a two-story, five bedroom mansion nestled in the Hollywood hills, with an Olympic-sized swimming pool, a tennis court, a hot tub, a dozen acres of sprawling greenery that featured an antique gazebo . . .

. . . and none of it belonged to her, of course.

At the moment, Suzannah Raines had exactly one hundred and seventy-nine dollars and fifty-three cents in her bank account. She was the not exactly proud, but at least uncomplaining, owner of a rustbucket Volkswagen, a tiny apartment in a quaint but rundown area of San Francisco, and one battered though trustworthy Singer sewing machine on which she was beginning (knock on wood) to earn a more decent livelihood.

Suzannah owed her sudden good fortune to six obese

cats—or rather, to their Fairy Godmother-like owner, the infamous Aunt Lucille. Aunt Lucille loved those fat felines. And because she liked Suzannah, Aunt Lucille had entrusted her with the care of them, while she herself went off to Europe to look for a new home with her latest beau. Lucille was like that.

As deals went, Suzannah reflected, peering through the windshield at the darkness of Canyon Drive, this was a once in a lifetime one. She could scarcely believe her good fortune. She had always loved the house—on the infrequent occasions that she had stayed there. She had never expected to have it for an entire vacation—and all to herself. Sort of. For the next three to four weeks, all she had to do was show the house to prospective buyers—Lucille's realtor was coming by the following morning to appraise the place—and stuff more food into the mouths of six animals that were already the size of little furry Sherman tanks. And Aunt Lucille had insisted that she use the car, too. To keep it in shape, she'd told Suzannah, right before she left.

And what a shape it was. As she eased the glossy Rolls into the street from her aunt's winding driveway, she felt a heady rush of excitement. She'd never driven a car like this in her life. It had the oversized, streamlined charm of its era, the early Fifties: wide running boards, giant super-white whitewalls, four huge headlights flanking the high silver grill, and, of course, the little silver lady poised for flight on the hood's shiny tip. Sitting bolt upright on the soft upholstery, Suzannah was too wound up to relax. She signaled, nervously scanning the road, and turned.

She'd been too agitated to move in properly. Her little ragtag canvas bags were still incongruously perched at the foot of the house's gargantuan staircase. She'd been too restless to sit around the cavernous kitchen once the cats were fed. And the car had beckoned her when she explored the garage, its glossy grillwork seeming to flash her a sly, inviting grin: Try me! it gleamed. Let's go for a spin!

After all, the Volkswagen, parked in the circular driveway with her other bags and sewing machine in the trunk, would have been anticlimactic. So here she was . . . spinning.

Suzannah rolled her window down. Leaning over to adjust the side mirror, she saw that she was grinning from ear to ear like a happy idiot. She relaxed her facial muscles, trying for a more dignified expression. But dignity was difficult when she felt like Cinderella in a pumpkin-turned-coach and besides, the lines of her face weren't well-suited for solemnity. She had full, round cheeks with a natural touch of rosiness and dimples that she disliked, though men seemed to admire them. Her full mouth almost pouted, and the soft rounded tip of her nose nearly tilted upward. Her eyes of hazel-green were offset by thick, shapely brows and her hard-to-manage curly light brown hair swept back from her forehead in a decidedly unsultry manner. On the whole her features, to her mind, were hopelessly wholesome.

Suzannah glanced down self-consciously at the outfit she was wearing, one she had designed herself and was hoping to sell, along with others, in the time Aunt Lucille had estimated it would take to find a buyer for the house. Would the inexpensive simplicity of her dolman-sleeved white lambswool sweater and her camel-colored knit circle skirt give her away as an imposter to any passing motorists, who were likely to be the truly rich residents of the Hollywood hills? Well, really rich people liked to "dress down," she reminded herself, and besides, she wasn't going anywhere in particular, and it was after ten in the evening.

Perched apprehensively behind the wheel as she idled at an intersection, she tried to shake off the feeling she'd be mistaken for a thief. When the first pair of headlights blazed in the rearview mirror, she stiffened. As the car pulled up beside her, she kept her eyes ahead, afraid to see if it was, as her paranoia suggested, the police. The car revved and passed her. Suzannah was chagrined to see that it was a gleaming cherry-red Jaguar convertible, driven by a tanned, curly-maned woman in blue jeans and a T-shirt. There was the dressed-down look, all right.

And when, some time later, flanked by a Mercedes on one side and a silver Pierce Arrow on the other, she watched two BMWs race each other through the light ahead, Suzannah dropped her last vestiges of self-consciousness. It was ridiculous. She'd never seen so many status-mobiles congregated in one area. A part of her was vaguely sickened by the parade of calculated wealth on display. But more of her was deeply envious. After the few years of rock-bottom poverty she'd just endured in her abortive marriage to footloose Charlie, how could she not be?

And a Rolls Royce did drive like a dream. Suzannah settled back, pushing thoughts of her ex-husband out of her mind and allowing herself to revel, for once, in the feeling of luxurious comfort. She had no idea where she was going, just a vague sense of heading west, toward the beach. But it didn't matter. A strong breeze through the open window ruffled her hair. The silver lady on the hood led her, winged, into the starry night. The car's graceful ease gave new meaning to the phrase 'joy ride'. This was the life.

Lulled into sweet serenity by the wide, smooth black roads banking and swooping beneath her, Suzannah lost track of time. She had come far, all right; the beach and the Pacific lay only another stoplight beyond. Now that her objective had been reached, perhaps it was time to head back. She turned onto the highway, realizing too late she should have gone left and southward. Sighing, she drove on, looking for the next conceivable U-turn point. She was probably in Malibu by now.

At the next light there were no signs prohibiting her. She waited, checked traffic, found the proper moment, and turned. There, no problem—except... why was the car accelerating without her shifting into a higher gear? With a jolt of apprehension, Suzannah noticed the motor revving way too high. Something was wrong with the accelerator pedal!

She took her foot off it, but it stayed put. Her stomach plummeted as the car continued speeding down the highway. This was major. Fearfully, she scanned her mirrors. The car closest behind her was far back enough for her to chance the brake. Carefully, with a foot that was trembling, she attempted to slow the runaway Rolls. To no avail.

Adrenaline surged through her veins; Suzannah thought fast and moved faster. There was a road, unmarked, but a road—just a few yards ahead. Before the car could pick up any more speed, she abruptly steered it off the highway and onto that road, praying it was a short one and not too steep.

Gravel flew beneath her. The car lurched downward into darkness. Desperately fending off panic, she kept a firm grip on the wheel and began to brake the Rolls as it careened down a winding slope. Where would it end? And when? The narrow dirt drive continued twisting downward. She craned her neck, wincing as the front left fender grazed a row of bushes. Though she continued to brake, the car was carried onward by the incline and its own momentum. She braked harder, praying there would be nothing in her path—

—and heard a sickening crunch and thud as the car jolted to a halt in a shower of dust.

For a long moment she sat there, stunned, her heart and pulse pounding away. The engine had died and the sudden silence was filled with a distant thunderous rushing that she realized was the ocean. Suzannah stuck her head out the side window, peering into the darkness. The headlights were up against something that looked like a hedge. She switched them off. If she could manage to get the car going, there was no sense in wearing out the battery. Now she couldn't see much at all, though.

You and your great ideas, she thought ruefully. Joy ride, indeed! With a little groan of apprehension, Suzannah put her hand on the door handle. Opening the door, she nearly fell out of the car, having forgotten that the door opened out to the left. Stumbling into an upright position, she shut the door and looked around her. There was a break in the line of bushes surrounding her and she strode toward it.

In a moment she emerged from overhanging palm trees into a clearing, where the half-moon dimly illuminated miles of beach and the glint of ocean waves over the curving sand. The only domicile visible, yards to her left, was a tiny, hutlike beach house nestled into the slope of some large dunes.

Lights shining from its little windows indicated it was inhabited. Suzannah marched up the gravel path that meandered on to two ramshackle slate steps. The door to the cottage was weather-beaten, mottled with patches of peeling paint. Whoever lived here was obviously not well-to-do. But as long as they had a phone . . . Suzannah knocked on the wood. Hearing no response from within, she knocked again, harder and louder.

The door swung open suddenly and she froze, fist raised for another knock. She was looking at a face that was strikingly handsome, with high, strong cheekbones, dark piercing eyes, an acquiline nose, and a chiseled, jutting chin. His hair was dark, wavy, and unkempt in an appealing way; he looked as if he might have just gotten out of bed. He looked, she realized, with her heart suddenly lurching into a faster speed, like one of those sexy, muscular, tall, and tanned models in a magazine ad for men's fashions. But this man was potently, skin-tinglingly three dimensional—and nearly naked, she realized, with an inner jolt. Only the whitish gleam of some scanty cut-off shorts broke the dark lines of his rugged frame.

As he returned her stare with an appraising one of his own, she felt herself coloring. The look on his face wasn't exactly one of welcome. As she couldn't think, immediately, of what to say, thrown off as she was by his devastatingly attractive features, his eyes narrowed, sweeping across her face and body. He put his hands on his hips, his chin jutting higher.

"Are you looking for someone?" he asked abruptly.

"No," she began, clearing her throat. "I . . ."

"Good," he interrupted. "Then you haven't found him." With a curt nod, he began to shut the door.

"Wait a second!" she cried, indignant. "My car is in your driveway . . ."

He raised an eyebrow. "Really? Then you'd better move it." And nodding an insolently polite good night, he shut the door in her face.

Shocked, Suzannah stared at the door. Then she banged her fist on it again. Immediately, it opened, and the man peered out at her warily.

"You're still here," he noted. His voice was deep, with a slight rasp and an accent she instinctively pegged as New York.

"Of course I am," Suzannah said. "My car . . ."

". . . is in my driveway," he finished for her, patiently. "And it really can't stay."

"I can't move it," she said grimly.

He cocked his head, puzzled. "Why not?"

"There's something wrong with it!" she retorted. "Why do you think I ended up here in the first place?"

His eyes widened. Then he leaned against the door frame,

folding his arms, the hint of an amused smile on his ruggedly handsome, albeit unshaven, face. "You made a wrong turn, then," he said laconically. "The nearest service station is about ten miles down the highway."

"Fine!" she exploded in exasperation. "But I'm here, now!"

"I see that," he said mildly. "But do I look like a mechanic?"

Yes! she nearly shouted in her frustration. He could have been, for all she knew; with his unkempt appearance, ragged-edged shorts, bare feet, and tanned musculature he wouldn't have looked at all out of place with toolbox in hand. But that was beside the point.

"Listen," she said, mustering the last of her patience. "There's something wrong with my accelerator pedal—it's busted, jammed, I don't know. I'm sorry to barge in on your privacy like this, but I took the first road off the highway I could..." She trailed off lamely, unnerved by the way he was looking at her. She read, for no reason she could think of, suspicion and mistrust in the man's face.

"Where were you going?" he asked abruptly.

"Nowhere—I mean, to my Aunt's," she said.

"Your Aunt's?" He sounded incredulous. "Do you always drop in on her at this time of night?"

"She's not there!" Suzannah blurted. "*I* am!"

He narrowed his eyes. "You are?" His tone was openly mocking.

"Look, mister," she began, fuming. "I'm sorry to bother you, really—I'm sorry I ever left the house!" she added, more to herself. "But as long as I did... Can I use your phone?"

"Don't have one," was his swift reply. He seemed almost proud of this.

"You don't?" she cried, bewildered. "But how can you live without..."

She stopped in midsentence, suddenly more acutely embarrassed than ever. From what she could glimpse of the man's little shack through the open doorway, it was obvious his existense was spartan. The shack itself seemed likely to blow away in a stiff gale, and judging from the man's appearance, he undoubtedly had very little money. Remembering the dark days of her marriage when the phone had often been disconnected due to unpaid bills, she felt ashamed of her brazen, unthinking exclamation.

"I'm sorry," she muttered, feeling doubly like a bumbling fool beneath the man's mute examination. "Skip it," she sighed, and as all seemed suddenly hopeless, she turned away from him to scan the beach. "Maybe there's another place nearby . . ."

As she squinted at the dimly visible horizon, she sensed him leave the doorway. She stiffened as he stepped up behind her. "Hold on," he said quietly, and she turned around to face him again.

"You really are lost . . . and you've had car trouble," he murmured, as if testing this premise out for credibility. His gaze no longer antagonistic, he seemed to size her up in the light from the doorway. His eyes traveled from her face to her breasts, which were clearly outlined beneath the clinging sweater—she hadn't worn a bra. His penetrating gaze roved over her hips, lingered briefly on her legs, then returned to meet her eyes.

"Yes," she said uneasily, feeling her skin tingle beneath his sensually speculative look. "That's what I've been trying to tell you."

He nodded, and extended his hand. "My name's Craig."

"Suzannah," she told him, and after a moment's hesitation, she gingerly took his hand. His grip was firm, but gentle, and warm. She felt an unexpected jolt of sensuous arousal at the feel of his surprisingly soft skin against hers. Newly aware of his scanty attire and his now more intimate proximity, she took her hand from his and stepped back. She wondered suddenly if she really preferred this stranger's friendliness to his rudeness.

He turned, and began walking down the path toward the bushes where the car was. Suzannah followed, perplexed by his mercurial change in attitude, but not about to protest, if he could manage to fix the car. "I don't know exactly how it happened," she called, having to speak louder over the distance between them; no doubt the noise of the ocean had kept him from hearing her arrival. "It was running fine until I made a turn on the highway."

"Uh-huh," he said noncommitally. "I'll see if there's

anything I can do," he muttered. "But if it turns out you just happen to work for some maga—" Craig halted, stopping in midsentence and emitting a low whistle as he first viewed the stalled Rolls Royce. He looked then from the car to her, and shook his head. "My mistake," he murmured.

"Excuse me?" she said, confused.

He shook his head again, and walked slowly up to the car. "Keys?"

"In the ignition," she said. "Oh, careful, the door..." But he was already opening the driver's door, apparently unfazed that it opened unconventionally. He slid into the seat and turned the key with the door still ajar.

"Headlights are fine," he muttered, blinking them. "Fenders probably absorbed your landing..." He turned on the engine, listened to its accelerating revving, tested the pedal, then turned the engine off. As she hovered nearby, he bent beneath her line of vision to examine the pedal, then sat up. "What I need is a flashlight. To look under the hood," he added, at her questioning look. But instead of getting out, he sat in the seat, idly running his hand over the upholstery. "Nice," he muttered.

"Does that service station you mentioned stay open late?" she asked nervously.

The man shrugged. "How long have you had this?"

"A couple of hours," she said with a wry smile.

He stared at her. Then his features relaxed into a look of faintly contemptuous amusement. "I suppose you've got a few of these to play around in."

"I do not," she said, defensive. "Look, it's not even mine."

He raised his eyebrows. "Oh," he said slowly, imbuing the one word with a significance she didn't like. "Does your friend know you're out with it?"

"I don't have a friend," she said quickly. "I mean..."

His eyebrows rose another notch.

"...it's my aunt's," she finished crossly.

"Oh," he said again, and again she bridled at his knowing air.

"What do you mean, 'oh'?"

He shrugged. "Just, oh," he said innocently, and smiled.

Suzannah pursed her lips in vexation. From the way he

was looking at her now, she felt she was being sized up as the sort of air-headed rich girl that she herself despised.

"Look," she began. "You've got me all wrong. I don't usually crash Rolls Royces into strangers' back yards in the middle of the night. I can barely afford gasoline for my *own* car, if you want to know the truth. Believe me, I've got better things to do, and at the moment, I'm just intent on getting home again—"

"Which is where?" he interrupted.

"Canyon Drive," she said distractedly. "Don't you want to get that flashlight?"

"Canyon Drive," he repeated. "Well, now—that *is* an underprivileged area, isn't it?"

Suzannah opened her mouth, then shut it. His insolently mocking tone infuriated her, and she decided it wasn't even worth explaining the details of her living arrangements to him. He could think whatever he wanted to think. "Listen, mister"—

"Craig," he said pleasantly.

—"you've been giving me a hard time ever since I got here"—

"Sorry," he interjected, with a dollop of sarcasm.

—"and seeing as my being here is inconveniencing both of us, don't you think the best thing would be for you to help me get going?"

Craig sat listening to her little tirade, relaxed and attentive. His amusement appeared to increase in direct proportion to her annoyance. "I guess so," he said slowly, still not moving.

"Flashlight?" she suggested tersely.

He shook his head. "Don't have one."

"But . . . you said . . ."

"I said that what I needed was a flashlight," he said, with exasperating patience. "And I'm thinking that what I'd better do is take a run up the road to that station."

"In what?" she asked. She hadn't noticed a car in the vicinity.

"Motorbike," he said. "You can ride with me if you like. Or you can wait here."

The idea of wrapping herself around this arrogant but undeniably attractive man on a motorbike seemed more alarming than enticing at the moment. "Wait . . . here?" she said dubiously, looking in the direction of the little beach house.

"I realize it's a touch less luxurious than a house on Canyon Drive," he said dryly.

"I'm not knocking it," she snapped, bristling. "I appreciate your hospitality."

"The butler's out at the moment," he went on, with an insouciant grin. "But I believe there's some wine in the fridge, if you don't mind serving yourself."

"Look, buddy, just because you're—down on your luck, doesn't mean you have to carry a mountain-sized chip on your shoulder!" she retorted. "Lay off the sardonic wit, will you? You've got the wrong girl."

"Down on my luck?" he repeated, a puzzled expression on his face. He stared at her, and she steeled herself for another round of sarcastic invective. But to her surprise, the man merely smiled, his mouth broadening into a wider grin as he shook his head, apparently amused at some private joke. "Oh, yes . . . times are tough," he said, with ironic flippancy, and chuckled. "But you're right—whatever dire straits we're in," he continued in a more serious tone, "we really shouldn't take our troubles out on each other, should we?"

"That's right," Suzannah said uncertainly. The man's quixotic mood changes were starting to really bewilder her. It was hard to tell when he was on the level. But he was, at any rate, getting out of the car at last. She moved out of the way as he closed the door behind him. Arms folded across her chest, she watched warily as he walked around the car, running his hand over its glossy contours with an appreciative air. Reaching the other side, he paused, frowning.

"That's odd," he said. "My bike was . . ."

The thought hit them both simultaneously. Suzannah's stomach sank swiftly as the man's frown deepened.

"Oh, no," she murmured. "I didn't . . ."

The man disappeared from sight as he knelt down. Suzannah apprehensively walked around the back of the Rolls.

"Well, it could have been worse," he said quietly, looking up at her.

Apprehensively, Suzannah lowered her gaze. She'd knocked the bike down and rather neatly flattened its front tire. Her front right wheel was still resting on the misshapen half. "Oh, no," she murmured.

"I've never owned a unicycle before," he mused, inspecting the damage.

Suzannah passed her hand over her eyes. The evening was turning more nightmarish by the moment. And there was no telling how this truly strange stranger was going to react. "Is it . . . really bad?" she asked.

"Salvageable." He shrugged. "It's not major."

"Oh," she said wanly, visions of repair bills she'd be unable to afford swimming before her eyes.

"Shouldn't cost more than a hundred, maybe less," he said. "The frame isn't twisted much, far as I can see."

He didn't seem as upset as she'd feared he'd be. But the thought of putting up a hundred dollars was certainly upsetting to her. A little moan escaped her lips. "A hundred," she echoed, nodding. "I'm really sorry . . . Craig," she added awkwardly. "If course I'll . . . I'll take care of it . . ."

"Of course you will," he said amiably. "But that's not what's worrying me just now."

"No?" she croaked.

Craig rose from his kneeling position to face her. Dimly, her mind registered that he was awfully tall, taller than her five feet ten inches. Her body instinctively reacted to the warmth his virile frame generated, and the authoritative power implicit in his solid build. She was suddenly vividly aware of her own vulnerable femininity as he looked at her, his face quite close to hers, his expression inscrutable. The blood rose in her own face, seeming to rush in her ears.

"The thing is," he said, "that service station is a nine mile walk, and most motorists on the Coast Highway aren't inclined to pick up hitchhikers at this time of night. The nearest house to here, so far as I know, is three and half miles down the beach to the north, and four miles or so to the south. So . . ." He raised his palms with mute eloquence.

". . . so here we are," she finished for him, slowly. "You mean, we're sort of stuck."

"Not sort of," he acknowledged, with a rueful smile. "Stuck-stuck."

Suzannah looked to the heavens, returned her gaze to his face, then stared forlornly at her feet. "Great," she muttered.

"It could be worse," he said.

She looked up at him again. "How's that?"

"I could be out of wine," he replied, with a twinkle in his eye. "Come on inside. I think this situation calls for a drink."

Craig was indicating, politely, that he'd follow her. Something in the man's manner suggested he was used to giving directions and having them carried out. Suzannah shrugged, resigning herself to the evening's twists of fate. "All right," she said.

As she walked back toward the little beach cottage with her companion close behind her, she reflected that he was taking this newest disaster in stride with admirable good cheer. But at this point she'd given up being surprised by him, and was merely grateful he wasn't bellowing with rage at having his sole means of transport demolished.

"Coming in?"

Suzannah realized she was still hovering on the step outside as he held the door open for her. For some reason the idea of being sequestered in closer quarters with Craig gave her a feeling of queasily apprehensive excitement. What was the matter with her? She seemed to lose her equilibrium every time she looked directly into those seductive eyes . . . "Not much choice, is there?" she managed, coolly, and stepped inside, quickly looking away from Craig to take in his house.

As abodes went, this one was truly humble. It was really only one room, though a loft platform erected at one end formed a makeshift elevated bedroom. The ceiling was high, and there were two latticed wooden doors that stretched the full height to meet it, opening out onto the beach. She could see the distant glint of moonlight on the ocean through the glass panes in the doors. The room was orderly and clean, but its lack of furniture, wallhangings—any touches of more homey, or feminine nature—gave it a woefully unlived-in air. There was one worn, faded armchair, a dime-store folding beach chair, a table made of an industrial spool, and a beat-up-looking lamp.

"How long have you . . . lived here?" she asked, trying to keep her tone free of any value judgment.

"Just a little while," he said, crossing to the half-sized refrigerator in the corner under the loft bed. Along the bare wall was a counter bearing toaster oven, hot plate, percolator, and a sink with a few dishes, pots, and pans piled in it.

"It's . . . nice," was all she could think of to say.

Craig greeted her noncommital remark with a wry chuckle. "I've decided to get down to basics," he said, removing a bottle of white wine from the small refrigerator. "You know, the minimal look—it's very fashionable these days."

She had to hand it to the guy. He was taking his destitute state in stride. Had he lived this poor and transient life for many years? Observing him as he applied a corkscrew to the wine bottle she somehow doubted that; his face had too much character, and his bearing of quiet authority didn't suggest indolence or vagrancy.

As she was mentally formulating a polite way to ask him what, if anything, he did for a living, she noticed a little easel set up by the windowed doors. There was a watercolor of the beach pinned to its wooden frame, and a sketch pad with a jar of crayons and brushes lay beneath it. Maybe that was it—although Craig didn't look like the stereotypical struggling artist. "Is that your work?" she asked, pointing to the watercolor.

"My . . . ?" He looked up quizzically, then followed her gesture. "Why, yes," he said slowly, as she walked over to take a closer look.

"It's good," she said, and it was an honest response. So he was an artist. "Do . . . you do any commercial stuff?" Are you able to sell your work was the blunter version of the question.

Craig cleared his throat, rubbing his cheek thoughtfully with his hand covering his mouth. "Well, I . . . I'd like to," he said. "But, most of the time I have to . . . do other things," he finished vaguely.

Suzannah nodded. She knew all too many people who had artistic skills, but drifted from odd job to odd job, unable to support themselves fully on their talent. Some lacked the gifts to really make it; others lacked the courage to really commit to trying. She wondered what Craig's problem was. He didn't look as if he would lack courage.

But then, Charlie hadn't seemed as weak-willed as he'd turned out to be, either. He'd had a headful of dreams that sounded wonderful, and a ring of conviction in his voice and face that she'd fallen for completely. How was she to know, until the dreams started folding like a house of cards, that he'd had nothing to back those convictions up . . . ?

Craig was approaching. Suzannah snapped to. He was handing her a china mug. She stared at it a moment, then realized she was being rude. Of course she shouldn't have expected wine glasses—what was she thinking of? Quickly, she lifted the mug to meet his proffered toast, and stole a glance at his face. From the hint of amusement in his eyes she gathered he'd read her thoughts. "Cheers," she said, clinking her mug to his, and she swiftly downed a gulp of wine, hoping this action might dispel any further impression of snobbishness.

"Cheers," he echoed, and took a sip, watching her. Surprisingly, the wine tasted excellent. It had a light dry flavor, and obviously wasn't of the bargain basement variety.

"It's good," she said.

"Merely a domestic wine," he remarked, "but well-bred, nonetheless."

His eyes still held a trace of watchful amusement. Suzannah decided that two could play this game. "I'm used to a steady diet of Dom Perignon, of course," she said. "But I don't mind slumming. Just this once."

He nodded. "Even expensive champagnes can get tedious—I suppose," he added, smiling. "Everyone needs some variety. Keeps the palate sharp."

She found herself smiling back. For a long moment, it seemed to her, they smiled at each other, and a warmth that was only partially wine-induced spread slowly through her insides. His rich, masculine voice was still reverberating in her ears and it was hard to ignore the quickening beat of her heart as his eyes held hers. Fascinating eyes, she mused; so warm and sensuously inviting . . .

A little alarm bell rang shrilly in the recesses of her brain. Suzannah looked down at her cup and took another sip of wine, feeling his eyes still upon her. The room seemed awfully small suddenly. Something in the way he watched her made her feel exposed and vulnerable. Though at first it had seemed odd to be fully clothed when he was just in shorts, now it was she who felt naked.

"You've got a great view," she commented, stepping out of his line of vision to the doors.

"Yes," he said simply. "Natural air conditioning, too." He opened the doors as he spoke, and a cool wind entered the room, ruffling her hair. They gazed out at the sand and surf in the silence for a moment. Suzannah was conscious of his nearness, feeling a tingle of arousal as his bare shoulder lightly brushed hers. What was going on here? She wasn't used to being so affected by a man's physical presence. But then, she'd never met a man who radiated such a raw, potent sensuality. It was disquieting, to say the least.

She took a step back from the doors and turned to survey the room again. "What do you . . . do?" she asked carefully. "Besides painting, I mean."

"These days, nothing," he said.

"Nothing?" She hadn't meant for the question to sound moralistic, but he was giving her that mischievously mocking look again.

"Is that so horrible?" he asked. "Oh, that's right—doing nothing is a respectable occupation for only the idle rich. Well, I go fishing every day—does that redeem me?"

Suzannah glared at him. "I'm not rich and I'm not idle," she insisted. "So you can stop needling me. I don't care if you're a fisherman, really, I was just making conversation."

"I see," he said, but she didn't think he did.

"Look, I know how I must appear to you, but as I've tried to explain, the car and the house don't belong to me. I'm house-sitting for my aunt, who's moving to Europe. I'm supposed to show the house to prospective buyers while she's gone."

"Oh," he said. She still couldn't tell if he was convinced. "And what do you do, Suzannah?"

"I work for a living, just like . . . you do," she said uncertainly. "In a boutique, ten to six, four days a week." It occurred to her that she still wasn't sure if her host really did make a living, or if he was merely . . . a bum?

"A boutique?" He seemed genuinely interested. "What kind?"

"Women's clothes," she told him. "And I make some of them myself," she added, with a touch of pride. "I'm a designer."

Craig was coughing, having choked on his wine. Alarmed, she instinctively moved closer to him, thumping his back with her hand as he doubled over.

"'salright," he spluttered, standing upright again as she gave his broad back another good thwack. "Went down—wrong pipe."

Suzannah hovered by him uneasily. Her hand was tingling from the contact with his bare skin. She became aware that her heartbeat had risen again, and that she was staring, unaccountably, at the curls of matted hair on his muscular chest, at the way the muscles rippled down to—and below—his navel. And her face became as red as the palm of her hand.

"Go on," he was saying, running his hand over his lips, after clearing his throat again.

Suzannah addressed her wine mug, hoping he wouldn't notice the flush in her cheeks. "That's what I'm going to be doing while I'm here," she explained. "I plan to take some of my clothes to the stores in Beverly Hills, to see if I can sell them."

Craig had a peculiar look on his face that she could only assume indicated a typically male lack of understanding about the world of fashion. "Uh-huh," he said slowly.

"You see, there are a lot of places—on Rodeo Drive, on Melrose, Robertson—that sell stuff similar to mine, but much more expensive, I'm sure," she went on. "Designer names, you know. My things are just as good, and in some cases, better."

"Really," he commented, taking another sip of wine. "What sort of . . . things do you make? Is that yours?" He pointed at her skirt.

She nodded. Craig stepped closer, and before she could protest, he bent and lifted the hem of her skirt a foot in the air, rubbing the material between thumb and forefinger. His eyes roved over the knitted lambswool. "Nice," he murmured. "Very nice."

She wasn't sure if his comment was directed at the skirt or at the ample expanse of bare thigh turning to goosebumps at his gaze. "Thank you," she said stiffly, and firmly smoothed the skirt down with both hands.

Craig raised his mug again. "Well, I wish you luck."

"Thanks," she murmured, and took another sip, as he did. "Well, I really should be going, I guess."

He stared at her blankly. "Going? What do you mean?"

"Well, I . . ." She paused, confused. "I guess I should try to reach the nearest phone."

"Don't be silly," he scoffed. "Do you really feel like walking three miles down the beach right now?"

"No, not really," she admitted. "But if I don't get started now, when will I . . . I mean, how . . . ?"

"In the morning, of course," Craig said smoothly. "Don't you realize, Suzannah? You're spending the night with me."

His simple declaration sent a ticklish chill up her spine. Something deep inside her responded to the disturbingly erotic connotations of his remark. Her throat seemed tight as she stared at him and he stared back, his eyes gleaming with sensuous invitation. "But . . . I can't," she managed to say.

Craig shrugged. "What else can you do? It's nearly midnight, and I'm sure that station on the highway's closed by now. In daylight, I could take a thorough look under your hood and maybe do the job myself. I know a little about cars. But I don't recommend your tramping across the dunes in the dark to wake up a neighbor— if they did happen to be home."

"Why wouldn't they be?" she asked, hoping for a loophole in his logic.

"From what I hear, most of the houses in this area are summer houses," he said. "And seeing as it's April . . ."

Suzannah looked at him, stymied. The idea of spending the night with this mysterious, dangerously seductive man . . . Dare she? She could feel the pulse pounding in her throat, so hard it must be visible. Self-consciously she rested her hand on the base of her neck, covering it from Craig's steady, expectant gaze.

"But . . . I wouldn't think of imposing on you," she began. "I've caused you enough trouble already, and it doesn't look like you have the extra room . . ." Her eyes had been drawn to the loft behind her.

"Oh, I'm sure I could make room for you," he said.

Suzannah realized they were both standing, staring at his

bed. She could feel a flush reddening her cheeks as she deliberately turned back to look at Craig. He'd been watching her carefully, she sensed. Was he enjoying her discomfort?

"It's all yours," he said, with a faint smile. "I've been sleeping outside in the hammock the last few nights anyway." As she said nothing, but swallowed, her eyes nervously shifting back to the loft bed, he added: "You can lock the doors from the inside if you feel safer. But I can assure you," he went on, wryly, "I'm not the sort of guy to take advantage of a lady in distress."

"Oh, I didn't..." She paused awkwardly. "But, your own bed... I couldn't..."

"I realize I'm looking a little on the slovenly side this evening," he said with a grin. "But I do have some clean sheets on hand."

Suzannah looked at him in mute chagrin. Somehow every other thing she said or did, however unintentionally, gave the impression she was being condescending. "I didn't mean..." Suzannah sighed. There was no use stuffing more potential feet in her mouth.

"Might as well make yourself at home," Craig blithely continued. "After all, we've got a half bottle of wine left. Unless you'd like to go to bed right now."

Suzannah stared at him, narrowing her eyes. He had the knack of imbuing seemingly harmless remarks with an unmistakably sexual subtext. But his face wore a maddeningly innocent expression. "No, I'm not in that much of a hurry," she said dryly, then added: "But don't let me keep you up."

He smiled. "I'm happy to be kept up. Here, have a seat."

She looked at the armchair, feeling trapped. The man's self-assured demeanor both irked and attracted her. "I suppose I don't have much of a choice," she said with a resigned shrug. Then she realized that once again, her remark could be misconstrued. "And I'm very grateful that you're helping me out like this," she added quickly, and sat down in the armchair.

"Don't mention it." He held up the wine bottle, that hint of mischief glimmering in his eyes again. "Another glass? Or maybe you'd prefer a soft drink. I've got some soda in the fridge."

She thought she detected a subtle challenge in his words.

Was he insinuating she was too scared of him to drink with him—or too much of a snob? "No, I like the wine," she said firmly, and held out her cup.

When he'd filled her mug nearly to the brim and then his own, he toasted her again. "To new acquaintances." He smiled.

They drank.

CHAPTER TWO

THERE WERE TWO things she hadn't counted on, Suzannah mused woozily an hour or so later. One, was that Craig would turn out to be such good company, and two, that he would happen to have a second bottle of wine handy.

Suffused with a warm glow, she yawned, stretching her feet out over the arm of his soft, comfortable old chair. Her sandals dangled precariously as she flexed each foot. Impulsively, she kicked them off.

"I've been waiting for you to do that," Craig commented. He was lying on his back a few feet away, his body stretched out tantalizingly, his head resting in his crossed arms.

"Why?" Suzannah asked, lazily leaning her mug toward her lips for another sip.

"It shows that you're finally at ease with me," he said.

Suzannah swallowed. Carefully she put the mug down on the spool-table to her right. At ease? Hardly! "Well, you don't seem so much a weirdo," she hedged.

Craig laughed. "Was I a weirdo?"

Suzannah nodded. "I've never met anyone so unfriendly to strangers." She straightened up a little, and peered down at him. "What was all that about, anyway? Is somebody after you, or something?"

Craig smiled, gazing up at the ceiling. "No, I don't think so," he drawled. Once again, the low, sexy rumble of his voice seemed to tickle her inner ear. "I'm just a man who likes his privacy. I haven't seen another human being in . . . a while, and to tell you the truth, I've enjoyed the isolation."

Suzannah nodded. "You are a very private person, aren't you? Come to think of it, we've been talking about me and my work for the longest time . . . and we've barely talked about you."

Craig shrugged. "But I'm fascinated with you and your work." He sat up, and refilled his mug from the bottle at his side. Suzannah demurred as he offered her more. "Where were we, anyway? You were telling me about how you developed a style."

Suzannah frowned. Even through her congenial alcoholic haze she was well aware that the man was avoiding the issue. But then, she hadn't had such a flattering encounter in as long as she could remember. Craig had been asking her question after question about clothes and designing, and she was enjoying this rare opportunity to talk about her favorite subject with a willingly captive audience. He now knew all about her grand design to spend her vacation here in L.A., peddling her latest creations to all the famous stores. "You're sure you're not bored?" she asked.

"Impossible." He fixed his dark warm gaze on her face again. She was almost used to being bathed in the glow of that look of his—almost; it gave her a coveted, appreciated feeling that was sinfully titillating.

"You were saying."

"Well . . ." She squinted, reaching back through the tangled trains of thought to find her starting point. "Oh! What I realized, even before I went to grad school, was that I'd have to design for myself—not for the current fashion."

"That's very brave," he commented.

She checked his face for signs of mockery, and seeing none, went on. "No, just practical. Look at me."

His eyes glimmered with a slightly warmer intensity. "I have been."

"I don't look like a model, do I?"

He pursed his lips. "Well . . ."

"It's okay. I've accepted it long ago; I don't have that chic, high cheekboned look. I've accepted my unfashionable body . . ."

"I can't see it would be at all hard to accept," he said seriously. "You can't truly believe . . ." Suzannah felt the flush creeping back into her cheeks. His eyes were making her feel undressed again.

"What I mean is, I'm not fashionably thin," she said.

"I'd say . . . voluptuous," he murmured, his husky voice caressing each syllable of the word in a way that made her squirm in her seat. She sat up.

"Well, when I started making clothes the anorexic look was still around," she hurried on. "But I realized that there were plenty of other woman like me, so I designed for me, and them. So far, it seems to be working. You see of lot of, um, healthy, natural-looking women in the magazines now—"

"More like you," he suggested.

"Right," she acknowledged. "And I've sold some of my stuff at Veronique's. Where I work," she added, at his questioning look. "Now I'm ready to take over Los Angeles." Craig's persistent attention was at last beginning to make her feel too self-conscious.

"You know," she said, "I've never met a man in my life who could stand to talk about clothes for more than a minute . . . and you've had me going on this for . . . for . . . nearly an hour," she guessed, finding it difficult to read her watch.

"You've been very informative," Craig said.

"You've been very indulgent," Suzannah said wryly. Even from this angle—slightly sideways as she leaned back in the chair again—he was devastatingly attractive—some might say gorgeous—If only he would put on a shirt! She dragged her eyes from the tantalizing stretch of male muscle and sinew. "So, what's in your future?" she asked. "I mean, besides sketching . . . and fishing?"

Craig considered. "At the moment, whatever comes my way," he said vaguely, shrugging a beautifully muscled shoulder. "I'm . . . between jobs."

Between jobs. That was the polite euphemism she and Charlie had used when he was out of work. Suzannah shook her head. "That's too bad."

To her surprise, he chuckled. "No, it isn't," he assured her. "I'm enjoying my time off."

"How can you?" she blurted. "I mean, aren't you worried? About . . . well, what comes next?"

Craig sipped his wine thoughtfully. "A little bit," he admitted. "But I try to keep things separate. When I'm not working, I'm enjoying life—the simple things that make it all worthwhile. Of course, when I'm working, I give it my all."

"Those simple things," she mused. "They aren't always enough."

"No?" He looked up at her with a faint smile. "What are the important things, then?"

Suzannah considered. "A roof over your head. . . . clothes to wear . . . being able to eat out," she added suddenly. When she and Charlie had lived together such indulgence had been impossible. And eating out was one of the things Suzannah most enjoyed . . .

"You mean, all that money can buy," he observed.

"What's wrong with living decently?" she challenged him. "If a person works hard, he—or she—deserves it.

Craig nodded. "If you've earned it. I can respect that," he mused. "I've never been a freeloader, myself. But I think there's such a thing as living . . . too well."

"Too well?"

"Sometimes . . . " He paused, searching for the right way to say it. "People mistake having money for happiness. I know it sounds like a cliché, but I've seen it happen. I've known some people born into money who are miserable," he frowned, "and make others feel it. And I've seen other people get rich and get lost . . . in their possessions. It's easy for that to happen . . ." He stopped himself, shaking his head with a rueful grin. "Sorry. Didn't mean to moralize." He sipped his wine.

Suzannah studied him, touched by the fervor she'd heard in his little speech. He was obviously a man with strong opinions on these matters . . .

"Anyway, I try not to take what I do have for granted," he was saying. "What about this wine? And the ocean . . ." He pointed and her eyes followed. "What could be worth more than the way that half-moon looks, shining on the ocean . . . and the beautiful sound those waves make?"

A hush fell over them as they listened together to the ocean's swell. She turned to meet his gaze, which seemed to glint with a bit of that moon.

"Then there are life's little surprises," he went on, softly. "A beautiful woman—a perfect stranger—comes to share that magical view. What more could a man ask for? When I find I'm looking for more than this, I'll know I've lost my way."

Suzannah couldn't break the look that bound them now. A strange, quivering feeling seemed to fill her as the wind rustled and the waves pounded just beyond them. She swallowed, struggling to fend off the emotions that were threatening to overcome her, the yearning feeling of arousal his eyes were awakening within her.

"Well, you're quite the romantic, aren't you?" she said, with forced breeziness. "I had that point of view once, but I'm afraid I lost it . . ." She lifted her cup, then paused, finding it empty. Craig rose, bottle in hand.

"When was that?" He was refilling her mug.

"A few years back, I guess," she said. "Boy," she mused ruefully. "I learned my lesson."

"Which one?"

"I married a perfect stranger," she said. "And I thought love and romance was all we needed . . ." She shook her head. "He wasn't so perfect. And I found out you can't live on romance forever. I'll tell you, Craig, beware of marrying for love alone. I tried it, and some of those simple things you talk about lost their luster."

"Marry for what, then?" he asked, kneeling beside the chair, his sudden closeness making her stiffen slightly.

Suzannah shrugged. "I can't imagine," she smiled ruefully. "But I'm trying to convince myself to be more . . . pragmatic." She addressed her china mug sternly. "Next time," she admonished it. "You go on out there and find yourself a mate who's loaded."

"Loaded?" He cocked his head, smiling. "Like you?"

Suzannah giggled. "I am *not* loaded," she told him firmly. "Neither with drink, nor with diamonds, despite your . . . rude insinuations."

"Sorry," he said.

She was tired of looking at Craig sideways, and leaning back in the chair like this was making her feel a little dizzy. Suzannah struggled to sit upright, and as she did, the chair tilted dangerously. Craig was instantly at her side, his hands deftly gripping both the tottering chair and her shoulder. Off balance, Suzannah found herself lurching into his waiting arms.

"Oh, my," she gasped, breathless, as he held her steady. "Good save."

"Are you okay?" he asked.

His face was only inches from hers now, and his dark brown eyes seemed to loom before her, his brow furrowed in concern. "Sure," she said. But she wasn't okay. His arm cradling her, his hand steadying her shoulder, the warmth of his bare skin against her, the nearness of his slightly parted lips . . . all this seemed to take her breath away, even as she regained it . . .

"I'm surprised at your advice," he was murmuring. "Not marry for love? You can't be that cynical. I don't believe you."

He should have, by all rights, been releasing her now. But he was holding her still, as he knelt by the chair, and she felt hypnotized by his gaze, unable to begin to struggle free. "I . . . I told you . . ." she breathed, finding it difficult to think straight with his arms around her.

"Don't you believe in love conquering all?" he continued, his voice low and husky.

"No," she whispered.

"How about love at first sight?" he countered.

There was a warmth and strength in his embrace that made her feel wonderfully secure, but at the same time, the liquid velvet depths of his dark eyes were transmitting signals that turned her insides wobbly. "No," she whispered again, then shivered as he brushed his palm against her cheek in a tender caress.

"And what are your thoughts about love . . . at first kiss?" he murmured, his eyes melting her with unconcealed desire.

"I've never . . ." Her words faltered as he brought his mouth to hers. And then, as her lips parted of their own volition to meet his, she was aware of nothing but the feel of his warm lips against hers, softly teasing and caressing.

She yielded, unquestioning, in sweet surrender to the exquisite touch of his moist skin.

The heady pressure sent her senses reeling. Their tongues touched in a sensuous, fiery dance, and she lost herself in the deepening kiss, her hands instinctively tightening around his neck. The scent and taste of him was overpowering, intoxicating her even more. Without thinking, she pressed herself closer to him, hungry with spiraling desire.

But it was he who gently but firmly pulled back, slowly lifting his face from hers. Tenderly he brushed his lips lightly across hers once more, then leaned back, drinking in her expression of dazed arousal with evident pleasure. "There, you see?" he murmured. "There's some romance left in you yet."

"You . . . you shouldn't . . ." she faltered, breathless.

"You're right," he said softly. "I shouldn't. As I said, I'm not the kind of guy to take advantage . . ."

Suzannah cleared her throat, and at last found the strength to struggle from his arms into an upright position. She felt the hot flush in her cheeks and her heartbeat pulsing loud in her ears. The room was slightly swaying as she looked beyond Craig to the glimmering moonlit dunes outside the windowed doors. She took a deep breath.

"Too much wine," she murmured.

"Apparently," said Craig. He got up, slowly, and looked down at her with some concern. "Are you all right?"

"Fine," she lied, nodding. Her heartbeat was slowing at last.

"I'm sorry," he said. "I got carried away. It was a little easier to resist you when you were across the room, but when I found myself looking into those beautiful eyes of yours at such close range . . ."

"So, we're back to the flattery," she said wryly, trying to affect a careless air.

"You *do* have beautiful eyes," he said, frowning. "They're green and golden brown . . . intoxicatingly bright . . ."

"Hazel," she said. "They're hazel, that's all." Standing up seemed like a good idea, instead of having him tower above her, so she got to her feet and crossed quickly to the open doors, inhaling the fresh sea air. She sensed him behind her and stiffened as she felt his body brush hers.

"Suzannah," he said softly. She turned to face him, and somehow, gazing up into those smoldering dark eyes, she knew that no amount of fresh air was going to cool her off. If he kissed her again . . . a fiercely erotic flush seemed to suffuse her from inside out as wild images of sensual abandon glimmered briefly in her mind. She wouldn't—couldn't—but if he were the sort of man to ruthlessly take command . . .

"I think it's time . . ." he began quietly, and Suzannah held her breath. ". . . I let you get some rest," he finished.

Suzannah cleared her throat, only able to mutely nod. She realized, with an inner flinch of embarrassment, that she was not so much relieved as . . . disappointed? Craig seemed cool, calm, and collected. She was the one whose equilibrium had been shattered by the devastating power of his kiss.

"I'll . . . be out there," he said, gesturing at a palm tree a few yards from the shack. She could dimly make out the form of a white hammock strung between it and the eaves outside. "You do want . . . to be alone." It was a question, she understood, and a tactful one. Only his eyes still held a trace of lingering arousal, a hint of sensual invitation.

"Yes," she said softly. "Thank you. For being . . . a gentleman."

Craig smiled. "It is taking some will-power," he admitted. "But you've had more than your share of wine, and there are rules about that sort of thing . . ." His eyes held hers in pregnant silence a moment. Then he snapped his fingers. "Sheets," he announced.

"Sheets," she echoed, uncomprehending. Then, as Craig left her side to open his closet, she saw him removing some fresh linens. Suzannah turned away. She focused on the watercolor set up on his easel, still shaken by the intense feelings that had welled up inside her when she was in his arms. Come on, now, the man was right: Too much liquor on an empty stomach had accounted for her momentary madness. Right?

She busied herself in studying the painting. It wasn't bad at all, really. It showed a sensitivity to color she found surprising. But then, Craig was turning out to be a surprise in many ways . . .

Moments later, he was bidding her good night. Suzannah watched through the glass-paned doors as Craig stepped out in the dappled moonlight and climbed, a lithe and trim shadowy figure, into his hammock. Then she latched the doors, and was soon climbing up the short ladder to his loft bed.

She slept in her clothes; it felt more secure that way. But sleep wouldn't come. The pillow smelled subtly of a musky masculine scent. Images of Craig's body, half clothed as he slept in the hammock outside, plagued her. Sighing, she turned and turned again, unable to stop thinking about the man out there in the moonlight.

The idea that she'd come so close to losing control was both scary and shockingly titillating. Sleep! she commanded her restless body, knowing it was useless. She couldn't think of the last time a man had affected her so deeply . . . well, since Charlie, and even that had been different. And then, she *had* lost control, and . . . Get out of here fast in the morning, she told herself firmly. Learn from your mistakes.

Sighing once more, she lay on her back, contemplating the ceiling. Resigned to a long night, she began to count the rhythmically crashing waves.

Suzannah looked over the mechanic's shoulder as he filled in her address on the bill. Craig had offered to absorb the cost, but she wasn't hearing any of it. She'd pay the bill, though she wasn't sure how; the ninety dollar estimate might very well put her back on a diet of tuna fish and peanut butter and jelly sandwiches if she couldn't manage to peddle any of her designs. The mechanic handed it to her now, leaving a greasy thumbprint on the edge, and she pocketed the yellow slip quickly as Craig approached her.

"Well," she said brightly. "I guess that's taken care of."

"I guess so," he nodded, squinting at her in the bright sunlight as he emerged from inside the service station's garage.

"Thanks for your help with the car," she said. "That was sheer wizardry."

He shook his head, grinning. "Pure luck."

Craig had traced the problem with her accelerator to one small, simple little spring under the Rolls's hood that had come loose. He had re-coiled the tiny loop of metal into its proper position before she'd gotten blearily out of bed that morning. After a quick cup of coffee brewed on Craig's hot plate, they had loaded his bike into the trunk of the Rolls, and driven back up the dirt road to the highway. Suzannah was just feeling fully awake by the time they'd reached the service station, and now that the bike had been looked at, her imminent parting with Craig seemed to be coming much too abruptly.

"So," she said, feeling acutely awkward. "Thanks for . . . everything."

"It was a pleasure," he said, his eyes locking with hers. A subtle but palpably electric current seemed to pass between them in a wordless moment as their gazes lingered. Craig hadn't made any romantic advances in the hurried activities of the morning; something Suzannah was both grateful for and secretly disappointed by. The momentary madness of the night before might have been dreamed, for all she knew.

But as they looked into each other's eyes she knew full well it had been real. And when he held his hand out to shake hers in parting, a shiver of erotic arousal coursed through her at his oddly familiar touch. He held her hand for a moment too exquisitely long, and then let go, with a friendly nod.

"I'm glad I could be of help," he said simply.

"Me, too," she smiled. "I'm glad we met."

Once again they looked at each other in silence. "Well, if you ever have another yen to see how the other half lives," he drawled, breaking the pregnant pause with a slightly mocking grin, "do drop by."

For a wild, impulsive second, she nearly returned the invitation, but she held her tongue. Things were better left as they were. Instead, she said good-bye, and got back behind the wheel of the Rolls. Her last glimpse of Craig was in the rearview mirror. He was watching her drive away, his thumbs hooked in the belt loops of his tight, faded blue jeans, the wind gently riffling his longish chestnut hair, the sun making his bronzed skin seem to glow even brighter . . .

Then Craig's attention was distracted by a man at the wheel of a sports car, who'd pulled up beside him in the station. The man either knew Craig or, more likely, he was just a friendly fellow asking for directions. At any rate the two men were immersed in conversation when she tore her eyes from the mirror, alerted by a car's honk behind her that the light had changed. And then she left her somewhat imperfect stranger far behind.

CHAPTER THREE

"THE LIVING ROOM," Suzannah announced.

Mr. Ross, the gray-suited, balding realtor who had been waiting for her, six leviathan cats meowing piteously at his feet when Suzannah drove up, nodded pleasantly. As he roamed about the spacious, high-ceilinged room, she looked it over herself, awed. It felt odd to be playing hostess when she herself had only a passing acquaintance with the house.

On her first visit she had been just a child, and the place had intimidated her. On her second she'd been a teenager, and had almost taken the house in stride. But on this, her third time around, she fairly ached with envy. The estate contained everything a woman of means could want. As she toured the premises with Mr. Ross, Suzannah thought about how she loved the many rooms, which reflected her Aunt's eccentric and eclectic tastes. Clearly someone who enjoyed living really *lived* in the airy, many-windowed house: It wasn't at all a sterile showplace of wealth and status. She followed Mr. Ross around the upstairs, staggered once again by the size of the spacious bedrooms, and contented herself with listening to him make comments about shelving and moldings, as he made notes in a little pad.

Outside it was he who pointed out to her some of the assets of the grounds. "You've got a real lap pool here," he noted, evidently impressed. "Costs a fortune to heat," he mused, more to himself, and made another note. "Gorgeous, isn't it?"

Suzannah could only nod. The calm turquoise surface seemed a mile long as they stood at one end. Beautiful tall elms had been planted against the high white wall that surrounded it. Bleached Mexican tiles flanked the pool on all sides. At the far end was a small, white-columned pavilion with little doors that led to dressing rooms.

Suzannah had swum in the pool, one halycon sun-drenched weekend when she was a senior in high school. It seemed another lifetime. But she could vividly remember changing in that little white dressing room, and plunging into the icy-cold water—

"It's not heated," she said suddenly. Mr. Ross turned, startled. "Aunt Lucille swims laps every day of the year, rain or shine, and she refused to install a heater because she likes the natural temperature of the water."

"She sounds like quite a lady." Mr. Ross smiled, and continued up the steps leading out of the walled pool area. Outside was a rolling lawn, beautifully sculpted, its *pièce-de-resistance* a zigzagging lush row of bright red salia that led to a small gray gazebo at the property's far end. Suzannah sauntered slowly up its steps, luxuriating in the cool shade and fragrant flowers, as Mr. Ross puttered around outside. Sitting for a moment on the wicker circular bench, Suzannah found herself thinking suddenly of Craig.

What would *he* make of all this? The indulgence of it, and the money behind it, might madden the poor fellow. Still, how could he, the self-professed romantic, resist the charms of a spot like this? For a moment she allowed herself to fantasize that he was there in the gazebo, sitting opposite her, drinking . . . iced tea, she decided, rather than liquor. They could talk, and sip, and look out over the beautiful greenery, with the breeze and sun, and her head on his strong, warm shoulder . . .

Suzannah bolted upright, startled by her own imagination. What had gotten into her perverse brain? It was doubtful she'd ever see that man again, let alone sip tea with him in an intimate *tête-a-tête*. Her own wistful schoolgirlish naiveté brought a smile to her lips. All this fairy tale luxury plopped suddenly in her impoverished lap was getting the best of her. She had to force herself to remember, again, that in the real world, she had next to nothing, and a man such as Craig had even less. And it was in the real world that he belonged.

With a sigh, she rose, and left the little gazebo. But images of Craig—his laughing eyes, his tanned, soft skin, that mocking little smile on his full lips, the thrust of his defiant chin—stayed with her as she wandered back to the house, rejoining Mr. Ross. She couldn't shake that vagrant beachcomber from her mind. Odd, that in one brief encounter, he'd sparked so much arousal in her . . .

Suzannah shivered as she re-entered the sunlit den. That one experimental kiss hovered, ghostlike, on her lips, and she suddenly felt herself go weak inside, an echo of how she'd felt then. Ruefully, she shook her head. It was best that a brief encounter had been all there was between herself and Craig. That man was potentially dangerous; just the sort of person who could ruin her life all over again with his idealistic, wastrel's ways.

"Well, I think I've got a good idea of what we have on our hands here," Mr. Ross said, rising from the rattan armchair and closing his pad as she came in. "I'll be talking to your aunt's attorney within the next day or so about an asking price . . ." He paused, gazing out through the picture window of the den. "One thing I can tell you for sure, though—I can't possibly show the place yet."

"Why?" Suzannah asked, alarmed. It had been Lucille's intention to get the house sold with all possible speed—and Suzannah herself had to be back in San Francisco in less than four weeks. A vacation of even this length had been hard to come by.

"Frankly, the grounds are a mess," Mr. Ross said. "Shouldn't take more than a few days of gardening, but if Mrs. Eaton wants us to proceed quickly, it's got to be done."

"Gardening?" Suzannah followed Mr. Ross's gaze to the grassy slopes outside.

"Hedges need a trim, grass wants cutting, flower beds

could use some attention. It's not major," he said, with a kindly smile. "But you'd be surprised how little it takes to make the wrong impression on a prospective buyer. Your aunt's interior designing is . . . eccentric enough as it is. If the grounds look sloppy . . ." He shrugged.

"Well, I'll certainly have it attended to," Suzannah said worriedly. As she showed Mr. Ross out, she tried to figure logistics. Perhaps Preston, the attorney her aunt had mentioned on the phone, would be willing to pay for some landscaping.

The phone was ringing as she bid the realtor good-bye. She nearly drop-kicked a cat by accident, rushing to locate it. There was an old-fashioned antique replica on the table in the hall. "Hello?" she said breathlessly.

"Welcome to L.A.!" came a musical, British-accented voice.

"Lila!" Suzannah cried.

"Well, I must say you've gotten right into the swing of it. I was ringing you up till all hours last night. You did get in last night, didn't you? And what, hit the Sunset Strip clubs immediately?"

Suzannah laughed. "Not quite. Where are you?"

"I'm staying at the Château Marmont, on Sunset," said Lila. "Stars galore! You'd die." Suzannah smiled. She was used to her old friend's hyperbole, even if she was still awed by Lila's glamorous lifestyle. When they'd first met, in college, the young Englishwoman, transplanted with her diplomat father to America, had been an aspiring Shakespearean actress. But fate and her stunning looks had turned her into a television star on an Australian sit-com. Now she'd landed her first role in an American movie, and she'd written Suzannah a few weeks ago to say she was bound for Hollywood. The chance to spend some time with her friend had been a decisive factor in Suzannah's accepting Aunt Lucille's house-sitting offer.

"Do you want me to meet you at your hotel?" she asked.

"No, I'm dying to get out and come see your Auntie's digs," Lila replied. "Why don't I just drive on out? Any snacks in the house? Better yet, I'll pick something up. You know, they've got the most marvelous natural juice bars in this town . . ."

Suzannah smiled as Lila rattled on. She was used to her

friend's chatty exuberance; Lila was always fast talking and fast moving, a long-legged whirlwind who barely stopped long enough, it seemed, to have her pictures taken. Suzannah had always envied her striking looks and Continental, larger-than-life style. Now she looked forward to some headier than usual girl talk.

Lila, upon her arrival, didn't disappoint. No sooner was she in the door than she was launched on a spicy anecdote about her latest affair, which was with, naturally enough, the director of the film she was in. The vivacious actress added a bunch of grapes, a hunk of cheese, and a quart of some exotic fruit juice to the tray Suzannah had been preparing, already laden with a pasta salad she brought with her from San Francisco, and sourdough bread.

"I don't know why I'm always hooking up with Englishmen." She sighed, following Suzannah into the sunny den.

"Well, you're British," Suzannah reminded her.

"I know." Lila frowned. "But these American men are so cute. I've always wanted one. It just never seems to work out . . . God, your Aunt's got taste! I *need* this chair—d'you think she'd miss it?"

"She might." Suzannah smiled. The chair in question was an antique wicker armchair that matched the larger wicker windowseat in which she sat, beginning to cut up the cheese. Two cats nearby watched her with great interest.

"Too bad," Lila sighed. "Well, this place is fantastic. All yours, is it?"

"For a while," Suzannah said, offering her a plate. She was already munching on salad, ravenous, she realized, from lack of breakfast.

"I'll be visiting as often as I can," said Lila, gulping down some juice. "We start to shoot tomorrow—which reminds me! Where are your beautiful clothes? I want to look over the lot of them. Must have dibs on the best. Got any pale blue something-or-other? To match my eyes?"

"They're all out in the car," Suzannah remembered.

"What? You haven't even unpacked yet? Darling, what *did* you do with yourself last night? Come on, now, tell all."

Suzannah hesitated. For some reason, she wanted to keep

her little beach-house interlude to herself. She was already looking back at her night with Craig through a rose-tinted haze, as a romantic idyll with a mysterious stranger, and she felt that her worldly friend would find the drama of one chaste kiss relatively unimpressive.

So as Lila walked with her to the front, where Suzannah unloaded the Volkswagon, bringing in two garment bags full of her designs, she related a highly edited version of her night's encounter, stressing its more comic aspects. But Lila, with unerring instinct, went right for the most intimate angle. "So you slept with him?" she asked cheerily, as they re-entered the house. "Was it fantastic?"

"Of course not!" Suzannah exclaimed, feeling her cheeks turn crimson. "I mean, I didn't. Sleep with him. He was nice . . . but, honestly, Lila . . . a total stranger? A beach bum?"

Lila shrugged. "Sounds ideal to me," she smiled. "What do you people call it—a zipless encounter? No strings . . . just pure physical pleasure . . ."

Suzannah forced a laugh. "Not my idea of a good time," she said, though she couldn't deny there had been a moment last night when such a prospect had seemed alluring . . . "And that's why I didn't want to get involved with . . . that man. I'm not like you, Lila. If I sleep with a man I'm attracted to, I'm liable to fall head over heels, lose all perspective . . ."

"I lose perspective all the time," Lila murmured, inspecting a knitted jersey. "But I get it back before the church bells chime. This one!" she cried suddenly. "Perfect!"

Lila was already unzipping the dress she had on, having pounced upon a smocklike jersey of turquoise and white. For awhile, all conversation consisted of opinions on which of Suzannah's clothes suited her best. When the dust settled, Lila had claimed three different items, one of which she intended to wear in the film.

"You know, you've really got the goods here," she said thoughtfully, sitting on the edge of the bed with the clothes in hand.

"Thanks, Lila," Suzannah said, straightening out the disarray her friend's kamikaze attack had wrought. "I only hope the shop owners of Rodeo Drive agree with you."

"They will," Lila murmured. "Packaging. That's the important thing—packaging and promotion."

"What do you mean?"

"Sit," Lila commanded, patting the chair by the bed. "Now, listen up, Suzannah . . ." She waited for her to take a seat. "You've got an incredible opportunity here, and we're going to see to it that you reap all the rewards, for once. First off, I'm going to go through all your gear again and pick out a few for Jaqueline. I've a pretty good feel for her taste—"

"Really? You think she'd . . . ?" Suzannah's eyes widened. Jacqueline Terry was the lead in Lila's film, an American movie star who was a renowned fashion plate.

"Whether she buys one or not doesn't matter," Lila explained patiently. "The point is, you tell the people Jacqueline Terry has one of your dresses . . . or is interested in the line . . . or whatever . . ."

"But that's . . ." Suzannah paused uncertainly.

"Good promotion," Lila said. "Now, you've got this house, which is a plus, but better yet, that Rolls Royce. When you go to the boutiques, you go in style."

"But I couldn't," Suzannah said. "The Rolls isn't . . ."

"You must," Lila said firmly. "Honey, if you roll up to Maxanne's on Beverly in that rattletrap Volks of yours they won't even give you the time of day, let alone look at your dresses! Suzannah, try to understand: Money talks to money in this town. You see? If you're aspiring to wealth, then you have to *be* wealthy."

"But I'm not," Suzannah said, frowning.

"What do they know?" Lila cried. "Listen to me—you're getting the benefit of years of learning, here! Now. You arrive in a nice car. You drop the name of a prominent movie star. You yourself are dressed . . ." She squinted at Suzannah. ". . . in your own clothes, of course, but with . . . accessories."

"Now, wait a second," Suzannah began, already anticipating Lila's bent.

"Your Aunt has no doubt left some of her little knickknacks around," Lila went on, unheeding. "Don't look at me like that, listen! Hunt up some jewelry. She wouldn't mind, I'm sure. Maybe there are some bracelets, diamond earrings, whatever. Wear them. And when you talk of San

Francisco, talk of the poshest places, the best stores, the cream. Are you following me? You dress rich, you act rich, think rich—*voila!* Soon you'll *be* rich."

"But—my clothes," Suzannah began, shaking her head. "They're not Oscar de LaRenta formals. Why should I have to present them—and me—in a false light? Can't my clothes just speak for themselves?"

"Not false, dearie," Lila said impatiently. "Your clothes have to speak to *these* people in *their* language. They're a condescending breed, Suzannah, believe me. So you tell them it's casual wear for the young at heart, or some such nonsense . . ."

For another twenty minutes, Lila coached Suzannah on the proper pitch that would appeal to the snobbish store owners of Beverly Hills. By the time the actress had to leave, Suzannah's head was swimming with what seemed like outrageous, hucksterish schemes. But she had to admit her friend had a point.

"Trust me," Lila smiled, Suzannah's dresses under each of her arms as they stood together on the front steps. "I'll call you tomorrow after I've had a chance to get to Jackie. In the meantime . . ." Her words trailed off. Both women turned as a buzzing noise grew louder down the driveway. "Hullo, you've got company," Lila noted, with a new tone in her voice.

For a moment the ground seemed to tilt under Suzannah's feet, and her heart began going in double-time. There, his hair glinting in the sun, the supple musculature of his chest rippling beneath a tight white T-shirt, was Craig, his lean legs straddling the little red motorbike. As she watched, her mouth slightly agape, he pulled up right in front of them.

"Ummm," Lila murmured appreciatively.

Craig shut off his motor, kicked his kickstand down and rose from the bike. "Hello," he said simply, pausing at the bottom step.

Suzannah realized she was staring, and found her voice. "Hi," she said. unable to tear her gaze away from the soft darkness of his eyes, now seeking a sign of welcome in her own.

"Aren't you going to introduce . . . your friend?" said Lila.

"Oh!" Suzannah said. "This is . . . Craig . . ." She stopped, realizing she didn't even know his last name.

"Craig Jordan," he supplied, stepping up one step.

"Well, my last name is Raines. And this is my friend, Lila Claremont," Suzannah added, indicating Lila. She paused, her pulse pounding at an unnatural rate, uncertain of what to do or what to expect. Had he come about the bill? Or . . .

As usual, Lila was the one with practiced poise. "I was just on my way out." She smiled and gave a friendly nod in Craig's direction. "I'll ring you up," she said cheerily to Suzannah and, as she leaned in to give her cheek a peck, she whispered: "Wow!"

Suzannah cleared her throat. "So long," she said to Lila, coloring. "I . . . Thanks for everything."

Lila was already striding towards her car. With a wave, she got in. Craig and Suzannah watched in silence as she backed up, and then drove swiftly down the circular drive. When she was out of sight, they turned to each other again.

"So," Craig said, with a smile.

She realized she was still standing two steps above him, as if guarding the door. "Oh . . . would you like to come in?"

"Well, maybe," he drawled, glancing past her, his eyes taking in the majestic contours of Aunt Lucille's mansion. "That's actually what I've come to talk to you about."

"What?" she blurted, confused. She felt, ridiculously enough, as if she wanted to step in front of the luxurious house to shield it from his skeptical view.

"I'd like to ask a favor of you," he said slowly. "Or rather, have a favor returned."

"Yes?" she prodded him, nervously. Those deep velvet eyes of his were making her legs feel wobbly again.

"I'm in a tough spot," he said. "The guy who lent me his place—at the beach? Well, he's had to come back to town suddenly . . . and it seems I'm out on the street . . . temporarily."

As he paused, evidently uncomfortable, she suddenly remembered the man in the sports car she'd seen talking to Craig when she left the gas station. Craig's landlord, then?

"So, I thought that, ah, possibly . . ." Craig was saying. ". . . for just one night, seeing as you might have the extra room . . ."

His eyes left her face to briefly scan the exterior of the house again. Suzannah watched him, her own eyes sweeping from his hair to the frayed cuffs of his jeans, his bare ankles in worn-out sneakers. Unable to stop herself, her gaze lingered over his trim and manly chest, the fit of his tight jeans over firm hips and thighs. The feel of his strong arms around her came back with vivid, visceral clarity, and a feathery shiver stole up her spine. Another night? Another temptation . . .

Suzannah snapped to. Craig was waiting for an answer. "Of course, there's room," she said quickly. "I mean, it's the least I could do, after . . ." He was watching her intently. ". . . after last . . . after your help," she finished awkwardly.

He cocked his head. "You're sure it's okay?"

Suzannah nodded slowly, her heart beating double-time. She wasn't sure at all.

He sensed it. "I'd stay out of your way," he said. "You'd hardly know I was here."

Right. His mere presence galvanized her body and made the simple act of breathing difficult. Nervously she glanced beyond him, her attention caught by the glint of sun on the windows above the garage. Craig turned, following her gaze. "Maybe . . . there," she said, as the thought took shape. There was a little suite of rooms above the garage where Aunt Lucille had lodged a caretaker for a while, some years back.

"Servants' quarters?" he asked.

There was nothing accusatory in his casual question, but Suzannah suddenly felt put on the spot. With such a palatial abode at her disposal, it probably seemed absurd to him, this suggestion that he lodge over the garage. But how could she explain that the idea of him being under the same roof with her gave her goosebumps?

"Then again, maybe not," she said hurriedly. "I don't know what shape the rooms are in . . ."

But Craig was already taking a canvas bag from the back of his bike. "All I need is four walls and a bed," he said, and Suzannah's heart went out to the fellow. He wasn't the type to ask for favors. Clearly his dire straits had become even direr.

"I'm sure there's space in the house," she began, but he cut her off with a wave of his hand.

"That looks perfect to me," he said, smiling and gesturing at the garage.

"I'll . . . cook you a decent meal," she said, trying now to make the arrangement more attractive.

His eyes widened slightly. "Well, you don't have to, but that would be nice." Then that twinkle of amusement she'd seen before shone in his gaze. "Maybe I can even be . . . helpful," he said quietly, his eyes sweeping her body with a quick, sensual appraisal that felt like a ticklish caress. "Is that car of yours running okay?" he added, his innocent query belying the innuendo in his look.

"It's fine," she said. "I don't need any help, thanks." But as he nodded and turned toward the garage, another thought hit her. It was the kind of impulsive combustion of good intentions with leaps of logic she was prone to, often against her better judgment. But the words came out of her mouth before she could reconsider.

"Say, Craig," she began. He turned around. "Have you ever done any . . . gardening?"

"Gardening?" He stared at her, puzzled.

"I mean have you ever worked, you know, on someone's property . . . doing, well . . . stuff?"

She stopped, wondering if she'd done exactly the wrong thing. Craig was looking at her as if she were as mad as a hatter. "Stuff?" he repeated.

"Well, I just thought that since you were . . . between jobs, as you said, that maybe you'd like to make a little money . . . here," she said, uncertainly. "The grounds need some work."

Quite suddenly his look of perplexity vanished. She watched, bewildered, as a grin spread over his face. "Let me get this straight," he said, as if he had just been let in on some hugely amusing joke. "You want to hire me, as a gardener? To work here?"

"Yes," Suzannah said. "What's so funny about that?"

Craig shook his head, and then his smile faded. "Nothing," he told her solemnly. "In fact, I think it's a great idea."

"You do?" She couldn't figure him out at all.

"Miss Raines, I'm all yours," he said meaningfully, his gaze holding hers. "And I really appreciate your . . . generosity." he added, more formally.

"You . . . do?" she repeated, once more apprehensive.

"Yes, I do," he said, with apparent sincerity. "Why don't you show me around your, ah, humble abode?"

Suzannah sighed. "Not mine," she reminded him.

"No offense," he smiled. "Where's the garden?"

CHAPTER FOUR

"WELL, THE HEDGES, I guess," Suzannah mused, gesturing vaguely at the overgrown greenery as Craig stood beside her on the rolling lawn behind the house. "They are kind of . . . shapeless, aren't they?"

Craig nodded slowly, his dark brown eyes traveling leisurely over the expanse of grass, shrubbery, trees, and bushes that seemed to stretch for miles. At the far end of Aunt Lucille's property, tall elms and willows cut off any glimpse of the neighboring house.

"And that path to the gazebo," Suzannah went on. "It *is* a bit overgrown. Not the sort of thing I'd notice, but Mr. Ross thinks . . ."

Her words trailed off as she turned to face Craig again and realized he'd been watching her, not the view. There was a sparkle of amused interest in his eye that she'd begun to recognize as a signal he had other things on his mind than whatever she was talking about. "What?" she sighed. "What's bothering you? Does it look like too much work? Or are you resenting the fact that my Aunt owns all of this property to begin with?"

Craig shook his head with a faint smile. "Actually, I was just enjoying the sight of you in broad daylight," he said. "I haven't had much chance until now. I was noticing some lighter strands of brown in your hair . . ."

Suzannah self-consciously brought a hand up to her brow, feeling her cheeks burn under his admiring gaze. "Craig," she said, clearing her throat, "you're supposed to be looking at the grounds."

"The grounds," Craig repeated, still not taking his eyes from her face. "They bring out the green."

"Pardon?" She looked at him, confused, trying to maintain her composure as the soft, glimmering depths of his eyes threatened to pull her in deeper.

"The green in your eyes. They change in the light, don't they?"

"Well, sort of," she muttered. "But Craig—"

"The left one looks browner," he mused, stepping closer. "With a little patch of golden-green—"

"Craig!" she cried, growing exasperated. "Do you want the job or not? If you don't, you should tell me now, so I can start calling up gardeners, or what-do-you-call-them, landscapers."

She'd stepped back as he drew closer, and she felt a trailing branch of the wisteria by the pool courtyard's outer wall nudge her shoulder. Craig followed her glance to the obviously untrimmed tree. "I'd need a power saw to take care of that," he said, squinting up at the hanging branches.

"I think there are tools in the little shed behind the garage," Suzannah said, glad they were finally on the subject at hand. "But if there's something special you needed, I guess . . ." She frowned, considering. "Well, I have to talk to Mr. McGinty about your salary, anyway," she told him. "My aunt's lawyer. He could probably arrange to take care of any extra equipment rentals."

"I see," Craig said, in a noncommital tone. "What sort of salary did you have in mind?"

"I didn't. Don't," she said, flustered. "I've never had to hire a gardener before."

"No?" He sounded mockingly incredulous.

Suzannah shot him a withering look. "No," she said firmly. "All I've got in San Francisco is a window box, and

I've managed to take care of it all by myself, believe it or not."

"Oh," said Craig with a grin. He turned, looking around the pool area toward the gazebo. "So you've got a green thumb?"

"Half of one," Suzannah told him, following Craig as he began to walk across the lawn to the zigzagging red salia. "I've done pretty well with tomatoes, but I was a failure with the herbs."

"Herbs can be tricky," he acknowledged, bending briefly to examine the brilliant red flowers, then moving on. "Isn't there an herb garden here?"

"Other side of the pool, I think," she said. Craig was mounting the few steps to the little gray gazebo. Suddenly she found her heart beating unnaturally fast. Her brief fantasy of only hours earlier was actually coming true. As she slowly approached the wooden pavillion, she had an odd sense of déjà vu mingled with apprehension. Somehow, seeing Craig in the flesh, his tall, athletically graceful figure looming before her in the place she'd imagined him, was more difficult to deal with than an idle reverie. Suzannah hovered by the entrance as he seated himself, stretching his feet out.

"Nice little place," he noted, then leaned over, inspecting the woodwork. "Couple of nails need hammering in." He leaned back then, casting an eye over the sun-dappled grounds outside with a proprietory air. "Well, Suzannah, you certainly could use a man around here," he murmured. His husky, low voice seemed to reverberate abnormally loudly in her ears. She tried to avoid his gaze as he looked up at her from the bench. "Coming in?" he asked idly, when she didn't immediately respond.

Suzannah nodded and stepped beneath the gazebo's roof but kept her distance, lingering by the doorway. "Of course, if you think there's too much here for you to handle . . ." she said, beginning to think she might be better off if he turned the job down.

"Too much for me to handle?" His eyes had a mischievous twinkle. "No, I don't think so."

"I'm not sure how much Mr. McGinty will offer," she said, ignoring the obvious insinuation in his last remark.

"Can't be less than seven or eight dollars an hour," Craig mused, with a shrug. "Why don't you request sixty a day? That's cheap next to what a Beverly Hills landscape company would charge, I'm sure."

"I suppose . . ." she murmured, forcing her eyes to blink as he fixed his gaze on her again. "How many days do you think it would take?"

"Two, at least, probably three—maybe more," Craig ruminated. "Depends on how easily it goes. After all, with just these two hands . . ."

Her eyes were drawn to the hands in question, resting on his muscular thighs. They were beautiful hands, actually, she found herself thinking—long slender fingers, tanned—and certainly not a workman's hands. Exactly what did Craig Jordan do when he did . . . whatever he did? Feeling his gaze on her she lifted her eyes to meet his. Something seemed to move inside her as their gazes locked in the cool shadows of the gazebo. Her throat was suddenly tight. Three or four days, with those magnetic, velvety eyes caressing hers? She wondered if she could stand it. The days were one thing, but that meant three or four . . . nights. "Are you sure it's the sort of thing you'd like to do?" she managed.

Craig rose from his seat. "Well, beggars can't be choosers," he said nonchalantly. "After all, you're doing me a favor."

Instinctively she moved back against the wooden frame as he approached. "It might turn out to be a lot of work," she said uneasily.

Craig smiled, reaching out to pluck a leaf from her hair before she could move away. She felt a shiver run through her as his fingers grazed her forehead. "Actually, I don't think it'll be that much work at all," he drawled slowly. "It might even be fun."

There was no mistaking his meaning now. What had she gotten herself into? "Why?" she asked, narrowing her eyes and purposefully ignoring his innuendo. "Are you used to this kind of work? Have you done a lot of it?"

Thankfully, the sensual teasing look left his eyes, and he straightened up, shrugging. "I've done some," he said vaguely. "Years ago . . . I'm qualified, if that's what you mean. I don't have a landscaping license," he added, the beginnings of another impish grin deepening the little smile lines at the sides of his sensuous lips. "You know, Suzannah, I get the feeling you're reconsidering your invitation."

"I'm not," she said quickly. "I just . . ." She paused, befuddled. He seemed too close in this confined space, so she turned away, and descended the few steps to the path. Once out in the bright sunlight, glad to have the breathing room, she regained her composure. "I just want you to know what you're getting into," she said, squinting up at his silhouette, and went on, pointedly: "It will be *work.*"

"Hey, I like to work," he said, affronted. "I take it I don't strike you as the industrious sort?"

"No, I'm sure you are," Suzannah said, chagrined. She'd only been trying to make it clear that she was hiring him for a job, not inviting him to stay with her for some romantic liason. But he'd taken her words the wrong way. "Well," she continued hurriedly. "I suppose I could call Mr. McGinty now, to arrange things . . . that is, if you . . ."

"Sounds good to me," Craig said, emerging into the sunlight. "I'll miss my ocean view, but I guess I could get used to this."

From the way he was looking at her, he seemed too much at ease already. "Aren't you afraid of getting spoiled here?" she asked wryly.

"No, all of this doesn't faze me," he said breezily, his eyes sweeping the grounds. "*You* wouldn't spoil me, now, would you?"

She met the provocative challenge in his eyes square on. "No," she said. "Why don't you see what's in the tool shed while I make that call, then? I'll let you know if we've got the go ahead."

"You're the boss." Craig grinned.

Suzannah paced the kitchen with a phone at her ear, followed by a striped cat who couldn't imagine what she was doing there if she wasn't feeding him. Mr. McGinty's secretary had her on hold. "Tell me to forget it," she muttered aloud into the silent receiver. "Tell me I'd be better off hiring a fleet of Hollywood gardeners than taking that . . . vagrant hunk for a handyman." She sighed. "I'm a fool, aren't I? Just tell me I am. It'd make things so much easier . . ."

"Well, I will if you want me to, Miss Raines—" Preston McGinty's sandpapery voice suddenly broke in, causing her to nearly drop the phone. "—but any more complex advice might prove to be expensive. This is Miss Raines, isn't it?"

"Yes," Suzannah said, wincing, and feeling truly foolish now, she barreled on, explaining the situation to the attorney.

"I have a message from Mr. Ross, from earlier this morning," he told her. "Well, if he wants the place put right, I'll be happy to authorize the necessary payments. Your aunt's in a hurry to sell. Just speak to my secretary . . ."

In all of a minute, the matter was taken care of, and Suzannah was left holding a once more silent receiver with a somewhat stricken look on her face. "Guess I've hired him," she informed the striped cat, still standing expectantly at her feet. "Well, I've made my bed, so I might as well . . ." She stopped, not liking the sound of that particular axiom, and hung up the phone. "I really shouldn't talk to myself," she murmured, and then, realizing what she'd said, sighed in exasperation and marched out of the kitchen into the sunny greenery out back.

Craig wasn't in the tool shed, but the door was open, showing evidence of his inspection. Suzannah scanned the property. A muffled clatter from the garage indicated her new employee's whereabouts. She walked around the large white edifice to the stairs that ascended its side.

"Craig?" she called.

"Come on up."

The door at the landing above was ajar. Suzannah grasped the rickety wood railing and bounded upstairs. "I talked to McGinty," she began, as she reached the landing. "Everything is . . ."

Her words trailed off. Through the open doorway she had a perfectly framed view of Craig Jordan, clad only in a skimpy, paint-spattered pair of shorts, stretching his supple musculature in an attempt to hang a suit bag from the rafters. For a moment she stared dumbly at his smooth bronze skin, the sculptured brawn of his shoulders. Then he turned, and she couldn't quite lift her eyes fast enough from the whorls of fine dark hair that covered his chest, descending in a spiraling line down his trim, flat stomach to the band of his shorts.

"Everything is what?" he asked.

"What?" she repeated, then felt the blood rise in her cheeks as she saw the amusement in his eyes. "Oh . . . it's fine. Everything's just fine with Mr. McGinty," she went on, tearing her eyes away to gaze with feigned interest at the little room. What on earth was the matter with her? She'd never known the sight of a half-naked man to . . . discombobulate her so!

"So, the salary . . . ?"

"Seventy-five a day," she said, her eyes drawn to the bag he'd hung up. A few shirts were visible on its enclosed hangers.

"That's great," Craig said. His eyes followed hers to the suit bag. "Oh," he began sheepishly. "I brought along some overnight things, just in case you did say yes . . ."

"You figured I would," she said, meeting his gaze again.

"I hoped," he answered simply.

The pregnant pause that followed was threatening to lengthen as he held her gaze with those soft dark orbs. "Well!" she said brightly, with a forced air of carelessness that sounded idiotic to her own ears. "We're all set, then. I mean, you are . . ." She looked around him, sighting an unmade bed and shelves that were empty but for dust. "I'll get you some sheets and things from the house. Anything else you need?"

He considered the question a beat too long, his eyes leisurely raking her body from head to foot. "At the moment, no, thanks," he said slowly. "But when I do, I'll be sure to let you know."

Suzannah cleared her throat, and turned abruptly to the doorway. "Well, you just go on making yourself at home," she said. "I'll . . . see you later, I guess," she finished, and walked back onto the landing.

"Bye now," Craig called after her congenially.

At the bottom of the stairs Suzannah resolved to put Craig Jordan out of her mind for the time being. It seemed that when she did think about him, or spend too much time with him, her mind tended to short circuit. And she had a lot of other things to think about.

For example, she had some homemaking chores before her. She hadn't set up her sewing machine; she hadn't really even unpacked. And then, there was the list of boutiques she'd put together and then amended slightly with Lila's input. The fashion-minded actress knew of a few more trendy places San Fransicans had yet to hear about, and Suzannah had promised her she'd make some calls. Lila had sensed her friend's unwillingness to impersonate someone other than her natural self, and was bound to check up on her progress fairly soon.

Suzannah walked slowly back into the kitchen. Well, it was a good a time as any. She drew the list of boutiques out of her back pocket, unfolded it, and resolutely strode to the telephone.

A salesgirl answered, but she was soon in touch with Annabella herself. As per Lila's instructions, she quickly introduced herself with as much highbrow affectation as she could manage. She dropped Jaqueline's name, and peppered her recital with references to prominent stores that catered to the monied crowd in San Francisco.

Annabella, if not overwhelmed by this pitch, was at least friendly, and seemed interested in seeing her dresses. "You know, I don't usually like to look at things from designers I'm not acquainted with," she told Suzannah, in a European accent. "But I suppose if Miss Terry likes your work . . ." Her laugh was a tittery tinkle. "I'll take my chances. After all, even Alfonso D'Ottorino—are you familiar with his line?"

"Of course," Suzannah said quickly. She'd never heard of him.

"Well, even he looks to the movie crowd for guidance. So, perhaps if you're free, say"—There was a rustle of papers—"sometime tomorrow in the late afternoon?"

"Anytime," Suzannah blurted out, then realized immediately she'd dropped her role too quickly. "That is," she added, "After three or so. I've got a luncheon date at . . . Ma Maison," she invented, her imagination supplying her with a fashionably chic locale.

"Ah," said Annabella, with the proper note of understanding. "Well, there's no hurry, after all. Perhaps Friday would be better for you."

"Oh, no," Suzannah said hurriedly. "I have . . . my tennis lesson. And . . . a massage. So tomorrow is the best, really. And I would so like to show you the things I have on hand before . . . you know, there *is* a lot of interest . . ."

"I see. Well, I'll expect you towards four then, Suzanne, is it?"

"Suzannah. Suzannah Raines."

"Suzannah. I look forward to meeting you."

When she'd hung up, Suzannah stood where she was, her heart beating fast. That hadn't been so bad. Lila would be proud of her. Now, if she could bring off the actual appointment with some style . . .

Someone cleared his throat behind her. Suzannah whirled around. Craig was standing in the kitchen's alcove by the pantry, a long black cord looped over and around one shoulder, a toolbox in his hand. He was looking at her in a way that made her suspect he'd been eavesdropping, and she reddened, thinking of how affected and hoity-toity her end of the phone conversation had probably sounded.

"Sounds like a busy week around here," he said, with a faint smile. "Lots of company."

"No," she said. "What do you mean?"

"Tennis instructors? A masseuse?"

Suzannah swallowed. "No, I was just . . . saying that."

"And here you almost had me convinced you didn't go in for such idle pastimes," he said, shaking his head.

"I don't," she said, her blush deepening. "I was only, ah . . . trying to get out of an appointment."

Craig shrugged. "I just work here," he said amiably, and he crossed the kitchen, toolbox jangling. "Say, that reminds me." He paused at the door to the back. "Is there board involved? With the room?"

"Oh!" Suzannah looked at him, flustered. "I'm going to make us dinner."

"We're eating together?"

"Of course," she said, narrowing her eyes at him.

"Very liberal of you," he said, with an insouciant grin. "Well, I'm back to the trenches." With a nod, he turned the doorknob, leaving her to silently fume. Why did he take every opportunity to tease her about their apparent difference in status? It was really unfair.

She turned to face the luxurious kitchen. She was surounded by accoutrements galore: pots and pans hanging from ceiling racks above her, copper and silver, bowls and baskets. It was enough to make any aspiring gourmet drool.

Suzannah pushed her annoyance at Craig's attitude from her mind, and began to prepare the evening's meal.

Some time later, having lost herself in the joy of cooking in a style she could never have carried out at home, she was contemplating a trip to her aunt's little wine cellar when Craig re-entered the kitchen.

"Something smells fantastic," he said.

Suzannah looked up from the pot of rice. Her eyes widened as she took in Craig's fresh, scrubbed, and decidedly more formal attire. He had on a pair of fashionably loose-fitting khaki pants and a well-tailored shirt that, although frayed, had the look of a Perry Ellis or a C.J. Young. Its tan and rust design brought out the highlights in his now not-quite-as-mussed-up hair. For a moment she forgot herself completely and merely stared at him.

"It's the best I've got," he said apologetically, apparently misinterpreting her stare.

"You look . . . very nice," she said, and was suddenly conscious that she herself hadn't thought to change for dinner. "You really didn't have to . . ."

"I was covered in dirt." He grinned. "So as long as I was showering, I thought I'd dress for dinner. That's a great tub up there, by the way—an old fashioned procelain job, and an attachment that you hold over your head? Very rustic."

This vivid image of Craig in a bathtub disquieted her. "I've never been up there," she said abruptly, checking the rice. "Glad you like it."

"Anything I can help with?"

"You could set the table," she suggested. "It's just about ready. Oh, and in the basement—"

"Yes, I saw your aunt's racks," Craig said. "Some great vintages. How about the Château Haut Brion? That would really make the meal."

Suzannah stared at him, unable to figure out if he was teasing. The wine in question cost over thirty dollars a bottle. "You've certainly got expensive tastes for someone who frowns on indulgence. Is that what you usually drink?"

"Well, I . . ." He stopped, about to say something but obviously thinking better of it. "I'd settle for some club soda," he amended himself, smiling. "But you know, when in Rome . . ."

"You're right," Suzannah agreed impulsively. She didn't want to appear miserly, and besides, she wouldn't mind tasting a good wine herself. Why not? "Go ahead. I'm just going to wash up—"

"Leave the rest to me, madame," said Craig, with a mock bow.

When she returned to the dining room, he held her chair out for her, obviously enjoying his role as impromptu waiter. When she took her seat, he continued to hover nearby. "Chicken *à citron?*" he suggested courteously, in a ridiculously affected accent.

"You don't have to do this." She smiled in spite of herself as he grandly proffered her the chicken.

"Well if you're used to Ma Maison . . ." he said, serving her rice and peas as well.

Suzannah sighed. "Craig, I've never been to Ma Maison. I don't even know where it is."

Craig shrugged, uncorking the wine. "I hear it's not at all what it used to be, anyway," he said, his eyes twinkling as he poured her a glass.

"Really?" She stared at him. "Where did you hear that?"

"Just kidding," he said. "So—who were you trying to impress? On the phone before?"

"Some woman who owns a fancy boutique," she admitted, looking down in embarrassment at her plate. "According to this friend of mine who's an actress, it's the only way to get in the door. The exclusive people want to deal with other exclusives. You can't seem like you're, ah, hungry," she finished, her delicate nostrils flaring as the scent of her chicken rose from the plate. "Do you know what I mean?"

"I get the picture," he said. But his voice sounded distant. Suzannah looked up. While she'd been talking, Craig had left her side to stride down the length of the dining room. At the far end of the table, which was a good ten feet of oak away, he'd set his own place. As she watched, her mouth dropping open in disbelief, he took his seat. Seeing her stare, he gave her a friendly wave. "If you need anything, send up a flare," he called, his voice echoing absurdly in the oversized room.

"I think you've made your point, Craig," she said dryly. "Now why don't you pull your chair down to this side of the table?"

"Point?" he queried innocently, and shrugged. "Well, if you want me to be closer to you, I'm flattered . . ."

"Look," she said. "I think a dining room this size is ridiculous, myself. But Aunt Lucille likes to have big dinner parties. She enjoys entertaining. What's wrong with that?"

Craig was involved in the process of sliding his placemat and food down the table. "Nothing," he said. "I was only joking around." He leaned over for the salt. "Of course, I grew up in an apartment smaller than this room."

He'd said it matter-of-factly, without a trace of resentment, but Suzannah felt the implied barb. She said nothing, serving herself another piece of chicken. She wasn't about to defend Lucille, or try to explain her own modest upbringing. In a certain way, she reflected, Craig sounded like her father. Poor Dad: Jealous of his wife's sister; too proud to ever accept her impulsive attempts at charity; too terminally middle class to ever ascend the heights Lucille had so cavalierly vaulted by marrying a banker. Well, with Mom working, too, Suzannah hadn't grown up one-room-apartment poor. Her childhood hadn't been in the kind of poverty Craig had apparently known.

"Maybe I should have stayed down at the other end of the table."

Suzannah refocused on Craig, snapping out of her reverie. "Oh, I'm sorry. So—you grew up in the city, then? Wrong side of the tracks?"

"Wrong end of a subway line is more like it," Craig said ruefully. "And I grew up fast. There's nothing like the streets of New York to educate a kid." He chuckled as he sliced another piece of chicken. "You're a good cook," he said, and bit into it with obvious relish.

"Thanks," she murmured. Suzannah couldn't help but picture this self-assured, full-grown man as a cocksure teenager. His hair had probably always had that one unruly curl over his left eye, his lips, that slightly insolent pout. Had he belonged to a gang? She'd read all about the gang problem in New York.

"Tell me, Suzannah," he went on, before she could form another question. "Are you sure your friend knows what she's talking about? Putting on airs to make your sale?"

Suzannah shrugged. "She should know about images. Mine apparently needs some work—to go over in Hollywood, that is."

"I don't see anything wrong with your natural image," he said quietly.

She shuddered slightly as his hand gently closed over hers. The touch of his skin on hers, much warmer than she'd expected, set her heart racing. When she looked up into his eyes, the heat she saw there was even more unnerving. "That's nice of you to say, Craig," she managed, and pulled her hand away. "But I think Lila knows what she's talking about. When I show up there tomorrow, I have to make a good—no, an elegant—impression."

"Are you taking the Rolls?"

Suzannah nodded slowly. "I suppose I have to. It still makes me nervous to drive it, but . . ."

"Don't worry about a thing. If there's any trouble, your chauffeur can take care of it."

"Right," Suzannah said. "My . . ." She stared at him then, comprehending. "Wait a second—"

"I'm at your service," Craig smiled. "Every Rolls should have a driver. And if you want Annabella to think you're a high class operation, what would be better than your driver delivering you and picking you up? Just think, you won't even have to worry about parking."

"But, that's . . . I couldn't," she said uncomfortably. "Besides, don't you have a lot of gardening to do?"

"Well," Craig said, leaning forward conspiratorially. "I have heard rumors that the not-quite-richest-of-the-rich in these parts occasionally require their servants to double up. You know, cook-and-cleaning woman? Caretaker-chauffeur?"

"I'm not the not-quite-richest!" she exclaimed, in a plaintive wail. "And our . . . relationship is getting stranger by the minute."

"Stranger?" He shrugged. "More interesting, if you asked me. I don't mind helping you out, Suzannah. Not at all. In fact, I don't feel I've had enough time with you as it is."

Once again, there was no mistaking the decidedly sensuous undertone to Craig's words as his eyes caressed her face. Suzannah tried to hold her ground under the force of that openly appreciative gaze. "This is nuts," she said firmly. "I don't want a chauffeur. I didn't even want a gardener—"

"No?" He looked at her in mock confusion.

"At least not a live-in one. My good nature got the better of me, I guess—"

"You *are* good-natured."

"And before things go any further, let's just keep—"

"Where are things going, by the way?" he asked, smiling.

"Nowhere," she said abruptly. "I wish you'd stop looking at me like that."

"Like what?"

"Like I was . . . something on the dessert menu," she said, reddening as his grin broadened.

"Well, you do look good enough to eat," he drawled.

"Hold it," she muttered, and rose from her seat. "Craig, I appreciate all the flattery, and the . . . everything, but, let's get things straight. I barely know you. You did me a favor, and now I'm returning it, okay? We're even. All you have to do around here is your job. Let's let the rest of it slide."

"But the rest of it really interests me," he said, his eyes making a leisurely survey of her figure. She tried to ignore the flutter of arousal she felt rising within her, unbidden, as he looked at her.

"I don't think we share the same interests," she said.

Craig merely looked at her, clearly thinking something to the contrary. "No?" he asked mildly, at last. "But I have taken an interest in you . . . and your career. I'd like to see you accomplish the mission you came here to do. And if having an expensive car and a driver at your disposal is good business, then why fight it? It's not a big deal to me, honestly."

"I can't figure you out," she said, exasperated. "It seems like making fun of me is your idea of a good time."

"I'm not making fun," he said gently. "I just want to help."

He seemed sincere. His face wore none of the mockery she'd seen earlier. In fact, the earnestness of his glimmering eyes and upthrust jaw was quite endearing. "I guess it would be a plus," she said, still dubious. "Arriving on Rodeo Drive in style."

"Absolutely."

"But, then," she thought aloud, "you'll have to let me help you. Maybe I'll do a little work on the grounds or something. I want us to be . . . fair and square. Even trade-offs, you know what I mean?"

"Trade-offs," he murmured. "Yes, I'd like that. I'm sure we could work something out."

Suzannah cleared her throat. She knew too well what he was insinuating by the predatory look that had returned to his eyes. "We can negotiate terms," she said dryly. "Tomorrow. Right now I'd like to clean up and get to bed early."

"That sounds like a great idea," he said, his smile lines deepening.

"I'll get you your sheets and your pillow—for your bed," she said pointedly. "Before I make my own. In the meantime—"

"I'll do the dishes," he volunteered. "That's fair and square, isn't it? After all, you cooked."

"Right," she said. "Excuse me." Navigating a clear path around him, she left the diningroom, and went upstairs to get the linen.

Craig was already finished when she came back, and she deposited the little pile of sheets and pillows in his arms.

"If I don't see you up bright and early in the morning," he said, looking significantly into her eyes. "I'll come and get you out of bed. There *is* a lot of work to do before your appointment."

"I'll get up," she said warily. The idea of Craig in her bedroom was disturbingly titillating. Unthinkingly, she ran her tongue across her lips. Craig's half-hooded eyes watched her. She swallowed nervously, and backed away. The air between them seemed charged with a subtle current. "Well, good night," she said abruptly.

His gaze held hers a skin-prickling beat too long. "Sleep tight," he murmured, and then turned, at last, to leave.

Heading upstairs, she tried to shake off the resultant off-balance feeling—a mixture of physical and heady desire—that undermined her stability whenever Craig Jordan's soulful eyes gazed into hers. Suddenly, she was exhausted. It was the tension, she realized, that his presence—or rather, resisting his presence—created in her.

Never had a bed looked so inviting. Suzannah undressed

quickly, washed her face, brushed her teeth, and had the lights out in a matter of minutes. Even the unfamiliar surroundings didn't daunt her. The bed was soft, the night air breezes from the open window warm and soothing. She closed her eyes, beckoned sleep to overtake her.

That was when she heard the splash. Suzannah's eyes flew open. She could hear the turbulence of the water, only yards away from her window. Someone was in the swimming pool, she realized with an inward groan, and she knew who it was.

The stillness of the night only seemed to highlight every splash and trickle from the water below. Sighing, Suzannah sat up in bed. He couldn't stay in very long. It was too cold. She turned to the window, considering calling out a request that he confine his aquatic frolicking to the morning hours. Then she rose, and walked over to the window, thinking she might close it.

The moon was three-quarters full, and once her eyes adjusted to the light she could clearly see the figure of Craig Jordan in the pool below. Her window overlooked the pool's back wall. She watched him swim a rapid lap, and then emerge directly beneath her.

For a moment, her heart thudded to a halt as a liquid weakness invaded her every limb. Craig hadn't worn a suit. He was standing, mere yards away, in glorious, statuesque nudity. Every line and supple curve of his naked body was clearly visible to her in the moonlight. She couldn't help but see what his skimpy shorts had left to her imagination, now revealed.

A throb of pure unadulterated desire went through her like a quake as he turned to the pool again, rivulets of water glistening all over his supple frame. Riveted, she took the physical beauty of the man in, her mouth feeling dry. Then he arched through the air, diving with athletic grace into the water.

Suzannah turned from the window, feeling weak-kneed. She climbed slowly back into the bed, suddenly wide awake. As the noises continued to float in through the open window, she lay back, eyes screwed shut. Unfair, she thought, with a grind of teeth. For the second consecutive night, that infernal man was going to keep her from a good night's sleep.

CHAPTER FIVE

HE WAS BENT over the lawn mower just a few yards away. She had to stretch to reach the top of the hedge, and as she did so, she couldn't help noticing the fit of his jeans. Perfect. In fact, he had the kind of body jeans had been invented for . . .

Snip.

But then again, he looked just as good in shorts. For that matter, clothes weren't really the crucial factor . . .

Snip. Snip.

As she knew all too well, after last night's glimpse of . . .

Snip-snip-snip-snip-snip-snip . . .

Hold it.

Suzannah lifted the shears from the hedge and stepped back, realizing she'd just trimmed a little *V* where a straight line should have been. Biting her lower lip, she squinted at the hedge, and wiped a bead of sweat from her forehead with the back of her hand.

Damn the man. How was she supposed to concentrate on hedgetrimming when he insisted on . . . well, being there, so close by? Unfair.

You hired him, remember? she told herself, exasperated, and forced herself to stare at the hedge, even though out of the corner of her eye Craig was clearly visible. He was ambling around an elm tree, the sun glinting off the highlights of his wavy hair, and tiny sparkles of perspiration on his muscular forearms . . .

Snip.

She funneled her field of vision down to the shears in her hand, narrowing her eyes. She had a feeling he was looking at her, so she did her best to appear immersed in studying the top of the hedge: a little crooked, yes, but certainly . . . trim. Self-consciously she pulled the bottom edge of her bathing suit down with one hand as she held the shears aloft. Of course, he couldn't see the bottom of her bathing suit from where he stood. She glanced down, noting that her own perspiration was causing the top of the blue one-piece maillot to cling to her breasts, vividly outlining each curve. Time to put a shirt on? But it was too hot. Besides, the hedge was still shielding . . .

Good God, Suzannah! she groaned inwardly. What is the matter with you?

Snip. Snip-snip-snip-snip-snip-*snip!*

She felt, she realized, with a shudder of chagrin, as if she were back in high school again. Not since then had she been so painfully aware of every move she made in the presence of a man. But then, when he looked at her, she reflected, the feelings she experienced went far beyond the scope of a high school crush. No, she felt more like a full-grown—and sinfully lascivious—female. He looked at her then, and her body responded with a subtle, inward unfurling, as if she were a slowly blossoming jungle flower, full of moist, heated petals turning scarlet as his gaze caressed them . . .

"What are you doing?"

Suzannah dropped the shears, which, by a fortuitous miracle, missed her bare feet as it sunk, blades downward, into the grass. Craig wasn't talking to her, she saw, whirling in the direction of his voice. He was standing at the base of the elm, staring at a branch just above his head, which latter he was shaking with an expression of incredulity. Suzannah stepped around the hedge, looking up at the tree in curiosity as the branch rustled. Then a plaintive yowl rent the air.

It was one of the little leviathans, who had somehow clawed its way up the trunk and was perched now, fur bristling, and eyes wide in hysteria, a few feet above Craig's head. How did you get me into this mess? the cat seemed to be saying, looking for all the world as if someone else had just deposited it there as a practical joke.

"Hold this, will you?" Craig asked, handing her his rake as she joined him, looking up.

"Oh, poor thing!" she exclaimed. The cat meowed again, ears straight up, eyes comically widening as Craig put a foot up against the trunk and readied himself for the rescue.

"That poor thing better have had her nails trimmed," Craig grumbled.

Suzannah suppressed a giggle as she watched him carefully, gingerly balance himself against the trunk, slowly reaching both arms up with the painstaking caution of someone defusing a bomb. The cat dug into the branch, stiffening as Craig stretched and his hands crept closer. For a suspended moment, neither cat nor man moved—and then, with the lithe, lightning grace of a high-jumping athlete, Craig was in the air—and a yowling ball of fur streaked from the branch.

For the next brief moment, Craig was Davy Crockett sporting a live coonskin cap. With a yelp of pain, he grabbed his hair, executing a second swift ballet jump into the air. And then, as Suzannah bent over, convulsed in helpless laughter, he was sitting on the ground, hands clapped to his temples, the cat a distant scurrying blur, zooming to safety in the house.

"Are you all right?" she managed, as he glared at her from the ground.

"I'll live," he muttered, inspecting his fingers for blood.

"That was brave of you," she said, unable to stop smiling.

"Uh-huh," he said, gingerly feeling his ear. She could see the drops of blood on his fingers. With an involuntary exclamation of concern, Suzannah knelt by him in the grass, inspecting his wounded ear.

"It doesn't look too bad," she murmured, her fingers brushing the hair away from the reddened scratch behind his earlobe. The scent of him, a blending of fresh shaving and soap smells and the musky, sweet-salty scent of his sweat, seemed to linger in the air as she stepped back, suddenly self-conscious again.

His look was one of wry amusement. "Glad I could provide some entertainment," he said.

She smiled again. "You should have seen yourself," she murmured, shaking her head. "You looked so . . ."

Lovable, was the word that sprang, unbidden, to the tip of her tongue. Blushing, she closed her mouth, as he gazed at her expectantly. The air between them seemed to tingle as his eyes held hers. Suzannah straightened up, folding her arms across her chest. "Funny," she said, awkwardly, and stepped back.

Craig squinted up at the sky, then returned his gaze to her, his eyes raking her body with a seemingly casual glance that gave her that budding flower feeling again. "It's getting hot," he noted. "You've got the right idea—I should have worn my suit."

"Yes," she said, still covering herself protectively with her arms. "I . . . I was thinking of taking a quick dip. When I'm done," she added.

"That's the advantage of being both management and employee, I guess," Craig said. "It's not every gardener who can jump into the pool they've just tended, you know."

His tone was light, but Suzannah still felt irked by his reference to her supposed higher status. "Really? I know another one who's certainly been taking advantage of the facilities here."

Craig chuckled. "Touché. Say, I hope I didn't keep you up with all that splashing around."

She turned to look at him. Did he have any idea of the effect his midnight skinny-dip had had on her? She could almost imagine, by the twinkle of amusement in his dark eyes, that he did. And a few other ideas, as well.

"I barely noticed," she said. "Must've been cold, though."

"Invigorating," he said. "Your hedge is a little lopsided."

Suzannah followed his eyes to the place where she'd left off clipping. She had cut it down too low on one side. "Whoops," she muttered. "Well, I'll balance it out."

She lifted her shears but Craig stopped her, his hand gently arresting her arm. A tiny current of electricity seemed to pass from his soft fingertips to her skin, and she found herself allowing the familiar contact to continue. She merely looked at him, waiting, somehow not intent on pulling away, though she knew she should be.

"I'll take care of it," he said. "You've done enough . . . more than an hour's work, I'm sure. It was nice of you to help."

"It's okay," she said. "I'm enjoying myself."

"You are?" His hand slid up her arm to come to rest on her bare shoulder. It was tempting, as he gently turned her to face him, to drop the shears into the soft grass and just let herself melt into his strong arms. Her so-called resistance was nonexistent when he touched her like this. "I'm surprised," he continued. "Wouldn't you rather be on the tennis courts? Or getting your massage?"

His mocking words brought her back to reality. Suzannah stepped back, politely but firmly removing his hand from her shoulder. "I don't play tennis," she said evenly. "And I've never had a massage in my life."

"No?" His look was playfully sorrowful. "That's terrible. No wonder you seem so tense."

"I am not tense," she told him tersely. The smile he gave her at those words didn't help.

"You should really let me loosen you up," he suggested. "I know where all the standard tension spots are located—"

"I bet you do."

"And I'm very good with my hands."

"I'm sure you are," she said dryly. "But listen, if we're going to be together for a while, do me a favor: Stop needling me about what you imagine to be my corrupt upper class values. I'm not a Rockefeller or a Vanderbilt, I'm a person just like . . . you," she finished uncertainly. "Kind of. I mean . . ."

"You don't have to explain," he said.

"I've been trying to explain," she went on. "What you heard on the phone yesterday was an act. I'm just trying to make a sale, remember?"

"I remember," he said cheerfully. "Sorry to get on your case."

"Okay," she said, flexing her shears. "So let me straighten out this hedge."

"Fine," said Craig, and he stepped aside for her as she brandished the shears.

Suzannah had managed to reclip only a few little branches before his words, still sticking in her craw, caused her to whirl around again. "Besides," she called, halting Craig in midstride as he headed for his abandoned mower, "What's wrong with playing tennis, anyway? Or being able to get a massage if you need one? Wouldn't you like that option in your life?"

Craig considered this, arms folded, gazing at the wisteria beyond her. Suzannah was struck with an entirely inappropriate sense of admiration for the graceful lines of his body as he struck his casual pose. She shook the thought from her head.

"There's nothing wrong with it, I suppose," he said quietly. "I guess I just associate that kind of a life with a certain kind of . . . superficiality. And you don't strike me as a superficial person."

"Well, even us deeper sorts have to eat," she joked, flattered in spite of herself by his assessment.

"At Ma Maison?" he asked, with a raised eyebrow.

Suzannah sighed, and put down her shears. "Listen," she began, walking over to him. "I like this house. I like the pool, the grounds, even that ridiculously plush car. And I appreciate every bit of it. It doesn't mean that's what I'd do with my money if I had that kind of money, though. I'd live more simply, but with style, that's all. Is it so wrong to aspire to that?"

"No," said Craig.

"Then what's the problem?" she demanded.

Craig gave her a long look, his velvet brown eyes searching and intense. "It's just a shame," he said quietly, after a moment, "that you have to try so hard to be something you're not in order to get what you want."

His words had the ring of truth. Suzannah looked away. "It's only a game," she said. "If I can get into the so-called right places, soon enough I'll be free to act any way I please—once I've made a name for myself. Isn't that the way it goes?"

"Sometimes," Craig said slowly. He obviously had more to say on the subject, but she saw him rein in his seriousness, shaking his head with a self-deprecating smile. "But who am I to say?" he said breezily. "You know a lot more about this sort of thing."

"That's right," she said, but she was suddenly not quite as sure that she did.

A few hours later she felt anything but sure. Sitting in the back of the Rolls Royce, she nervously checked her reflection in her hand mirror. Had she struck the right balance between casual and chic? She was wearing her most expensive design—a subtly striped gray and white knit skirt and matching pullover that hugged her body's lines snugly, set off with a loose, oversized jacquard jacket in the same taupe and white tones in a different pattern. With the simple white blouse showing under the V-neck of the pullover, the outfit gave her an air of sophistication and casual elegance that pleased—she fervently hoped—by its very simplicity. The clothes she was planning to show had more daring patterns, brighter colors, but they were dresses and skirts, variations on the same three cuts. What she had on, she imagined, made her seem more businesslike and monied.

Normally, in San Francisco, she might have added a loose tie or her favorite worn and slightly battered gray felt fedora, for the fun of it. But this wasn't a fun-oriented trip. Checking her natural pearl earrings—a pair borrowed from Aunt Lucille's dressing table drawer—and then running a comb through her bangs, Suzannah closed the mirror with a snap and looked at the delicate Tiffany watch—Aunt Lucille's of course—on her wrist.

"How's the weather back there?" Craig called from up front.

"Fine," she called, with an attempt at bravado. But in truth, she was dreading having to go into her act, and having to ride with Craig up front and her back here made her all the more self-conscious. "How do people do this?" she mused aloud. "It's so *weird*..." She looked at the overly large back seat next to her. "Do they just... ignore the driver?"

"Of course, ma'am," Craig said, poker-faced in the rear-view mirror.

"Would you stop calling me ma'am?" she asked testily. "At least until we get there, please?"

"Yes, ma'am," Craig said.

"You're having a grand old time, you are," she muttered.

A better time than she was, she suspected.

"It's a great little buggy," he said, patting the wheel.

"I'm glad you—oh! There it is! Rodeo Drive," she exclaimed.

Craig nodded, and turned when they reached the light. Suzannah leaned back, her face pressed up near her window, watching the procession of expensive looking shops as they moved in slower traffic down the famous thoroughfare. Jewelry, clothes, chocolates, clothes, a restaurant, clothes . . .

"Good God," she murmured. "Every other store here's a clothing store! There's Giorgio Armani . . . and a Gucci store . . . and, hmmm . . . something new is opening up here . . ."

"C.J. Young," said Craig, following her gaze.

"Really? Oh, yes, I'd heard he was opening a store in Beverly Hills!" She craned her neck for a better look. "Are you sure? Where do you see a sign?"

From what she could tell, the store, whose windows were still brown-papered, could have belonged to any number of designers. Two burly workmen were loading a naked mannequin, carried casually under their arms, a sight that didn't seem to faze any of the wealthy looking pedestrians that peppered the sidewalk.

"It's . . . ah, on that crate there, isn't it?" Craig said, but as the car accelerated suddenly, she couldn't get a look. "Sorry," he said. "We were holding up traffic."

"Hope it opens while I'm still here," Suzannah mused.

"Why?" Craig asked casually. "Is he any good?"

"C.J. Young? Sure," she said. "He's one of the best . . . well, in America, at least."

"Oh," Craig said. "The Europeans are better?"

"Some would say," she mused, noncommital.

"What do you like about his clothes?"

Suzannah glanced at the rearview mirror. She didn't really comprehend why someone with Craig's philosophy would be so interested in designer styles. He was probably keeping her talking to put her at ease. She appreciated it. "Well, he doesn't go in for all that overexpensive, fancy stuff," she told him. "It's quality materials but relatively reasonable. Functional, but smart."

"I like the sound of that," Craig said.

"And I guess I like him," Suzannah rambled on, nervously smoothing her skirt, "because he's not one of those jetsetters. You don't see pictures of him hobnobbing with Jackie O. You don't see him at all, actually. Apparently the guy shuns publicity. He likes to let his work speak for itself. I admire that."

"I see," said Craig.

"But then again, maybe he's as bad as all the rest. Only he's horribly ugly," she mused, "so he hides himself. Who knows?"

Craig cleared his throat. "Here we are," he announced. "Annabella's."

He pulled the car over to the curb as Suzannah's pulse accelerated. He quickly hopped out, and walked around the hood in front to reach her passenger door. Suzannah watched him, noting that in black trousers and a white button down shirt with a tie, he passed for a chauffeur quite easily—an incredibly handsome chauffeur, of course, but that wasn't in itself suspicious.

"Here you go, ma'am," he said, holding out a hand to help her from the car. And then, dropping his servant's demeanor for a split second, he whispered, "Good luck."

Suzannah shot a glance at the plate-glass front of Annabella's. The brightly lit interior revealed a salesgirl, two customers, and an older woman hovering in the dressing room area—all looking out at them. Suzannah quickly turned away. Craig had shut the door, and was standing by. He looked at her expectantly.

"Should I wait here, ma'am? Or—"

"The clothes," she whispered nervously. "You're supposed to get the clothes out of the trunk and bring them in for me."

Craig stared at her, a peculiar look on his face. "Oh," he muttered. "I hadn't thought about that."

"Craig!" she implored. "They're watching!" What was wrong with him?

Craig was looking around him uneasily. Suddenly he snapped to, and reached into his pocket. "Right," he muttered, and put on a pair of large, black-rimmed sunglasses. As she stared, perplexed, he smoothly moved to the trunk, and got out the two suit bags. She stole another look at the window of Annabella's, feeling a little rush of self-consciousness. Was she making a complete fool out of herself—or making the right impression?

"After you, ma'am," Craig said pleasantly, his voice muffled a bit by the suit bag he was holding in front of his face.

"Are you okay?" she whispered, still not understanding why one would put sunglasses on to enter a building.

"After you, ma'am," he repeated.

Maybe he was feeling as self-conscious as she was, and awkward about acting like a servant. Shrugging, Suzannah took a deep breath, then walked resolutely to the open glass door of the boutique.

Inside, she headed directly for Annabella. It could only be she, wafting perfume and waving long fingernails as she came forward, her long lashes fluttering with a quizzical air.

"Hello," Suzannah said brightly. "I'm Suzannah Raines. We spoke on the phone yesterday . . . ?"

"Of course," Annabella said, crinkling her heavily made-up face into the facsimile of a smile. "So glad you could drop by."

Suzannah turned to Craig, who still seemed to be shielding himself with one of the two suit bags. "You can just leave those there . . . Craig," she told him.

"Yes, ma'am," he murmured, and put the bags down on the high stool nearby. "Will that be all?"

It was still disorienting to have him ma'am-ing her. For a moment, Suzannah just stared at him, even more disoriented by the sunglasses. "Oh, yes . . . that's fine," she said, recovering herself.

"What time would you like me back, Miss Raines?" he asked. "Or should I wait?"

As Suzannah hesitated, not used to making such decisions, Annabella stepped in. "It shouldn't take too long," she said. "Why don't we just take these into the back . . . ?"

It didn't take very long at all. Craig hurried over to relieve her of the suit bag as she emerged from the boutique less than fifteen minutes later. As he deposited her clothing in the trunk, Suzannah tried to keep up her carefree front, nodding pleasantly as he held her door open for her. Only when they were easing back into traffic did she close her eyes and let out a long and shaky sigh.

"No luck?" Craig asked.

"Nope," said Suzannah.

"Bag didn't feel much lighter," he observed. "She wasn't interested?"

"Oh, she was interested," Suzannah said grimly. "In Jacqueline Terry. What she wears, where she eats, who she sees . . . and she was interested in a whole lot of people I certainly don't know anything about," she went on, leaning back against the plush upholstery and wincing. "I must've invented more gossip than Louella Parsons ever did on a good day. But I didn't sell any clothes."

"Your style wasn't to her taste?"

"I guess that was it," Suzannah reflected. "But you know, she barely *looked* at the things I brought her. She just pumped me. Who did she think I was, *People* magazine?"

"She thought you were rich and famous," Craig said. "Or at least a friend of such. Wasn't that the idea?"

"Well, sort of, but . . ." Suzannah let out another sigh. "So much for beginner's luck."

"Don't get discouraged," Craig said sympathetically. "You're just scratching the surface. There are tons of places here, you were just saying so."

"I know," Suzannah said glumly. The thought of carrying on this charade with myriad store owners over the next few weeks was not at all appealing. "Craig," she said, leaning forward. "Why don't you pull over?"

"Ready to try another?" he asked, surprised. "Now, that's showing some spunk."

"No," she said. "I'm just tired of looking at the back of your neck. Couldn't I ride up front now?"

She could see the smile spread across his face in the rearview mirror. "You know, Miss Raines, I believe that's one of the nicest things you've ever said to me," he drawled. "At least, since I've been in your employ. But really, what would people think?"

"Very funny," she growled. A moment ago, she'd felt he was on her side. She'd wanted to be closer to him. But once again, he was reminding her of the differences that separated them.

"Got to keep up appearances," he was continuing. "So I wouldn't advise it. But if you'd like to look at the rest of me . . ."

His eyes met hers in the rearview mirror. For a split second, a vivid memory of his handsome naked male form darting through the moonlit water made her squirm uncomfortably in her seat.

"I'll be glad to oblige you in the privacy of Canyon Drive," he finished.

Suzannah cleared her throat. "Thanks, but no thanks," she told him stiffly, and leaning over, she pulled the glass divider between front and back seats shut. Turning her eyes to the vista of cars and palm trees on all sides of her, she tried to concentrate on something other than the driver. Riding in a chauffeured Rolls suddenly seemed to have limited charms.

CHAPTER SIX

"NOT TO WORRY, COOKIE," Lila said. "The woman obviously has no taste. But I have excellent news for you."

"Oh?" Suzannah looked warily at the receiver in her hand.

"Steven's wife has fallen in love with that back-buttoned thingy you gave me, and she wants to come by and see some more."

"Who's she?"

"Deidre Mills," Lila said. "The director's wife. Isn't that fantastic?"

"Is it?" Suzannah asked, afraid to get her hopes up.

"Oh, it is. Now, let's arrange a lunch for tomorrow . . . ?"

Craig was rummaging through the massive refrigerator when she came back into the kitchen. He'd already changed from his tie and pants to his gardener's outfit, and she was once again slowed by the sight of his bronzed body in motion. "Everything in the world but mustard," he muttered, straightening up. "What did your guardian angel of fashion have to say?"

"I've got a prospective buyer coming over," she said

worriedly. "Here, tomorrow . . . for, I don't know, high tea or something."

"A Lila connection?"

She nodded. "The director's wife. I can't figure out if I should be insulted or not."

"Insulted? Why?" He paused in the act of putting a swiss cheese and ham sandwich together.

"Well, she said something about my clothes having a wonderfully unrefined look to them," Suzannah said. "Is that a backhanded compliment or what?"

Craig raised an eyebrow. "She does sound sort of snooty."

"I think so." Suzannah frowned. "Well, if she's got cash to burn I guess I can put up with some condescension. At any rate, I've got a lot of work to do."

"Work? What do you mean?"

"I noticed some loose buttons when I showed the clothes today. And there's one dress that has to be restitched up one side, it's hanging wrong. Plus, I'm in the middle of a skirt—"

"Hold it, hold it," Craig said, waving his sandwhich at her. "What you need is a little rest and relaxation. You're working yourself into an unnecessary panic here."

"I am not," she said defensively. "I just want to show the best stuff I've got."

"You're showing your nervousness," he said, shaking his head. "That won't attract customers."

"Do I seem that . . . ah, high-strung?" she asked, taken aback.

Craig put his sandwich down, slapped his hands free of crumbs, and walked over to her. "Turn around," he commanded.

"What are you doing?" she said uneasily, as she turned.

"Relaxing you," he muttered, and before she could protest, she felt his hands grasp her shoulders, beginning a gentle kneading that instantly sent delicious waves of soothing sensation through her tensed-up muscles.

"You don't have to . . ." she began, but the words faltered. His strong, nimble fingers seemed to hone in with unerring instinct on the sore spots at the base of her neck. "Ooooh," she breathed, giving in with a slump of delighted surrender. "That's . . . good."

"You're all knots," he murmured. "Does this hurt?"

He'd begun a more forceful rotation with his thumbs at the top of her spine. Suzannah was unable to reply for a moment. Wonderfully near-painful yet exquisite feelings were coursing through the muscles around her shoulder blades. "Umph," she managed. "Hurts good."

"Ah-ha," he pronounced, and he began slowly massaging a path down her back, then up again, with efficient, constantly moving strokes. Suzannah closed her eyes, leaning back into the pleasurable pressure of his strong hands. A fantastic warmth trailed in the wake of his fingers. She was a limp lump of malleable clay in his expert grip.

"You are . . . good at this," she mumbled. She could feel the length of him close behind her, smell the musky-clean masculine scent of him surrounding her. As he gently but forcefully circled the tender tension points at the sides of her neck, Suzannah fclt she was ascending to some higher plane of pure physical delight. Her skin tingled where his fingertips pressed. An intense inward shiver traveled the length of her body.

"See?" he murmured at her ear, his voice low and husky, his warm breath delightfully ticklish. "You do need to relax more."

"Where . . . did you learn to do this . . . so well?"

"I've had a few massages myself," he said. "Not professional ones, of course," he added quickly. "That's for the higher-bracket crowd."

Briefly, Suzannah wondered who had ministered such masterful touches to the man who held her captive in the palms of his hands. Was he referring to some lessons learned in the bedroom? The undeniably sensual aspect of the way he was molding and melting her body brought a flush to her cheeks as the thought flitted across her happily muddled mind. Tell him to stop, she told herself dreamily. But when she parted her moistened lips, no sound came out.

"Now, before you go back to work," he said softly, rubbing a firm path down both slopes of her shoulders. "Why don't you take a break? I was thinking of going out to the beach for an hour or so. You should come with me."

At the moment, she would have followed him into the Sahara. Suzannah forced her eyes open. It was a deliciously inviting prospect, like playing hookey on a day when there were tests to take in school. "An hour?" she whispered, her head rolling to one side.

"Sure," he said. "Fresh ocean air's just the thing to clear your head. And there's nothing like a sunset for colorful inspiration . . ."

It sounded heavenly. "I shouldn't," she sighed.

"You must," he said.

"Okay," Craig said, looking back at her as he revved his motor. "Hop on."

Suzannah hovered on the driveway curb, struck with a nervous foreboding. At first, taking a ride on Craig's motorbike had seemed like an enjoyable way to travel. But now, the prospect of having to wrap herself around him gave her pause. Apprehensive, she readjusted the strap of her helmet. "You're sure it's big enough for two?"

"Don't be silly," he scoffed. "Come on."

Suzannah steeled herself, then climbed onto the little seat behind Craig as the motor puttered and revved beneath her. Gingerly at first, she put her arms around Craig, trembling as her bare knees and thighs locked into place around his jeans-clad legs.

"Hold on tighter than that," he said. "I don't want to lose you when we hit the open road."

Suzannah swallowed, shifted her weight slightly, and then hugged Craig's firm midriff tighter. His taut, trim muscles were warm to her touch beneath the thin T-shirt he wore. Try as she might, there was no way to avoid pressing her chest against his back as they pulled away from the curb.

"Don't be afraid to squeeze!" he called, as the motor roared louder.

"Right," she muttered, her heart pounding.

Then they were moving fast, faster, and the wind whipped her hair clean out of her face and the road flew out from beneath her. With a little gasp she held on tighter, her pulse accelerating as Craig picked up speed. It was scary, but exhilarating, being exposed like this—a first for her, who had shunned motorbikes all her life. Now, as they whizzed down Canyon toward Sunset, she began to understand their attraction.

Craig took some chances that made her breath catch,

snaking his way around slower moving cars and zooming into the fast lane. The wind was a loud whistle in her ears. Her eyes were tearing. She held his taut, solid frame as tight as she could, no longer wary of hugging his thighs with her own. She found herself reveling in the protective warmth of his body, that was shielding her from the stronger wind. Her own softer curves seemed to mold effortlessly and perfectly to his firmer lines. Her whole body hummed with the steady vibrations of the motor and her inner zinging happiness.

"It's great!" she shouted, as they rounded a curve, leaning together to one side at the road's slope.

"I know!" he called back.

A goofy grin spread over her face. When they slowed to stop at a light, her body was still vibrating and she felt abnormally light-headed. There was an ostentatiously gleaming silver-gray Bentley alongside them. Suzannah glanced over at the driver, who looked ridiculously stiff in his impeccable suit, and his companion, dressed in an incongruous safari-like outfit. Instead of young and beautiful, they struck her as pompous and old before their time, in the confines of their airtight luxury auto. She suddenly felt years younger, herself, out in the open air, with disheveled hair and the flush of unrestricted velocity in her cheeks.

"Hold on!" Craig called.

They were off again. She began to vicariously enjoy the game he played, of trying for an unbroken series of lights, speeding up and slowing to make it work, dodging and darting between the cars. When he narrowly avoided an accident running a red light, instead of screaming as her heart jumped into her throat, she found herself giggling, wildly, caught up in his devil-may-care sport.

Soon she smelled the ocean in the wind. The road had flattened, and there was less greenery, only the ubiquitous palm trees. Relaxed now, she held on less tightly as they struck a consistent speed. At first she'd found it odd to be in such physical contact with Craig and not be able to carry on a conversation, but she'd gotten used to it. She felt connected with him in a more intimate way, joined with him in the adventure of the open road.

They were on the highway now. She recognized the scene of her crisis, only a scant few nights before. Craig was driving them to his former home. As they turned down the unmarked driveway, and he slowed to a snail's pace, she tapped him on the shoulder. "Is it okay to go down here?" she called.

"My friend won't mind," he assured her. "The beach is big enough for all of us."

When they reached the bottom of the drive, there wasn't any sign of habitation anyway. Climbing off the bike, Suzannah felt dizzy. Her feet were on the ground but her body seemed to still be traveling at a faster speed. "Doesn't look like he's here," she noted, wiping the tears from her cheeks.

"Who?" said Craig, as he put the kickstand down, leaning his bike against the hedge for extra support.

"Your friend—the guy who came back?"

"Oh." Craig glanced towards the little beach house. "I guess not. Come on."

He swung his little pack over his shoulder, a canvas bag she'd seen him load onto the back of the bike before they took off. Suzannah followed Craig to the beginning of the white sand, and, as he paused to take his sneakers off, she did the same. The sun was a big orange ball over to the left as they started over the dunes. The sand felt wonderfully warm around her bare feet, and although the wind was fairly strong, she still felt warm all over from the still-lingering imprint of his body against hers.

"This is my favorite time of day," Craig said, as she fell into step alongside him. "Well, this and sunrise. Look at those colors."

Suzannah followed his gaze to the gently sloping line of little dunes, where purpling crevasses, shadowy blue bluffs, and golden sand competed with the ocean's foamy green and the deep blue of the sky for the eyes' attention.

"Gorgeous," she murmured, stopping to take it all in. Gulls circled the breaking waves a little farther out from shore. The only people visible were distant sticks and dots where the shoreline formed a little cove, big cliffs of dirt and rock jutting out into the breakwater. She took a deep breath of salt-sea air, listening to the falling and rise of the waves and the calling of the gulls. Then a rustle of canvas behind her caused her to turn around.

"No, don't move," said Craig. "I want to get this . . ."

He was removing his sketch pad and a bundle of colored pencils from his sack. As she watched, nonplussed, he sat down abruptly in the sand, squinting up at her with a crooked smile.

"You can't be serious," she said, looking down at herself, embarrassed. She'd dressed casually, for comfort, in lightweight khaki walking shorts and a soft, ribbed peach tank top, a simple, asymmetrical thin brown leather belt her only accessory. Her hair was no doubt in complete disarray.

"You look lovely," he said, with a simple earnestness that made her heart beat a little more forcefully. He gazed up at her, pulling one pencil from the bunch. "Those soft earth tones, and the rose in your cheeks, with that sunset alongside . . ." He shook his head. "A vision. Don't worry, this will only take a few minutes."

Suzannah shrugged, feeling completely self-conscious, albeit flattered. She didn't know what to do with her hands, so she shoved them into her shorts pockets, and looked away from him, trying to concentrate on the gulls.

"Perfect," Criag murmured. From the corner of her eye she could see his hand moving quickly over the broad white page. Flexing her toes in the warm white sand, she shivered as the wind rose briefly, then relaxed again, feeling bathed in the warm rays of the dying sun.

"You're fast," she said, stealing a glance at his work in progress. She could see there was already a lot of color on the sheet. Four different pencils lay discarded at his feet. "Do you do this a lot?"

Craig nodded, his eyes darting from her to his lap and back again, the colored pencil moving even when his gaze was elsewhere. "All my life," he murmured. "And of course, I still do my own drawing when we've got a new—" he broke off suddenly. "Whoops. Broke a point." He leaned over to rummage in his sack.

Suzannah stared at him. "What were you saying?" she asked. "Who's we?"

"We?" He frowned, picking up another pencil. "Did I say, we?" His hand flew over the pad. "Oh . . . it's just an expression I use," he said smiling sheepishly. "Referring to my muse. We—she and I. I meant to say, I do a drawing when my muse and I get a new idea . . . for, ah, an image. Like now, for example. Here we go." He dropped his pencil and held the pad out in front of him to look at it.

"I'm afraid to see," she said. He certainly was the romantic sort, she reflected. Few men she'd met believed in muses.

"Just a quick sketch," he said gruffly. "Bare outlines."

Suzannah knelt down next to him, letting out an involuntary exclamation as she saw the paper. There was no mistaking her—her posture, her profile. He'd captured the essence of her with a bare minimum of lines, drawn with surprising deftness. The colors were impressionistic, brighter and bolder than the realistic sunset hues. Suzannah couldn't deny there was something charming in the way she was portrayed, seemingly carefree with bare shoulders raised slightly, hands shoved in pockets, a wisp of hair caught in her lips, which were just two perfectly proportioned red lines and . . .

"A hat!" she cried. "But . . . that's amazing!"

"Just an old fedora," he said mildly. "You don't mind, do you? A little artistic license."

"You don't understand," she said. "I have a hat like that, at home. It's just the sort of thing I'd wear, with this outfit. . . . I mean, if I'd thought of it . . ." She shook her head. "You're good," she told him. "You've really got a flair for this sort of thing. Has anyone ever told you ?"

Craig looked at her, his smile lines deepening. There was a look in his eye she didn't quite know how to interpret. "Well, I've never really taken it that seriously," he said. "You think I have talent? You're not just being friendly?"

"Not at all. You've got an eye. And for a man, you've got something even more surprising," she said thoughtfully, studying the drawing. "A sense of lines . . . of the clothing. And that hat, it's a very professional touch."

"Just an idea," he said, folding the pad. "Actually, with a subject like you . . ." His eyes glimmered with a sensuous, teasing look. "Just the hat would be enough. No clothes at all—now, *there's* an idea."

"I told you I wasn't a model," she said, pouting. She was trying to hide the wicked shiver of excitement racing up her spine as he looked at her, his provocative gaze seeming to strip the clothes from her body. Craig chuckled, collecting his pencils.

"Wait," she said. "Don't I get to keep it?"

"The drawing?" He shrugged. "Not one of my best. A trifle."

"Well, don't throw it away," she said. "Give it to me."

"If you insist." He nodded. "When we get back."

"You should keep at this," she said thoughtfully, as he packed his pencils up. "I know you . . . artist types often have a prejudice against it. But maybe you could try some commercial work."

"You really think so?" He smiled. "No, I'm sure someone with your talents would be able to get work easier than I would. Clothing's more practical."

"Not necessarily," Suzannah said, getting up as Craig rose. She dusted the sand off her knees and walked with him toward the water. "Of course, if you were going to do some kind of graphic design work you'd have to practice certain things."

"Oh? What sort of things?"

"Well, you left out my feet," she mused.

"I've never liked to bother with them," he admitted, smiling. "But it hasn't stopped me."

"Well, maybe not from drawing for fun, but . . ." She narrowed her eyes at the horizon, considering. "I don't know, maybe there's somebody I know from design school who could give me some names . . . you know, some agencies here in town that hire free-lancers. Would you be interested in trying your hand at something like that?"

Craig looked at her, amused. "Well, I don't know. But I appreciate your being . . . so supportive."

Suzannah shrugged. "I think you're good."

"Thank you. And I think you're . . . a special kind of woman," he said quietly, his gaze holding hers. "One in a million, I'd say."

"How's that?" she laughed, feeling embarrassed by the frankly admiring look in his eyes.

"A lot of people wouldn't extend themselves to strangers, the way you have," he said. "You hardly know me, but you've done a lot, and not for any ulterior motives, either."

"Ulterior motives?" She looked at him, confused. "What does that mean?"

"Well, in my experience, most people want something in return for the favors they give. Most people don't take an interest in you for who you are, but for what you can do for them."

"What could you do for me?" she blurted, in genuine puzzlement. Then, realizing her words might have been unintentionally offensive, she added, hurriedly: "I mean, beyond what you already did—that first night, remember? You were the one being friendly to a stranger."

"Ah," he said quietly, with an ironic smile. "So you think I'm good for nothing."

"No," she said, feeling her cheeks redden. "That's not what I meant."

"I'm good for something?" he asked, the sunset picking up the teasing twinkle in his eye.

"Well, I . . ." She paused, feeling stuck on the spot. As he stepped toward her, she felt her pulse quicken. His eyes were gazing into hers with that soft magnetic pull she'd come to know so well, that she'd been trying to resist for so long now. "You . . . you've been a great help," she managed.

"You don't mind having me around?" Clearly, he was enjoying teasing her.

Suzannah met his gaze straight on, knowing he was flirting, but for once, unable to keep herself from flirting back. "No," she said, a smile playing about her lips. "You're not a *complete* nuisance."

"Then you think I'm a useful sort of guy," he said. "But you've barely tapped my resources, you know."

"No?" He was stepping closer. She stood her ground. "What talents have I overlooked?" she asked wryly.

"This," he said softly, pulling her closer. Then his soft and supple mouth was touching hers with feather lightness. As she felt his fingers moving through her hair, drifting across her bare shoulders, it was she who increased the urgency of their kiss, without thinking, swept up in the moment.

She was feeling a hot flush of excitement surge through her, filling her every cell with a fiery life, and she didn't think to question what was happening. His mouth drank in the sweetness of her parted lips and then he deepened his kiss, his tongue teasing at hers. She was acutely aware of her breasts straining against the thin cotton tank top as he pulled her against his chest, conscious of his hands slipping possessively down her back, caressing the lines of her spine, then resting gently on the curve of her hip.

Yes. It was the only word that filled her mind, a word that didn't need to be spoken. There was a yes in the way she arched her body up to meet him, her arms locking around his neck, her fingers seeking the soft thick hair. There was a yes implicit in the hungry seeking of her tongue as it meshed with his, and it was echoed, in silent agreement, by his taut muscles against her, the rough heat of his demanding mouth.

She heard a sighing moan as he molded her pliant body closer to him, but couldn't tell if it was she or he who'd made the sound. A rushing noise was filling her ears, the sound of wind and sea and passion. The virile, masculine scent of him filled her nostrils, mixed with the salty ocean air. His hands were gently cupping the curves of her buttocks and she could feel the evidence of his arousal against her loins. The warmth of spiraling desire rose from the center of her in waves. Her heart was pounding at a dizzying rate.

Suzannah felt the smooth muscles of his shoulders move beneath her tightening fingers, felt the heat and strength of his taut thighs pressing hers. Time seemed suspended as his lips' satin softness covered hers, his rougher, sweet-salty tongue more languorously exploring the wet recesses of her mouth. She felt herself melting against him, her resistance replaced by a delirious surrender to the yearnings she'd felt from the moment they had met. Hazily she realized just how much she had wanted this, ached for his kiss and his caress for days on end now.

The unexpected shock of icy water splashing over her feet and ankles ended her moment of blissful infinity. Rudely awakened, her eyes flew open and she pulled away from Craig, shivering. He caught her wrists as they slid from around his neck, though, and held onto her as the wave turned to froth on the sand behind them, then retreated.

"Suzannah," he murmured. The look of glowing desire in his dark eyes was suddenly somehow fearful to behold. What had she done? How could she be giving in to him so recklessly?

"You're right," she said, her voice shaky. "You do have

other talents. That was quite a demonstration."

"We were just beginning," he said quietly, emphasizing the *we*. He tried to draw her back to him but she resisted now, shaking her head.

"No, that's . . . quite enough."

Craig let go of her wrists. He cocked his head to one side, eyes narrowing. "Why are you afraid of me?" he asked simply.

Suzannah stared at him, biting her lower lip. It was herself she was afraid of, she knew, more than him. It had been over a year since Charlie had left, a year since she'd been intimate with a man. She felt as if she was an untapped well of unrequited emotions, firmly sealed passions. Now this man who was not much more than an acquaintance was threatening to plumb that well, release those pent-up desires with the searing strokes of his commanding tongue. When she'd thought she had her inner vulnerabilities hidden under lock and key, it was much easier to forge ahead, live day to day. The thought of losing all control was overwhelming. And the last time she'd given herself over to her feelings, lost herself in unthinking love . . . pure disaster. But how could she explain all this to Craig?

"I'm just not used to . . . casual flirtations," she said, avoiding his eye. Another wave of icy froth was dancing inches beyond their feet. "It's not that I'm afraid, I'm not . . . interested."

"No?" His tone was frankly incredulous. "And what makes you classify this as a casual flirtation?"

She met his eyes again, inwardly flinching at the fiery defiance she saw in them. "Well, really, Craig . . . we don't know each other at all." She forced a little laugh. "I guess I'm an old-fashioned girl. You're going too fast for me."

"I see," he said. His gaze was searching now, penetrating. For a long moment he merely studied her in silence, the setting sun giving his face a deep, rusty-red glow. "Well, that's encouraging, at least," he finally said, his tone lighter. "You're not ruling out a future for us."

Suzannah cleared her throat. "A future? Well, as . . . friends, I guess."

"Friends?" He seemed to weigh the word on his tongue, testing it, savoring it for taste. A frown indicated that he found it wanting. "That's awfully limiting, as futures go."

Was it only physical pleasure he was after, then? Suzannah had never found it conceivable to have sex divorced from feelings. "It's the only sort of future I can see," she said. She knew that if she accepted him as a friend and a lover, she'd be lost. She already liked him too much as it was. What sort of a future could she hope for with a man like Craig? He represented exactly the aimless sort that she was striving to get away from.

"Well, I hope your vision improves," he said, with a smile. "Because I don't intend to hide the fact that I want you, Suzannah—and in more than a friendly way."

Again the water splashed over her bare feet. She stepped back, unable to stop her trembling. Hugging herself, she turned away, trying to project a more careless air. "You're making things difficult," she called over her shoulder.

"No, you are," he retorted easily, falling into step alongside her. "But if you're intent on putting up barriers I'll just have to scale right over them—or coax them down," he added, thoughtfully. "That's probably a better approach with you."

His badly reasoned logic brought a smile to her lips in spite of herself. "You seem to think you know me well," she said.

"Enough to want to know you much, much better," he said, with a breezy confidence that brought a different kind of shiver to her body.

Suzannah stopped in her tracks, gazing at the molten rim of sun as it descended into purple-gray clouds that formed a jagged line above the ocean. "It's cold," she murmured abruptly. "Shouldn't we be heading back?"

"If you want," Craig said. "But I could warm you up . . ."

She felt him behind her, and then his arms slid gently around her waist. The firm, hard lines of his body felt wonderfully warm and protective against her softer curves, but she forced herself to step away. "No, thanks," she said, with a warning in her voice.

"Stubborn Suzannah." He chuckled. "All right, then, we'll go." He pointed to the sand where their sneakers and his pack and pad rested. The rising tide was only inches away. "Not a moment too soon, I guess."

She trudged up the sandy slope after him and they gathered up their belongings. Still, she couldn't resist taking a moment longer to watch the sky deepening in a dramatic vista of purple, navy blue, and wispy gray and red wisps of cloud.

"Now there's a valuable thing," Craig murmured at her side. "That doesn't cost a penny. You can't get those colors, you know—not framed, blown up, or in a piece of yarn. Though we can always try."

Suzannah nodded, understanding him perfectly. There was a blue in the morning skies of San Francisco she always wished she could somehow cut right from the air to put into a patchwork dress. And a view like this was truly priceless; elemental, raw, and wild, nature's most casual feats could easily overshadow the gilded canvases any wealthy art patron might collect.

"Ocean sunsets head your list, I suppose," she said. "Of those best things in life . . . ?"

Craig smiled, nodding. "Although the feeling of riding a motorbike with Suzannah Raines wrapped around me might nudge sunset watching from the top. Sunsets only engage one or two senses. But you—"

"Then put your sneakers on," she interrupted, not wanting to hear more. His flattery had a way of undermining her antiseduction stance. "If the ride's any colder than this, I'm liable to bruise your ribs with a wrestle hold," she joked.

"I can take it as tight as you give it," he grinned.

She did have to cling to him more forcefully on the way back. Without the sun, the wind whipped right through her bare skin. By the time they'd reached Aunt Lucille's in the deepening dusk, her teeth were chattering. They headed directly into the kitchen for some hot coffee. Suzannah was glad to see that Craig was keeping his distance now, and keeping up a less aggressive banter as well. Maybe he'd taken her words on the beach to heart.

"What's for dinner?" he asked, as the teakettle began whistling.

"Pot luck," Suzannah said. "Every man for himself. Now that you've forced me to waste so much time in blissful relaxation, I have to get right back to work. I'm just going to grab a sandwich and head upstairs."

Craig clucked his tongue. "I see I'm a bad influence. Tell you what . . . you go ahead. I'll put some sandwiches together and bring them up. You know, as a butler might . . ."

Suzannah shot him a withering look, but the friendliness in his face dispelled the sting of what might have been sarcasm. "Actually, that would be nice," she said. "Could you bring up the coffee, too?"

"Of course, ma'am," was his poker-faced reply.

In her makeshift workroom, Suzannah forced herself to get organized with all due haste. A part of her wanted to linger lazily over that sunset, and the devastating kiss that had briefly inflamed her . . . before she came to her senses, Suzannah remembered. And the sensible thing to do now was to get her sewing materials in order, fast.

She was immersed in running a test spool of thread through the cranky Singer—it always resisted being carted and shoved around, and its needle holder was out of alignment, as if in protest—when a soft knock on the door to the little bedroom distracted her. "Come on in," she called, but couldn't look up, busy as she was adjusting the tiny screws in the silver machinery.

But of course, once Craig was in the room, concentration became difficult. The now-familiar masculine scent of him close by and the delicious aroma of freshly brewed coffee were enough to cause her to abandon, for a moment, her repair work.

"Where do you want it, lady?" Craig drawled, in the manner of a mock furniture mover.

"Wow," she exclaimed, catching sight of the tray he'd prepared. "Put it, oh, I don't know, on that little card table."

He'd made a giant, triple decker sandwich out of cold cuts, lettuce, and tomatoes, hunted up some potato chips, and poured sparkling mineral water into a cut glass tumbler. The tray, a gargantuan mahogony job obviously ferreted from one of Lucille's cupboards, was decorated with a tiny bouquet of freshly cut daisies next to the steaming coffee.

"You really do have a designer's eye," she said, shaking her head. "And where did you get the vegetables? From out back?"

Craig nodded. "Will that be all, ma'am?"

Suzannah smiled. "Quite," she said, in her best imitation

of a British dowager. "In fact, Craig, you've done more than enough—rilly, you have."

Craig smiled. "There's more coffee if you need it later. Planning to burn the midnight oil?"

"Could be." She stood by the tray, shaking her head. "Seriously, I really appreciate this. Thanks for going to all the trouble . . ."

"Well, I made an identical plate for myself." He shrugged. "So it wasn't entirely altruistic." He turned, heading for the door. "Good luck with your work. I'll see you in the morning."

"Oh." She looked at him. Ironically, after her big speech at the beach, his more distant manner was oddly disappointing. She was tempted to ask him to stay, so they could eat together, and be . . . together. With an inward sigh, she looked back to her sewing machine. "Okay," she said. "Well, goodnight, then. Thanks, again."

He nodded pleasantly, and opened the door. She nearly had to bite her tongue to keep from detaining him. Suzannah watched the door open, and his handsome frame go through it. When the door shut quietly behind him, she stood, bewildered by her feelings.

So that's it? a voice in her head asked plaintatively. No goodnight kiss? No more attempts at melting away resistances with those strong, warm arms . . . ?

"That's it," she murmured aloud. The phrase came out more forlorn than firm. But it was for the best . . . wasn't it?

CHAPTER SEVEN

"THANK YOU," said Deidre Mills. "How lovely." She picked a sandwich from the silver tray and deposited it daintily with long fingernailed fingers on the plate in front of her. Then, smoothing the napkin in her lap, she leaned forward to inspect the tea service on the wicker table, as the tray moved on.

"Fabulous," Lila said, shaking her head. "You really do know how to do a tea, Suzannah."

Suzannah had no idea how to "do" a tea. She was piloting blind, with the help of stalwart copilot, Craig Jordan. He was standing before her now, tray in hand, bending slightly to proffer her little sandwiches, his face serene and seemingly remote.

"Ma'am?" he said politely, deadpan, as she merely looked from the tray to him and back.

"Oh," she said, snapping to. "Thank you." Suzannah picked up one of the sandwiches, noting with rising admiration for this man's hidden talents, that the crusts had all been trimmed, as she gathered they were supposed to be.

"A pleasure," Craig murmured, so softly, and so close that she was sure neither of her two guests in the sunlit den had heard. Suzannah smiled at him, then quickly dropped the smile, befuddled again as she'd been for quite some time. She couldn't get the hang of it. How were you supposed to act toward a butler? She'd never had the occasion to figure this particular bit of social politesse out. And then, how were you supposed to act toward a butler who wasn't a butler, really, but a sensually magnetic hunk of masculinity whose very presence raised your body temperature an extra ten degrees? That was a question she didn't think could be looked up in Miss Manners.

"Excuse me, ah..." Deidre Mills was trying to attract Craig's attention.

"It's... Craig, isn't it?" said Lila.

He was already at the older woman's side, head cocked in a perfect pose of subservient expectation. "Yes, ma'am."

"Do you have any skimmed milk?" Deidre asked. "I really would prefer it to this cream."

Without thinking, Suzannah began to rise from her seat, fully prepared to dash into the kitchen. But Craig was already nodding, and moving in a sort of sideways-and-backward step to the door. Flustered, Suzannah sat down again, her eyes riveted to his retreating figure. Head held high as if it weren't quite attached to his body, Craig had somehow managed to navigate a path out of the room without looking where he was going. His absolute equanimity in this role was amazing. She was almost ready to believe he really *was* a butler.

Then, out of the corner of her eye, she caught him balancing the silver tray on top of his head as he went through the doorway. Mortified, Suzannah stole a glance at Lila and Deidre. They were intent on sipping their tea. Suzannah cleared her throat and picked up her own teacup, exhaling a deep breath.

"How long will you be in L.A.?" she asked Deidre. "Lila tells me—"

A crash from the hall interrupted her. Suzannah winced as her guests looked to the doorway, then she barreled on. "—principal photography is supposed to be completed within the next few weeks. Do you plan to stay any longer?"

"Well, Mitchell usually likes to do some wheeling and dealing while the editing begins," Deidre began. "And of course, I like to shop."

Suzannah smiled, as Lila laughed and raised her teacup in salutory agreement. But as the director's wife continued to talk, Suzannah's mind was down the hall, listening for the sounds of sandwich platcs and tray being picked up off the floor. Funny guy, she muttered silently. He was having a grand old time.

It had been Craig's idea to play butler at this afternoon tea. She wondered now if he'd offered to help more as a chance to make fun of her than to make things easy. Suzannah had been nervous, running late due to oversleeping after a long night's seamstressing, and woefully unprepared for the arrival of the famous film director's wife. Craig had volunteered for service, saying he'd take care of everything, which he had. But she sensed a subtle subtext to his charade, aware as she was of every move that he made. This is how the idle rich live, he seemed to be saying to her, as he served and bowed, and made himself so visibly invisible: ridiculous, isn't it?

"She's not the Queen," he'd reminded her, when she'd begun running about in a panic, twenty minutes before Deidre's arrival.

"No, but she could probably afford to buy all of my clothes, and Canyon Drive, if she took a liking to it," Suzannah had told him.

"Maybe she'd like to buy a used Rolls," he'd joked. "Or a recently repaired motorbike . . ."

"Maybe you could put a shirt on," she'd said dryly.

"Or maybe a tux?" he'd suggested, looking down at his T-shirt and bare feet. It was then, as Suzannah groaned in mock despair, that he'd gotten his bright idea. Shooing her out of the kitchen, he'd taken command.

And now here he was again, composed as before, bearing a little milk pitcher on his tray. Suzannah forced herself to ignore him as he came in, and tried instead to pick up the thread of Deidre's discourse.

". . . and so many parties," she was saying, pulling back a lock of carefully coiffed blonde hair from her ear to reveal the sparkle of a small diamond earring. "There seems to be one every night."

Suzannah nodded in what she hoped was the properly sympathetic mode. She felt Craig's gaze upon her and tried to ignore his lifted eyebrow.

"But then your shopping pays off perfectly," Lila said. "Without the parties, where would you wear your new clothes?"

"How true." Deidre smiled.

"And darling, speaking of new clothes," Lila said, giving Suzannah a quick little wink. "Bolt down the rest of your tea, will you? Suzannah's got some things here that are . . . to die!" she said, with a dramatic flailing of wrists.

But Deidre Mills did not expire. She hemmed and hawed—complimenting, appreciating, but not buying—for the better part of a half hour. She seemed to be a woman who could not make up her mind. Everything Suzannah showed her was perfect, absolutely, but . . . too . . . something-or-other for her. Suzannah found her spirits flagging in the home stretch, as she despaired of pleasing the woman. When she left Suzannah and Lila alone for a moment, to wash up before departing, Suzannah was convinced the tea had been a fiasco.

"Sweetie, not at all," Lila said consolingly. "She's like that. But she may come round. She's got things on hold at practically every store in Los Angeles. Then when the mood strikes her, she pounces on something she remembered seeing somewhere. Don't worry . . . just give the old girl some time."

"Will that be all, ma'am?"

Suzannah looked up. Craig was standing expectantly close by. Oh, come on, she nearly said, the party's over. But the look of tacit compassion for her situation she saw in his eye stopped the beginnings of crankiness.

"Yes, Craig," she said quietly, unable to suppress a small sigh. "Thank you . . . very much."

He nodded politely, averting his gaze, and began clearing the table.

"Besides," Lila said, "you'll be coming to Reggie's tonight, won't you? I'll introduce you to some more folks."

Deidre had invited her to a soirée being held at another director's home that night in the Hollywood hills. "Oh, I don't know," Suzannah said worriedly. "I'm not sure I'm up for it. Besides, I'd really have to dress up, and none of my own stuff is really formal or extravagant . . ."

"You must come," Lila said firmly. "Don't you have one evening dress sort of thingy?"

"Not really," Suzannah answered, frowning.

"Come anyway," Lila said. "I'm sure you can fix something up. There's more than one reason to go . . ." She paused significantly, turning to watch Craig, who was gathering the last silverware on his tray. Only when he'd left the room, moments later, did she speak again. "There are some very interesting people you could meet," she said, *sotto voce*. "Some eligible bachelors, for example."

Suzannah laughed. "You're not setting me up, are you?" she scoffed. "Do I look lonely to you?"

"Well, now that you mention it, not exactly," Lila said, with a meaningful glance toward the door. "You certainly can't complain about how difficult it is to find good help these days."

"Lila," Suzannah began, reddening. "I told you. Craig's just doing some gardening. There's nothing going on between us."

"Like hell," Lila said sweetly. "If I lit a match around you two the room would explode. You're positively combustible."

"Don't be silly," Suzannah said. "Craig and I . . ." She couldn't think of how to finish the sentence, though.

"Don't *you* be silly," Lila said, narrowing her eyes. "Honey, he's gorgeous, and I'm sure he's simply mounds of fun, but you should be meeting men who are going places, or better yet, have already arrived. Reggie's will be full of them and gorgeous women such as yourself . . ." She snapped her fingers. "Bingo! So you're coming tonight. I don't care if you wrap yourself in a drape like Scarlett O'Hara did."

Deidre had re-entered the room. Lila did one of those social hairpin turns she was so good at. "Deidre, Suze and I were just discussing the crowd who'll be over at Reggie's. Don't you think she should meet Daryl Brady? He's coming, isn't he?"

Deidre gave Suzannah a shrewd once-over and nodded. Suzannah, embarrassed, tried to steer the conversation back onto clothing. Deidre expressed interest in one particular dress that she wanted Suzannah to put aside for her, thus confirming Lila's prediction, and then the two women were on their way. When she'd seen them out, promising Lila she'd make an appearance at the party that evening, Suzannah shut the door and then leaned back against it, suddenly exhausted.

"Craig?" she called. Her voice echoed through an empty house. Suzannah took a quick tour of the downstairs environs, then stepped out into the back. There was no sign of her gardener-cum-butler, and a quick inspection of the garage area told her he was off the premises completely, since the motorbike was gone. She assumed he'd gone into town on some errand or another, and she walked slowly back into the house.

She realized it was the first time she'd been alone—but for the cats—since she'd come to Lucille's. Restlessly, she paced around the spacious living room, suddenly at a loss as to what to do with herself. The idea of trying to figure out what she could possibly wear to Lila's chic soirée was very anxiety producing. She'd brought mainly casual stuff with her to L.A., and half of it needed ironing or cleaning . . .

Laundry. That was the thing to do, a good, healthy, and mindless task. One of the great advantages of Lucille's was its on-the-premises washer and dryer. It was a luxury someone from a walk-up in San Francisco who spent too many hours at the laundromat could really appreciate. Suzannah quickly gathered a bagful of items upstairs and then marched down to the basement, trailed by a couple of curious cats.

As she loaded the spic-and-span oversized modern washer, Suzannah kept thinking about what Lila had said. Was it so obvious that she felt . . . something for Craig, and he for her? Was it written all over her, that when he was around, she found it hard to concentrate on anything else?

About to turn the machine on, she remembered that what she was wearing needed washing as well. Suzannah took off her jeans, socks, and shirt, added them to the load, and began the cycle. Clad only in panties and a white T-shirt that was merely wrinkled, not dirty, she slowly ascended the basement stairs, trying to sort out her feelings.

There was no denying her attraction to Craig. Yesterday on the beach, it had taken a great deal of willpower to resist his seductive advances. And he certainly hadn't made any secret of his wanting her . . . Images of that sunset and the glow that suffused her when she was in his arms made her knees go a little wobbly as she rummaged about the kitchen for a snack. Thinking about how he'd held her, and brought long-dormant feelings to life with his lips and tongue had made it doubly difficult to sit in that sunny den and be served by him. It had seemed too absurd, when all she wanted to do, really, was be held in his arms again...

But Lila was right. It was Charlie, all over again, a great physical attraction for a man who had little else to offer, in the long run. Craig seemed more solid, somehow, confident and aggressive, but... he was a drifter, wasn't he? Sometimes artist, sometimes... whatever, moving aimlessly from odd job to odd job. Suzannah sighed. If only she were more like Lila, if she were capable of having fun with a man and letting it go, letting herself go! But if she let herself go with Craig, she had a sneaky feeling she'd be truly a goner. She was already missing him when he wasn't around...

Charlie, Craig, Craig, Charlie, Suzannah mused, peering into the cupboard for some crackers. Now Charlie was simply a case of a man who couldn't make up his mind. He'd gone from unsuccessful job to unsuccessful job, promising each time that the *next* was his true calling. And when failure had started to get to him, going from one little flirtation to another had seemed a good idea... and finally going, period, when Suzannah couldn't stand his being unfaithful and his unwillingness to try to change things. But Craig... all he needed was to set his sights. She felt that very strongly. And he'd succeed. After all, she mused wryly, he'd set his sights on wearing her resistance down. And hadn't it worked?

A persistent buzzing from beneath her stopped her reverie. Was the wash done already? Suzannah looked up at the kitchen clock. How long had she been sitting here, aimlessly toying with a piece of cheese and some crackers, thinking about that man? Too long. She rose, and walked into the pantry, then down the basement stairs. She transferred the load from washer to dryer, and then started up the steps again.

"There you are."

Suzannah froze in midstep. Craig was standing at the top of the stairs, the undisguised interest in his gaze making her feel more naked than she actually was. Heart thudding unnaturally loudly in her ears, she paused, acutely aware that her thin T-shirt left little to the imagination. She did not know whether to retreat or move forward.

"What . . . Where did you go?" she managed, trying to sound casual.

"Ran out of shaving cream," he said, his eyes making a languidly appreciative tour of her body from ankles to thighs and beyond.

"Oh," she said, feeling absurd, perched midway up the stairs. "I was . . . doing laundry. I have to go to some party tonight," she rambled on, not knowing why she felt a need to explain. "And I don't have anything to wear."

"I see," he said, his eyes twinkling with amusement. "Yes, I couldn't help overhearing . . . the fabulous Reggie's."

Suzannah folded her arms protectively, nudging the edge of the T-shirt down to more modestly cover her midriff. "I don't really want to go," she told him. "But I feel like I should."

"Of course you should," he said. "But from what I gather, you would want to wear something more . . . glamorous. Say . . ." He cocked his head, as if struck by a thought. "Have you checked upstairs? Maybe there's something in your aunt's wardrobe you could borrow."

Suzannah stared at him, thinking. "Well, I couldn't . . ." Actually, she reflected, Lucille was tall, too, and while somewhat heavier was still—more-or-less—Suzannah's size. With some careful belting here and there . . . It wasn't such a farfetched idea. "Maybe I could," she said. "I'll take a look."

Craig nodded. "Want a beer? I picked up a few odds and ends."

"No thanks," she said, waiting for him to clear a path. He did, with an amiable nod, and Suzannah quickly vaulted the remaining steps, hurrying through the kitchen as Craig unloaded a grocery bag behind her. She went directly to her room upstairs and donned her robe, then padded down the thick carpeted hall to Aunt Lucille's bedroom.

Her aunt had one of those great old-fashioned walk-in closets full of clothes, as well as a mirrored armoire bulging with sweaters and accessories that included some lingerie Suzannah would have thought too provocative for a woman her aunt's age . . . or perhaps even her own. But that was Lucille.

In the closet was an embarrassment of riches. Most of the stuff, however, just wasn't to Suzannah's taste. The more expensive dresses and gowns were either too flamboyant or too out of style. Stepping back, her eyes growing confused by the riot of color and fabric, she suddenly noticed a hanger right in front with something on it that caught her attention.

It was a bright red cardigan of silk crepe over a hip-stitched pleated skirt that had a look of absolute up-to-the-minute, drop-dead chic about it. At first she couldn't believe such a thing possible; she'd drooled over this outfit in *The Times* fashion issue just a few weeks ago with an ache of unrequited desire. It was C.J. Young's most extravagant creation, at the top of his line and miles beyond her price range. But it was that very ensemble, she'd recognize it anywhere. Suzannah felt the material with fingers trembling with excitement.

"Lucille," she breathed, in a tone of reverent awe. "You've outdone yourself."

Still unable to believe her good fortune, she searched for the tag indicating the size. She'd noted that many of Lucille's clothes were a size or more too large. If fate were cruel, and this particular one . . . but, no. It was perfect! And the price tag was still on it. The outfit hadn't even been worn. Would Lucille . . . could Lucille . . . Dare Suzannah . . . wear it?

She let out a low whistle when she saw the price, only a dozen dollars higher than the current year. Seeing those four figures in a magazine was one thing, but actually having the item in front of you, and knowing you could really wear it, was something else. Pulse racing, almost afraid the silk would evaporate like a dream before she had a chance to put it on, Suzannah eased the dress off its hanger. She dared. She had to. She would treat it with utmost care, have it dry-cleaned at Hollywood's finest establishment—Lucille would understand. Suzannah just knew it.

With trembling hands she discarded her T-shirt and slipped the skirt on, luxuriating in the feel of the fine material. Perfect fit. Fingers still trembling, she unbuttoned the matching cardigan and put it on. She'd never felt so sheathed in sweet luxury. She knew most of C.J. Young's clothing was more casual, understated and unflashy than this. The reclusive designer prided himself on making clothes that were worth more for their craftsmanship and durability than for their frills. But for his new spring line he'd introduced a few choice things that were transcendant in their simple elegance. And this was the pick of the lot.

Sweater buttoned to the sexily plunging V-neck, Suzannah stepped out of the closet area to view herself in the standing mirrors. The hem of the skirt was resting on the floor as she posed, but that was because the dress obviously called for heels. She pulled the skirt up so the line of it was unbroken, then struck a modellike position, hands demurely clasped behind her back, head tilted slightly with chin to shoulder. Batting her eyelashes at the brilliantly red, red figure before her, Suzannah had to admit she looked—

"Fantastic."

Suzannah whirled round in a rustle of silk crepe. Craig was standing in the doorway of Lucille's bedroom. Feeling like a child caught with her hand in a cookie jar, she dropped her pose, and nervously clapped a hand to the soft cardigan's V, covering her cleavage.

Craig was striding slowly across the carpet now, his eyes traveling with undisguised admiration over every curve and pleat of the red dress. Her mouth suddenly dry, Suzannah bit her lip, self-conscious under his intense scrutiny, and turned back to the mirror, her hand still lingering around the top button of the sweater.

"It's something, isn't it?" she said, shivering slightly as he kept coming, stopping only a foot behind her. "I had no idea Aunt Lucille was so up on current fashion. What do you think?" She sounded girlish to herself, but there was no way she could mask her excitement at the dress and her nervousness at his silent appreciation.

"You're a beautiful woman," he said quietly.

Suzannah shook her head. "It's a beautiful dress," she corrected.

"No," Craig said simply. "You know what the French say? When you compliment a woman's dress, you mean that she herself is not attractive, or the dress doesn't really suit her. But to say the woman is beautiful is a compliment to both."

She saw him in the mirror, then, right behind her. A chill stole down her spine as her eyes met his in the reflection and he stepped closer. She felt the tall, supple strength of him against her, inhaled the subtle musky scent of him, felt his warm breath graze her ear. Spellbound by the picture before her, she didn't think to protest as his arms came forward, sliding past her waist. Gently his hand closed over hers, and he slid it from its modest perch, as his other hand lightly smoothed the pleated skirt.

Holding both her hands captive now at her side, he held her gaze a moment, the darkness of his eyes smoldering with a liquid intensity that quickened her breath. The soft silk-molded globes of her breasts rose and fell. She could see the pulse she felt beating at the base of her neck.

Then his lips covered that spot as he held her, a willing prisoner against him. The soft thickness of his hair tickled her cheek as he bent to claim the milky whiteness of her skin, kissing a wet and fiery trail from collarbone to the hollow beneath her ear. Suzannah closed her eyes, a breathless moan escaping her parted lips.

As he brought his tongue and teeth into play, nibbling at her earlobe, Craig slowly glided her hands up with his own, sliding them over the exquisitely soft material until her palms beneath his lightly cupped her breasts. Curling tendrils of arousal spread through her body as she felt the rosy tips of her breasts tingle and ache into hardness beneath her own hands, still held by his.

It was then, as the quiver of desire that coursed through her threatened to become a quake, that Suzannah opened her eyes once more. She was looking at a lovely woman in red . . . herself, as if through the gauze of fairy-tale vision. For a brief, magical moment, she was enchanted. But the prince . . .

. . . didn't look like a prince. A man, a too-real man in faded blue jeans and bare feet, his T-shirt stained with the green of grass and brown of earth—that was the handsome hero who held her, his forearms lightly dusted with a spray of dark hair now glistening with sweat. It was as if a wrong chord had been sounded in an ethereally wafting melody, or a spatter of mud had marred the silver perfection of a still pond's reflection. The spell was broken. For a jewellike moment she had been seeing herself transported to some higher realm of richness and royalty. But now she felt the hard floor beneath her feet.

"No," she whispered, and she stepped forward, freeing herself abruptly from his embrace. When she turned around to face him, breathless and upset, she didn't recognize the man for a second. Was it Craig who looked at her in mute, hurt resentment? Or had it been Charlie she'd expected to see . . . the man she'd thought to be her white knight, the man who promised her roses and rhapsodies, then dashed all of those dreams to harsh realities of sordid, sullen poverty and hopelessness?

"No?" he asked softly, his eyes clouding as they searched hers for an explanation.

"I'm sorry," she murmured. "But . . . it's wrong. I can't, Craig."

He was watching her hands, she realized, as she unconsciously smoothed and resmoothed the silk, as if she were trying to erase his touch. "Ah," he said slowly, his lips setting into an ironic smile tinged with a faint bitterness. "I spoiled the picture, didn't I?"

Again her eyes betrayed her, shifting to his wrinkled T-shirt and his faded jeans, as she shook her head helplessly. "I'm just . . ." she began, feeling her cheeks flush as he registered her gaze.

Craig chuckled. "I realize I'm not dressed for the occasion," he said, his smile broadening, though his eyes were devoid of amusement. "But you know, beneath it all, we're just a couple of humans . . . like creatures, with mutual desires."

"You're assuming a lot," she said, more stiffly than she'd intended. His words were striking too close to the truth.

Craig shrugged. "You're repressing even more, Suzannah."

Now the twinkle was back in his eye. His mocking tone was even harder to bear, though, and she turned away. "Maybe it's true that *men* are all alike," she said evenly. "Too smug to take no for an answer."

"Or too smart to accept it so easily," he retorted breezily.

Suzannah shot him a look. "I have to change, if you don't mind," she said. "In private?"

Craig nodded, his eyes sweeping over the outfit as if memorizing it for some future savoring. "The guy who designed that thing ought to see you in it," he said. "I have a feeling he'd think his work had been enhanced."

"Thank you," she said awkwardly.

"You're welcome," he answered, and he left her with her mirrors.

The techno-electro-pop that boomed from the large speakers at Reggie's party was still reverberating through her head as Suzannah navigated the twisting turns of Canyon Drive. She knew she was driving faster on her way home than she had when she left Lucille's hours earlier, and that this was possibly due to having imbibed three margaritas. But she felt masterfully in control of the vintage Rolls. All was right with the world. For the first time, the car felt like an old friend, and she, still radiant in her fire-red C.J. Young original, was the rightful driver of such a splendiforous chariot.

"Splen . . . diforous," she murmured, a little smile glazed on her face. There was the hedge indicating the beginning of Lucille's front property. Suzannah slowed the car and turned up the sloping driveway, switching on the brights as a warning to any vagrant felines on the lawn. Approaching the house, she squinted, trying to imagine it as a stranger might, or as Jack Baxter would. Jack was stopping by in the morning.

"Splen . . . did," she muttered, and reached over to fumble in the glove compartment for that remote control thingamajig. She found it, pointed, pressed, and watched, immensely pleased, as the garage door slid open like the door to Ali Baba's cave. As she pulled in, she noted some signs of unfinished business on the garage periphery—tools left out, garbage bags piled with cuts of foliage. That would have to be taken care of, she reflected. Things should look shipshape at sunup.

That last phrase lingered in her mind but proved too much of a tongue twister to pronounce. She found herself engaged in an unsuccessful and noisy struggle to get the door open.

"Ssssh," she whispered. "You'll wake the gardener." But the stubborn door handle wasn't responding, and a moment later, she decided, with a satisfying turnaround in logic, that waking the gardener was precisely the thing to do.

Suzannah poked the horn with her elbow, then grimaced in pain. Wasn't the horn. She found it protruding from the steering column, and gave it a series of loud blasts, short, short, short, and long. Then she sat back, closing her eyes a moment. Thinking that the car was still moving, she sat up straight, eyes flying open. Suzannah shook her head. Margaritas.

Footfalls on the stairs indicated that the gardener was now awake, if he had been asleep. Suzannah put on her most serious expression, facing the door. A moment later, Craig Jordan appeared, attired in the same pair of scanty cut-off shorts she'd seen him in the night they'd met. A familiar tug of arousal at the pit of her stomach made her squirm slightly in her seat as he approached, dark eyes wary, the soft, pinkish overhead garage light making his smooth, tanned skin look even darker. She pulled her eyes from the sexy swirl of fine dark hair on his broad chest to meet his questioning gaze.

"Why do you always walk around like that?" she asked, before she had time to edit herself. "Don't you think it's indecent?"

Craig paused by the front fender, peering in at her. "I thought I was alone," he said mildly.

"You're not," she said, and then, realizing she might be coming off haughty, she smiled. "Don't you like pajamas?"

He considered her question gravely, leaning against the fender, chin in hand. "Nope," he said at length. "I like to sleep naked."

"You would," she blurted.

He smiled. "You wouldn't?"

Suzannah narrowed her eyes. "I'll never tell."

Craig shrugged, and yawned. "Good party?"

"Yes, thanks," she said. "And you?"

Craig looked at her, leaning over to get a better view through the side window. "Just fine, thanks," he said slowly.

He was making her feel self-conscious. "Good," she said. "Well, good night."

Craig gave her a peculiar look, then straightened, smiling faintly. "Good night," he said, and with a casual wave, he turned and headed for the stairs.

It was then that Suzannah remembered there had been a reason for all this. "Oh. Craig . . ." she called.

He turned back at the door. "Yes, Miss Raines?"

Suzannah frowned at the formality. "I can't seem to get this door open."

"Oh," said Craig. "You need some assistance?"

"That would be nice."

He walked around the car to her side, and peered over the half-rolled window. "It's locked," he pronounced.

"Now, how did that happen?" she wondered aloud.

"I can't imagine," he said dryly, and deftly lifted the little knob. "I also can't imagine how you managed to arrive here in one piece."

"What's that supposed to mean?" she asked indignantly, as he opened the door for her.

"You're crocked," he said. "Sloshed. Snockered. Looped. And there are laws about driving like that, you know."

"Nonsense," she said, doing her best to retain her balance as her wobbly heels hit the cement floor. "I'm completely legal."

"Uh-huh," he said laconically. "But can you walk?"

Suzannah glared at him. She was holding onto the open door for support. She looked down at her feet; then, with a sigh, she sat back against the edge of the car seat and unstrapped her black shoes. "It's these heels," she explained. "You ever try walking in two-and-a-half-inch heels?"

"One-and-a-half's my limit," he said. "How did your dress go over?"

"Like wow," she said. "People stared. I was embarrassed." She sighed happily. "It was great."

"I'll bet," he smiled.

"Aunt Lucille won't mind—she can't. And oh, and Craig . . ." she said with renewed excitement. "I met this wonderful man who's coming to see the house tomorrow! He's a movie producer who's a friend of Lila's and he's . . ." She stopped, suddenly self-conscious.

"He's what?"

"He's, I don't know, some sort of big wheel here." Jack

Baxter had been smooth, suave, a little too handsome, and a little too aggressive. She wasn't even sure if she would have liked him without the margaritas, but she'd enjoyed his flattery and his attention for a good portion of the evening. Somehow discussing him with Craig made her feel vaguely guilty, though she wasn't sure why.

"A lot of big wheels? At Reggie's?"

There was a tone in his voice that smacked of cynicism, but she chose to ignore it. "Tons," she told him. "I met Ryan Peel, and George Morris, and . . ." She rattled off the many names, the first of which, a dashing young movie star she'd swooned over in her youth, had nearly induced the same reaction in her when he'd walked into the party. But after meeting half-a-dozen movie stars and some celebrities from many different arenas in the time it took to drink her first drink, she'd managed to conduct herself with what she'd hoped was sophisticated grace, only staring when she absolutely couldn't help herself.

"It was good promo," she told Craig, feeling the need to justify her obvious awe at mixing with such a crowd. "I talked to a lot of people about my clothes. They kept giving me their cards." She patted the front left pocket of the red silk cardigan.

"That's nice," he said, his expression impenetrable.

"And what a house!" She rolled her eyes. "You think this place is too much? This Reginald guy must be some kind of Rockefeller. In fact, there *was* a Rockefeller there."

Craig wasn't looking impressed. "Oh," he said.

His dour rain-sprinkling on her parade was starting to annoy her. "Look, I know you probably think it's all a big joke, but these people could be important to me," she said defensively. "Lila says that all the contacts that count get made at these parties and I've already gotten an invite to another one."

Craig yawned. "That's good," he said.

"It is," she said vehemently, wondering for a brief moment who it was she was trying to convince. "These are the kinds of people who dictate taste in this town—everywhere. If I can interest them in my clothes, and my best stuff catches on, well, the sky's the limit!"

He raised one eyebrow. "Is that so?"

"That's so!" she told him. "That's how the business works."

"Is it?" The mockery in his voice was more prominent now.

"Oh, you wouldn't understand," she said crossly, getting up. She half suspected he was purposely ridiculing her because of the way she had rejected him that afternoon in Lucille's bedroom.

"Maybe not," he said shortly, and he stepped back to let her pass him. The concrete was cold beneath her bare feet as, shoes in hand, she kept walking out of the garage. At the door she turned to face him again.

"Sorry I woke you up," she said, feeling hurt herself now at his coolness. She'd secretly been looking forward to seeing Craig when she got back, and telling him all the details of the evening. She'd hoped bygones would be bygones, and he'd be his usual friendly self. No luck there.

"No big deal," he said. He was staring at her in the dress again in a way that brought an unwelcome tingle to her skin.

"This Baxter guy's coming before noon," she said. "I guess we should get things tidied up." She gestured at the tools and bags outside the garage door, and Craig looked over there.

"Certainly, ma'am," he said.

"Oh—ma'am yourself!" she exclaimed, anger bubbling up like a sudden geyser inside of her. She turned and stalked from the garage, not wanting to look back. She wasn't sure if the soft laughter she heard was his or only her own imagination. Lifting the hem of her skirt over the damp grass, she hurried into the big, dark house. She should've known a man like Craig wouldn't appreciate the finer things that the fast crowd at Reggie's had a taste for—and those were the things she wanted.

CHAPTER EIGHT

"SO, ARE YOU in love, or what?"

"What?" Suzannah asked guardedly into the phone as she scanned the mail she'd just taken in from Aunt Lucille's box. She'd just ushered Jack Baxter out the front door.

"Jack!" Lila exclaimed. "Sweet pea, he's a dreamboat! And terminally loaded, to boot. When are you going out with him?"

"Lila," Suzannah sighed, gingerly pressing her still throbbing temple with one hand. "I don't want to go out with him." Briefly, she wondered if her friend was telepathic. The phone had rung as soon as Jack drove off in his silver Mercedes, and moments after he had, in fact, asked her out to dinner the following evening. Feeling both hung over and vaguely apprehensive about seeing this high powered, handsome, but slickly aggressive Hollywood tycoon again, she'd graciously declined.

"Why not?" asked Lila. "Oh . . . now don't tell me you're already head over heels with that . . . gardener of yours."

"No," Suzannah said quickly, shooting a quick glance down the hall. She hadn't seen Craig all morning. She'd been avoiding him. Had he been avoiding her? Certainly, while she gave Jack his brief tour of the house, Craig was nowhere to be seen.

"Good," Lila said. "That's the path to doom and destruction. Isn't the yard almost finished? He'll love you and leave you and where will you be, silly girl? Really, I don't see why Jack doesn't—hold the line a sec, will you, sweet?"

As Lila carried on a muffled conversation with someone else, Suzannah found a check from Aunt Lucille's lawyer made out to her amidst the mail. Craig's first week's salary, she realized. She'd have to tell him it had come, and cash it—

A shriek in her ear signaled Lila's return, her volume and excitement doubly increased. "Babycakes! It's a red letter day! You've made a sale!"

"I have?" Suzannah squeaked, her adrenalin shooting up.

"That was Deidre just now. When I told her I'd rung you up, she said, 'Make sure your friend sends that blue shift over, I want it for tonight, will she take a check?' 'Of course you will, I said—'" Here she let out another shriek of happiness. "And you will! Suzannah! Am I not the best friend you've ever had in the world?"

Suzannah assured her she was, her heart racing in excitement. As soon as she was off the phone, she ran straight through the house and out into the yard. There was Craig, visible at last near the gazebo, immersed in spading the salia flower beds.

"Craig!" she called. "Guess what! I've sold a dress!"

He looked up in astonishment, his face breaking into a broad grin as she ran breathlessly toward him. "Who to?"

"Mrs. Mills! Isn't it incredible?"

And without even thinking, she sailed right into his arms. Dizzy with her own exuberance, she nearly knocked him over. Craig hugged her close with a laugh. Only then, when she found herself looking up at him from the warm strength of his embrace, felt her heart beating furiously against his chest, did she stiffen in sudden embarrassment, and pull away.

"Sorry," she murmured, cheeks flushed, heart hammering.

"Don't be," he said, an affectionate smile on his tanned

face. "This is fantastic news. I knew you'd sell something soon."

"You did?" As she smiled back at him, she realized all her resentful feelings toward him seemed to have evaporated. She was too jubilant to hold grudges. And he seemed genuinely happy at her good fortune. "Lila just called," she told him. "They're sending a messenger over to pick up the dress and give me a check. Isn't it amazing? Oh, that reminds me . . ." Beaming, she quickly brandished the check from Mr. McGinty's office at him. "Your salary's here. I just have to cash this."

"Perfect timing," Craig said, slapping the dirt off his hands. "We'll have to go celebrate!"

"Great idea," she said, grinning uncontrollably. As they looked at each other, a pulse of happiness seemed to pass between them and then blossom almost palpably in the air. "Should I open some wine? Or let's go out to a bar or something. What do you think?"

"I think I know just the thing," he said. "Have I got the whole afternoon off, boss?"

"Sure," she said.

"Come on, then," Craig said, and he grabbed her hand. "Ever been to Santa Anna?"

CHAPTER NINE

"AND IN THE home stretch, it's Seafire by a length—Slapdash coming on strong—Houndtooth on the rail—Seafire—Slapdash, neck in neck—Seafire—Seafire, by a nose!"

Craning her neck, straining her ears to catch the whizzing commentary from the loudspeaker, Suzannah stood on tiptoe, crammed against the rail with Craig. As the crowd's screams peaked and died into a buzz, with knots of people on all sides already heading back to the winnings windows, she clutched his arm excitedly, pointing towards the finish line some twenty yards away.

"That's us!" she cried. "Seafire—"

"The results are now official," the loudspeaker overrode her. "In the seventh race, paying four-forty, three-forty and two-sixty, Seafire is the winner. In second place—"

Suzannah couldn't help letting out a little whoop of victory. After betting on two races—they'd arrived at the track midway through the afternoon's series of nine—this was her first win. She still didn't entirely comprehend the system of odds and betting, and didn't know enough inside information, which Craig seemed more aware of, but she knew enough to have lost a little money, and now, to collect some winnings.

"Ten dollars," Craig grinned, holding up their tickets. "Think you can handle it? Don't faint on me, now."

He offered her his arm. Suzannah hesitated, then took it, impulsively, letting him guide her through the milling crowd that was now leaving the rail. "I won't faint," she assured him. "But I will buy you a beer."

"I'm too well bred to refuse," he joked.

The sun was shining brightly over the oval field as she glanced back, catching a glimpse of Seafire in the distance, taking a desultory pose for the press in the winner's circle. She stole a look at Craig's rugged profile and a little shiver of arousal coursed through her as the crowd jostled her closer to him. Already suffused with the warm glow of winning after the rush of the race, she felt bold and almost wickedly audacious, letting him hold her, as they headed for the window to collect their winnings.

"I'm beginning to understand the attraction of this sport," she told him, looking around her at the broad spectrum of humanity out for a day at the races. Youngsters, old-timers, couples, men both polished and threadbare gesticulating in little semicircles in the grandstands, racing forms in hand—she'd had no idea this world existed. The track had been some nebulous gambler's coven, in her fantasy.

"It's very attractive when you're winning," Craig said, steering her round a knot in the crowd. "Here, you get on line . . ." He gave her his ticket. "I'll get the beers."

"But I said—"

"You can reimburse me," he said with a wave of his hand. "I'll meet you back here."

Still buzzing with the high spirits she'd felt all afternoon, Suzannah took her place, watching the tall, graceful figure of her escort weave his way through the colorful crowd. He seemed to stand out, somehow, she mused. Or maybe it was because . . .

Suzannah turned away, focusing on the window ahead. Come on, you know what you were thinking, the little demon voice in her head whispered. You know what that feeling you're feeling feels like, don't you? All the colors she saw were more vivid when she was with him, all the sounds more present, more musical. Everything she saw looked newer, somehow, when she saw them with Craig. She'd been feeling a bubbly, sparkling sensation all afternoon, an aliveness that seemed to swell up inside of her when he looked at her, or smiled or spoke...

He's fun... that's all, she told herself. Who else would think of taking a woman to the races for a giddy celebration like this? But that doesn't mean...

She stopped herself. The inner argument was becoming tiresome. Why was she so hellbent on convincing herself that this glow she felt wasn't some sort of, well... love? Because it couldn't be, she told herself firmly. Again, she conjured up the negatives. He was a vagrant, a drifter, an aimless... gambler, she added, smiling in spite of herself at how puritanical she was starting to sound.

Although, come to think of it, the only shadow cast on their sunny afternoon was her perplexity at his carefree attitude towards spending the little money she knew he had. So far, he'd lost more heavily than she, who only made conservative, two-dollar bets. But he kept betting even higher amounts.

Which was why, when they sat in the grandstand together, hunched over the racing form, she felt a grim foreboding as he explained his tack for the next race. "Trifecta?" she queried worriedly. "What's that mean?"

"It's a three way bet," he explained patiently. "Hold still," he murmured, and leaned forward to deftly wipe a little foam from her upper lip. Suzannah reflexively licked her lips, which tingled from his touch. He was still looking at her mouth. "Did I get it all?" he murmured, beginning to lean forward again, his eyes twinkling mischievously.

Suzannah's heart jumped. She started back to avoid his playful kiss. "Craig," she said warily. "Explain the tri... fecta to me."

"Okay," he said. "You see, you pick all three horses in the order you think they'll finish. Now, I'm betting that Lucky Breeze comes in first, Spring Shade places and Tall Saddler shows."

"But... what a long shot," she said. "How can you possibly be that accurate? You'll lose your shirt!"

Craig shrugged. "Sure, I'm taking a risk," he said, eyes

glittering with enthusiasm. "But that's what makes it interesting."

"Interesting?" she said dubiously. "But didn't you say you had a . . . a what is it . . . from your friend at the beer stand . . ."

"An inside line," he said. "A tip. That guy I know from Santa Monica says that number nine, that's Lucky Breeze, is the odds-on favorite. The smart money's going down on him, just watch the board. When it gets close to race time, the odds will shift from twenty to one, to say, eight to one."

"Okay," she reasoned. "So why not bet on Lucky Breeze, period? Why blow more money on a big risk?"

"Why not stay home in bed?" he grinned. "Lucky Breeze wins, fine, but where's the thrill? That's too easy."

Suzannah shook her head. "You're nuts," she said, but she was only half-joking. "I'm betting on Lucky Breeze. That's enough excitement for me."

Ten minutes later she was squeezed against the rail, anxiously scanning the crowd for signs of Craig. Just as he'd predicted, the odds board showed a sudden shift in Lucky Breeze's odds. She felt that twisting, queasy turn in her stomach increase as she looked down the field to where the horses were being lined up, each in their little metal closetlike quarters. She had five dollars on the new favorite, but it could have been fifty. Caught up in the excitement all around her, she waited impatiently for the race to start.

"It's post time," the loudspeaker crackled, with a burst of bugling. Craig had elbowed his way back to her at last.

"We're set," he murmured, with a grin.

"Where's Lucky Breeze?" She was straining to see.

"Second from us, yellow jockey . . . And I've got money on two and one, over by the inside rail."

"You're doing that trifecta thing? How much did you bet?" she asked worriedly.

"Seventy-five dollars," said Craig.

The gunshot sounded through the speakers. "And they're off!" intoned the announcer. "It's Papa Joe taking the lead, with Lucky Breeze a length behind . . ."

Suzannah's stomach had plummeted at Craig's nonchalant announcement. He was downright bonkers, she thought, shooting him an apprehensive glance. He'd already blown a third of his paycheck. If he lost this bet . . . Her heart was hammering. She focused on the colorful blur of jockeys as the horses sped by. The announcer spoke so fast she could barely understand his nonstop commentary.

"Come on, Saddler," Craig murmured at her ear.

The names of horses were on everybody's lips. Time seemed suspended as the brown and black, shiny and powerful figures turned a curve with thundering hooves. She'd never thought a minute and a half could seem so long. Dimly, she comprehended that Lucky Breeze was clearly in the lead, but by now she was absorbed in Craig's bet, and Craig's bet only. Spring Shade was close behind, as Craig had guessed. But Tall Saddler was straggling, no longer neck in neck with a fourth horse, but behind.

"It's Lucky Breeze, coming into the home stretch—Spring Shade—Quarter Moon coming up—Tall Saddler, by a length—Quarter Moon—"

Beads of sweat had broken out beneath her bangs. The horses seemed to be flying in slow motion on the straightaway, then on the curve they became a whizzing bunched mass of black and blue. Her throat was tight and dry.

"Lucky Breeze—Spring Shade—Lucky Breeze by nose—by a length—!"

The auctioneerlike drone of the announcer was incomprehensible above the buzz of the crowd crushed against the rail. Pushed back against Craig, she could feel his fast heartbeat matching her own.

"It's—Lucky Breeze, the winner in first—Spring Shade in second, and—ladies and gentlemen, a photo finish for third place!"

Suzannah turned to Craig, surprised to see him grinning when she felt all the color had left her own face. "Photo finish? What's that mean?"

"They've got a camera set up by the finish line," he explained. "When the race is too close for the eye to judge, they rush the photo into a minilab setup and consult the picture. Should take a few minutes, and then we'll know. Hey, you won!" he exclaimed, squeezing her shoulders. "How about that! You're going to clean up."

"I am?" she said worriedly. Her concern for Craig's reckless bet had almost completely overshadowed her own success.

"Five dollars with those odds should get you around seventy bucks," he told her.

"Great," she said, some of her enthusiasm returning. "But what about you?"

"We'll know in a minute," he said, glancing out at the track. In the distance, officials could be seen milling about the first horses being walked off the course. "If Tall Saddler took third, I collect eight to nine hundred."

"And if not . . . you lose your whole bet?"

Craig nodded. He didn't seem anxiety stricken, which to her was a wonder. She didn't know which was more disturbing, being tied in knots not knowing if he was about to become rich, or knotted the same way dreading the loss of the only money he had.

They hovered by the rail, where others who she supposed had made similar bets scanned the winning circle area. Craig was urging her to go ahead to the winnings windows, but she stood rooted to the spot, staring at the loudspeaker as if willing it speak. In a few moments, it did.

"The results are now official. In the eighth race, paying thirty-one-forty, thirteen-eighty, and four-eighty, Lucky Breeze is the winner . . ."

The voice droned on. But the only words that registered with a faint shock, was the name of the horse that had taken third place—not Tall Saddler, but Quarter Moon. She had her eyes on Craig's face. His eyes, at first narrowed in intense anticipation, opened wider in surprise as his money went up in smoke. Then his face relaxed into a rueful smile. He felt her gaze on him, and shook his head at her.

"Tough luck." He sighed. "Well, there's still one more race," he went on cheerfully, as if nothing of much importance had just happened. "Let's go in and collect your winnings."

The odd thing, Suzannah realized, as they slowly made their way to the arch in the grandstands, was that Craig's nonchalance didn't appear at all feigned. She was starting to know him well enough to at least detect when he was masking his emotions. In this case, she could tell that he'd been genuinely disappointed for a moment, but had taken the loss in stride. As they got in line his spirits seemed just as bouyant as when they'd first come in two hours earlier. She was the one who had suddenly lost her enthusiasm.

"I think we should check out Silvertone in the next one," Craig was saying. "He's looked good on his last three outs."

"Craig," Suzannah said. "I think I've had enough. Let's just cash in my ticket and go home."

"Really? There's just the one race—" He stopped, seeing the look in Suzannah's eyes. "All right," he said. "Though I wouldn't mind a shot at recouping some of my losses."

"Are you kidding?" She stared at him, horrified. He'd blown the bulk of his paycheck already. Just how foolhardy was he? "Look, I'll split what I'm getting with you, okay? And we'll call it a day."

"No way!" he scoffed. "It's your winnings. Why should you have to give up any of it on my bum bet?"

"I wouldn't have bet on Lucky Breeze if you hadn't tipped me off," she said. "So it seems only fair—"

"Don't be silly," he grinned. "That's charity, and I don't want it. If it makes you feel better you can buy me a hamburger, okay?"

Suzannah sighed. "I'll make us dinner, that's for sure. But I think you're being—"

She stopped, as he was humming the familiar opening bars of "Oh Suzannah." Pressing her lips tightly together in vexation, she turned away. Fine, she wouldn't cry for him. And, since her worst fears about his character were being justified, maybe it would be best if she didn't care for him as much as she was starting to, as well.

Craig set his wineglass down on the glass tabletop, the little ping! of glass against glass echoing against the walls that hid the pool. Since the night was warm, they'd elected to eat on the patio behind the house. The sun was already a mere band of hazy orange behind the trees, and crickets sang in the stillness of the shadowing lawn.

"You're being awfully quiet for a woman who's just launched her career in fashion," Craig said, looking at her thoughtfully.

Suzannah sipped her wine, avoiding his eyes. She had been quiet, she knew. Ever since they'd left the Santa Anna racetrack she'd withdrawn into herself. She was struggling with her feelings, trying to be clearheaded, trying, for once in her life, to give rationality the upperhand. It was painfully ironic, that just when she'd been allowing herself to admit she was falling in love, Craig had acted in a way that stopped her cold, had made her remove herself and run for cover. It's a good thing, she kept telling herself. You were starting to get involved. It was almost too late . . .

"Anybody home?"

Suzannah looked up, startled, feeling a flush fill her cheeks as Craig stared at her across the table. "I'm sorry," she said. "I was thinking . . ."

"Clearly you were," he said. "But what about?"

Stymied, she took another sip of wine, stalling, looking for an out. "Oh, plans," she said vaguely. "For the future."

"Got some?" he asked breezily.

"Maybe," she said, but his careless attitude was getting to her. "What about you?" she said abruptly, turning things around. "Craig, what are you going to do? With yourself?"

"Well, I've still got to move some rocks to dig out those beds," he said, gesturing toward the streak of salias behind him. "Got to lay some ground cover, first thing in the morning—"

"Seriously!" she exclaimed, more vehemently than she'd intended. "I mean, what are you going to do, after? Your job's almost done here, isn't it? Then what happens?"

Craig leaned back in his seat, cradling his head in his clasped hands. "Then I go elsewhere," he said slowly. "To another kind of job."

"What?" she asked, the slight buzz of wine and the more potent anger of her disappointment in him making her more confrontational than she'd allowed herself to be before. "Where? With who?"

"I've got something lined up," he said after a pause, his face darkening. "Why do you ask?"

"Because I . . . because, oh . . ." She drummed her fingers on the table in frustration. "There's so much you could do, a man like you!" she exploded. "You've got talent, you're smart, you're attractive. How can you live like this, drifting from one odd job to the next, throwing your money away as soon as you get it, never looking to the future—"

"Whoa, there, slow down," he began. "What makes you think—"

"It's a waste is what it is!" she barreled on hotly. "You're in the prime of your life, damn it. Why don't you make something of yourself? You're not like . . . like Charlie was, deep down, I know it! He was an outright failure because he never had it in him to do anything, he just dreamed he did! But you're a different kind of dreamer, aren't you? I know you could make it real—"

"Charlie?" he frowned. "Who is that?"

"My ex-husband!" she exclaimed. "Ex because he couldn't stand to face reality! He left me because my leaving him was inevitable, and he couldn't stand that either, if you want to know the truth!" she railed, too steamed up to stop. "And look at you! Why would I want to get involved with you, even if I did fall in love with you—" she blurted. "I wouldn't! That is, I couldn't let myself—oh, hell!"

Suzannah stood up abruptly, spilling over her glass of wine. With a little moan of frustration and embarrassment she kept right on moving, blindly rushing past the table onto the lawn, dimly aware that Craig had risen behind her. Her throat was tight, her stomach churning with the pent-up emotions that were now overflowing. She felt the sting of angry tears at the corners of her eyes as she half-walked, half-ran to the sanctuary of the little wooden gazebo.

Now she'd done it. That's what happened when you kept a lid on feelings too long. They exploded in a big mess all over you and you made a shrewish, shrieking fool of yourself! She clung to the rail of the gazebo's inner bench, taking a deep, shuddery breath.

"Suzannah." His voice from the doorway behind her was soft and low.

"Go away," she muttered, her face buried in the crook of her arm.

"Look at me," he said, quietly, but commanding.

Suzannah lifted her face. He was hard to see clearly in the gathering dusk, but he didn't appear to be angry. "I'm sorry, Craig," she said, trying to keep the tremor out of her voice. "I know I have no business telling you what to do. I shouldn't have said anything."

"Don't be sorry," he said. In two short strides he was at her side, taking hold of her arm with gentle but forceful fingers. "I'm glad you said it, Suzannah."

"Glad?" she said, confused to see the faint smile hovering at the edges of his mouth.

"So you admit it," he murmured, his eyes glittering in the fading light. "You care. You've fallen for me, the way I've fallen for you."

"No," she whispered. "That's not . . . I didn't . . ."

"You don't have to lie," he murmured, lifting her chin with forefinger and thumb. "The truth is . . . here."

The dark smoky velvet of his eyes held her, breathlessly expectant. And then his lips dipped down to meet hers, gently, lightly grazing her trembling softness. Instinctively she parted her lips to taste the sweetness of his mouth, a warm current of desire coursing through her from the exquisitely tender touch of her skin against his.

His mouth left hers, hovering mere inches away. "You see?" he breathed huskily. "This is what's true . . . this feeling . . ."

Now when he kissed her, his lips claimed hers more forcefully. As she pressed herself closer to meet him with an uncontrollable urgency of her own, his mouth ravished and possessed hers, exploring and then dominating her in shameless intimacy. She couldn't deny it, as a moan started and caught deep in her throat; she couldn't deny that she wanted this, wanted him, with a force that shook her from head to toe.

His body moved sensuously against hers. Suzannah slid her arms slowly up the tantalizingly warm hardness of his chest as their kiss lengthened and deepened. She felt his strong arms gather her against him, and trembled as his hands caressed her spine, fingers restlessly kneading the small of her back beneath the flimsy material of her cotton halter.

When his lips broke from hers at last, only to claim the hollow of her neck, she whispered his name, in a strangled, throaty whisper, a voice not her own. Craig was slowly planting a hot, moist trail of fiery kisses from her ear to the nape of her neck, and she arched her back, barely able to stand the ache of pleasure she was feeling, the soft lushness of her breasts pressed against his unyielding chest, her hips moving slowly against his.

"I can't . . . keep fighting it . . ." she murmured.

"The battle's over," he whispered, looking up with eyes hooded with desire. "Surrender . . ."

Her skin was tingling and hot beneath his lips and tongue

as he began to kiss a line from her neck to the hollow of her breasts. One hand pulled her hips even closer to his, gently molding the curve of her buttocks, as his other hand stole up from her hip to slowly stroke a warm circle on her side and abdomen with his palm. Every inch of skin was tingling to new life at his caress, the warmth spreading throughout her like a slow moving liquid fire.

Again he claimed her mouth, his tongue thrusting more urgently within the wet recess, seeking hers. With no thoughts of resistance, she eagerly met his tongue with hers, reveling in the taste and feel of him, quivering with arousal as his caresses brought the tips of her breasts to aching hardness. And she could feel the hardness of him, now, cradled between her loins. Suddenly their clothes seemed a bizarre constriction. She wanted to feel him against her, unbound and unrestricted.

As if reading her mind, Craig broke their kiss, and, leaning her back against the gazebo wall, he brought his hands up to slip, with tantalizing and deliberate slowness, the straps of her cotton halter from her shoulders. Neither of them spoke as he nudged the halter down, gently, and she was naked to the waist before him. His eyes roamed over the soft whiteness of her torso with the same slow deliberation, as if he'd waited too long for this moment to be hurried now. His gaze touched the quivering pulse at the base of her throat, lingered like a caress on the full roundness of each breast, and their stiffening pink tips.

She didn't move, couldn't move as he reached out to cup and cradle the full curve of one breast, his thumb slowly, lightly circling the swollen nipple, sending an exquisite quiver of arousal through her. Then his head dipped and she moaned softly as his tongue found that sensitive peak. She tangled her hands in his dark hair and felt the thick strands like an extra, feather-light caress as they fell forward, brushing the soft skin of her breasts.

The feelings that surged through her as he kissed and nibbled at one breast and then the other, his hands cupping and kneading each in turn, were indescribable and overpowering. She closed her eyes, her breath coming in deep, shuddery gasps. "Too long . . ." she murmured dreamily. "It's been too long . . ."

Too long since she had felt like this, though she realized, hazily, she had never felt quite like this, not with Charlie; she'd never felt such an exquisite welling of nearly painful arousal at a man's touch. When Craig lifted his mouth from her breast, she stiffened involuntarily, not wanting him to stop, her hands still tangled in his hair.

"For me," he whispered huskily, "the waiting's been an eternity."

She shook her head. "This isn't what I wanted to happen . . ." she began.

". . . but it's happening," he finished for her, lightly putting a finger across her lips. Then, as the straps of her fallen halter had pinned her arms to her sides, he lifted them gently, freeing her. He took both her hands in his. Gazing deeply into her eyes, keeping her locked in a shimmering current of desire, he pulled her gently toward him, walking back.

She moved with him as if sleepwalking down the steps of the little gazebo, unashamed of her half nakedness in the darkness and his smoldering gaze. For a moment they stood silently, facing each other in the short, soft grass. Then, as the moonlight broke through the gray clouds above them, he let go of her hands, and brought his own up to gently tug at the waistband of her skirt.

He slid the skirt slowly past her hips, and as he did, he bent and lowered himself to a kneeling position before her, his mouth kissing each inch of newly revealed skin. As the skirt fluttered to the grass his arms slid round her thighs, his hands lightly cupping the full curves of her buttocks, his lips covering the soft skin of her belly with moist, hot kisses that seemed to heat the warm center of her arousal to a higher flame. Before his thumbs could slip under the waistband of her panties, she stopped him, gently, kneeling down in front of him so they were face to face again.

"I want to . . ." she whispered, her hands reaching out to eagerly unbutton his shirt. With sudden brazenness, she quickly undid them all and pushed the shirt from his shoulders. Feasting her eyes on the sexy swirl of hair that had so tantalized her before, she leaned forward, kissing and sucking his nipples until it was he who groaned in pleasure.

With trembling hands she undid his belt, pulled down the zipper of his jeans, and impatiently tugged the tight fabric from his hips. He helped her, then, and in moments, the naked maleness of him was revealed, freed from the constraints of underwear. With matching eagerness he slipped her panties down and at last they were skin to skin in the sultry warmth of the moonlit night, moving together from knees to sides, lying on the cool, soft grass.

Their first embrace there was a savage molding of body to body, lips seeking lips, hands searching curves and secret hollows in a sudden surge of unrestrained passion. But then, as she lay back, he hovered above and at her side, slowly exploring every surface of her body with wondering eyes, as if his good fortune was hard to fathom.

"My God, Suzannah," he whispered, his voice thick with desire. "I've wanted to see you like this, to touch you, for forever..."

Suzannah didn't speak. She felt full to the brim with ineffable sensations. Boldly she let her eyes rove over his perfect male nudity, drinking in the strength of his long legs, firm-muscled thighs... the beautiful breadth of his chest, the strong molding of his shoulders. His fingers were lightly tracing a path from her shoulder to the softness of her inner thighs, then lingering there, tantalizing her with playful strokes that paused just before the silken inner skin, lightly tickling the curl of fine hair at her thighs' juncture.

He was watching her now, his eyes no longer surveying her pliant, supine body, but searching her eyes for signs and signals. She looked back at him, her lips parting soundlessly as he smiled with those velvet eyes, and his fingers found the silken core of her, eliciting a shuddering moan from her once again. She couldn't bear it any longer, having him beside her and yet so far away, the inches between them suddenly insufferable.

"Craig," she whispered. "Make love to me... now... please..."

"Now?" he murmured, his hand now cupping the moist mound, her legs twitching restlessly, parting at his lazy caress.

"Yes," she murmured, reaching out a hand to pull him over her.

"You want me, then?" he asked, his voice low and husky. "You do want this to happen?"

"Yes," she breathed, her hand still coaxing him to come to her. He was resisting, and staring into the glimmering depths of his dark eyes, she knew what it was he wanted. "Yes, I... I want you," she said, squirming beneath his persistent caress. "I want you!" she whispered, hoarse with desire.

Then, when he lay down beside her, wrapping her body with his own, she could hold nothing back. She was his. When his lips found her mouth again, she returned his kiss with an untamed passion that matched his own. She gloried in the weight of his hard, rugged body over hers, the wonderful roughness of his chest hair against her breasts. They rolled together in the grass, both murmuring wordless sounds of pleasure, as he fitted her body to his with increasingly powerful commands.

She hadn't thought such pleasure was possible. She'd never felt herself urged to a plateau of sweet, savage delight, only to hurtle forward, to a higher pleasure still. His lips were alternately tender and demanding, kissing the softness of her inner thighs with heartrending tenderness, then claiming the core of her quivering femininity with an urgent, masterful tongue. She cried out, again and again, not knowing what it was she said, but wanting him, feverishly, wanting him to join her, to merge with her as one in the soft grass, arching her body and pressing it to his more recklessly, until at last, he was above her, parting her legs, and then, with an exultant groan, within her at last.

Suzannah moved her body ecstatically, sinuously with his, savoring the exquisite feel of his hard strength within her yielding softness. She ran her hands over the powerful width of his back, loving the feel of his smooth skin over hard muscle. The throb of her pulse was mingling with his heartbeat as they moved as one in the fragrant darkness.

Slowly they sought the perfect rhythm, felt out and found the ultimate beat and tempo of their sensual song. Time was suspended, and all she knew was the thrilling thrust of him, and her answering, dancing hips. His hands and fingers teased her with knowing, gentle movements, then squeezed and caressed her more forcefully. His lips captured one rosy nipple, sucking its already taut peak to an ache of hardness, then nibbled their way across her swelling bosom to favor her other breast. He was prolonging every instant, every move, drawing from each touch and caress the pinnacle of pleasure.

But at last there was no stopping the passionate hurtle of their mutual desire. Wrapping herself around him, she flew with him, climbing higher and faster, the world receding, the stars above burning brighter, coming closer. She heard him whisper words of desire, of love, as their flight grew frenzied, bursting upward into light, plummeting to the very peak of ecstasy. And then she was spinning, falling, weightless through starlight, hearing only a long, low moan of pleasure and an answering groan before she felt the earth beneath her once again.

For a while they clung together in the damp grass, their bodies joined, moistness coating them, sharing a contentment that transcended happiness. She could have stayed like this forever, she imagined, saturated with satisfaction, huddled in his arms. The crickets were singing again, and the moon wore what she imagined to be an envious smile, clear and fullfaced in the sky above.

Then Craig slowly rolled onto his side, his arm slipping beneath her neck. Suzannah turned on her side, settling contentedly against him, breathing in his musky maleness mixed with the scent of the flowers of the garden all around them.

"Tell me," Craig murmured at her ear. "Now, that wasn't so bad, was it?"

She gave his arm a playful punch. "You know it wasn't," she said.

"Then what took you so long?"

Suzannah lifted her head, and propped her chin up on her elbow. Looking down at him, she frowned. "Have you always been this conceited? Or are you just letting it out more, now that . . . we're better acquainted?"

Craig let out a deep, throaty chuckle. Tracing a feathery trail with his fingers up her abdomen to the curve of her breasts, he merely shrugged. "I love the feel of you," he murmured. "I guess I'm only annoyed I haven't been able to do . . . this much sooner."

His hand was gently cupping her breast, his palm lightly pressing the tender ache of her still-taut nipple. "It's crazy," Suzannah muttered.

"Us not making love? I quite agree."

"No, you," Suzannah sighed, unable to resist moving sinuously to meet his seductive caress. "Stop that, will you? I'll overdose."

"Impossible, I'd say." Nevertheless, his hand left her breast, and he traced little circles on her hip instead. "Sorry, but I can't keep my hands off you."

"It's okay," she said softly. She saw the little smile lines at the sides of his full lips deepen, and felt a sudden surge of love for this man who'd made her feel so exquisitely womanly. She bent forward and impulsively gave him a quick but tasty kiss.

"Um," he said. "I'll take a dozen."

"Temporarily out of stock," she told him playfully. She wanted time to stop, she thought. She wanted just to lie naked on the grass with him under the moon and stars and not have to think the thoughts that still hovered around her now, like bothersome flies. Shouldn't have, buzzed one. Stupid you, taunted another. You're going to regret this . . .

"What's wrong?" he asked.

Were her expressions that transparent? "Nothing," she said. "Only I wish I had your attitude."

"Which is . . . ?"

"Live for today. Enjoy life's simple pleasures and don't worry about tomorrow's complications. That's the gist of it, isn't it?"

"Partially," he said. "And what's yours?"

Suzannah considered. "At the moment, I'm a blank slate. I'm feeling too good to think straight. But I know myself well enough to know . . ."

"What?" he asked softly, and she heard the seriousness in his tone.

"I know I'll feel like hell tomorrow," she said wryly.

"Why?"

She looked at him, wanting to share her fears with him but afraid of offending him at the same time. A little stab of longing went through her as she drank in his beautifully nude masculinity reposing on the grass. Again, she was reminded of those fantasy-feeding ads for the best designer clothes—although this particular pose would have been too X-rated for even the raciest—and it struck her that Craig looked even more attractive. He was like an archetypal model for the models themselves.

"Because . . . I'm not good at living for the moment," she admitted, quietly, looking away. "As soon as this . . . moon magic . . . wears off I'll be filled with fear and trembling."

"Afraid it won't last? This good feeling?" He reached his hand out to gently smooth her cheek. "It will," he said. "I'll see to that."

Suzannah smiled, but already she felt herself shifting, gathering herself for retreat. Anxious feelings undermined her afterglow, like a cloud covering the moon. Maybe he was sincere, she thought worriedly. But even so, even if he really cared for her as she knew she cared for him—that made it worse. Because she couldn't, wouldn't give her heart to a man like Craig, no matter how much it hurt to pull away. She'd let that kind of impulsive recklessness nearly ruin her life the last time. She'd vowed never to let it happen again.

Suzannah sat up, gazing off into the darkness. Tonight was all, she thought, with a little ache inside—it was all she could allow herself. If she got in any deeper, she might lose her resolve. Craig was stirring in the grass beside her. In a moment, he stood, stretching, his hands gently playing with her hair.

"Would you like some more wine?" he asked softly.

Suzannah nodded. Wine would help keep her from thinking, worrying . . . and panicking. She held her hand out and he helped her up. Standing naked beside him in the grass, she was surprised at how unashamed, how delightfully immodest she felt. "Where's my fig leaf?" she joked as he took her hand, and they began to walk back toward the patio.

"They're out of fashion." He grinned, casting an appreciative eye over her pale nudity. "This is the new minimal look—just a few blades of grass in the hair."

Suzannah felt the back of her head. Her hair, in wild disarray from the abandoned heat of their lovemaking, did indeed have bits of grass entangled in its curls. "It's a good thing we're not expecting company," she said, as they stepped onto the patio.

Craig uncorked the half-bottle on the table and began to pour. "This is an exclusively private party," he said gravely.

"Only the most elite of the elite." He handed her a glass. "To love," he said, holding up his own in a toast. "And the good life."

Suzannah clinked her glass against his, again feeling a bittersweet pull in her heart. It *was* love, wasn't it? But it couldn't go on. She couldn't let—Suzannah took a deep stinging gulp of wine, hurriedly trying to ward off those dark apprehensions. "The good life," she mused aloud, turning to face Aunt Lucille's grounds. "This is it, I guess."

"Absolutely," he said, following her gaze. "Too often wasted on those who don't appreciate it. I know what," he added suddenly. "Let's take a swim. It's a perfect night."

"All right," she said, smiling. "It's only fitting that I take a skinnydip with you. I've done it enough times in my mind already." She stopped, embarrassed by her honesty.

Craig laughed. "I've wanted you to join me since the first night," he said. "Come on—last one in is a party pooper."

He put his glass down, and sped off toward the pool area, with Suzannah in pursuit. It felt wonderful to run through the grass in the warm breezy darkness. Once through the gateway it was only a few running yards—and then she was flying, splashing into the cold water split seconds after Craig.

She came up sputtering, shivering in the bracing shock of the unheated pool. Craig surfaced a few feet away, his lean, taut musculature slicing the dark water with powerful strokes. Suzannah dove below, then came up in the shallow end, breathing heavily, content to rest against the side while he swam a briskly athletic lap.

Craig dove in a graceful arc below the surface. She waited, with tingling anticipation, the ripples in the dark signaling his approach. Then he was beside her, taking a few strides in the shallow water that came up even with the tan line cutting across his lower stomach. She leaned back against the smooth tile pool rim as his body met hers, deliciously wet and warm, and his lips and tongue claimed her mouth. She tasted the slightly chemical water taste and the sweet-salty taste of him, reveling in the feel of his wet, matted chest hair brushing her already taut breast tips.

"Hey, Princess," he murmured, when their kiss had gone

so deep and long that coming up for a breath was a necessity.

"Hey, yourself," she said, and she shivered happily as his arms closed around her. She could feel his hard arousal cushioned against her stomach beneath the water and she fitted herself, dreamily, to the taut leanness of his thighs. Craig bent his head, licking the soft upper swell of her breast with his hot, moist tongue, fanning the flames of desire that already flared in the pit of her stomach.

She wove her hands into the tangled dampness of his hair, pulling his head up to gaze into his eyes. His face, lit by the moonlight, was nearly painful for her to behold, with his eyes so openly adoring, glimmering so close to hers. "Oh, Craig," she whispered. "I do . . . want you, so . . ."

His smile was one of pleasure tinged with victory. His mouth took hers again, tongue greedily exploring her readily surrendered mouth. Their lips, slippery with desire, clung and melded. Then again, he bent to kiss and lick each trembling rosy tip of her breasts, until her breath came in short, shallow gasps. His circling tongue and gently nibbling teeth were driving her half-crazy with arousal.

"Love me," she whispered, her hands kneading the skin at the small of his back, fingers digging into the top of his firm buttocks. She wanted to be filled with him again in thoughtless frenzy, not caring, not worrying about tomorrow. Her hands went up to slide around his neck, and he gently parted her thighs with his knees in the shallow depths, slowly and tenderly beginning to seek the sensitive center of her desire.

"Oooh," she whispered, as his hands guided her hips to meld with his. "Can we . . . Is this . . . ?"

His chuckle was a deep throaty growl of amusement. "Sure," he murmured. He was gently but firmly leaning her back, lifting her legs, which she quickly wrapped around him, shuddering with arching arousal. He was nudging her up, his hands and lips filling her with dizzying sensations, and then, parting her, entering her with an exquisitely slow, sure thrust, his strong hands clutching her closer to him beneath the lapping water.

"Suzannah . . ." Craig moaned her name softly as she instinctively rotated her hips, bringing him even closer, deeper. She gazed into the dark eyes below thick lashes and saw the same delight tinged with awe that she was feeling as they moved slowly together.

Soon her head fell back. Trembling, sighing, her eyes closed, she moved with him in an undulating rhythm, increasing speed as he seemed to lift her higher, higher, the delirious hot, moist sensations unfurling within her and the cool wet water all around her nearly too pleasurable to bear.

Though their first time had been tender, wonderfully leisurely at first, a tender exploration of each other's every curve and hollow, there was a violent urgency now as she clung even more tightly to him. She was savage and demanding in the relentless heat of passion, shocking herself with her own unbridled enthusiasm. It was as if she wanted to lose herself in the shelter of his arms, to drive and be driven senseless in a frenzy of pure sensation.

When the moment came, and the height of pleasure burst, cometlike within her, she found herself wailing his name, face buried in the wet, salty hollow of his neck, her body shaking, rocked with ecstatic spasms. Even as their rhythm slowed, and he kissed her tenderly, his hands tangled in her hair, she clung to him, not wanting to let go, wanting the last moments to last forever. There was a desperation in the way she embraced him, and even Craig seemed troubled as he gazed at her upturned face in the flickering moonlight.

"Suzannah," he whispered. "You're crying . . . Have I hurt you?" His voice was tight with tender concern. "What's wrong?"

Wordlessly, she shook her head. Already the water seemed cold, the wind too sharp, and her shivering increased even as he soothed her with his hands and lips. "No," she whispered. "You haven't hurt me . . ."

It's you I have to hurt, she thought miserably. Too fast, too soon the harsh realities were breaking in. She realized that she had loved him so intensely now because she'd known it was for the last time. It would have to be. She couldn't make love to him again, couldn't be with him like this.

"Let's go inside," he murmured. "You're going to turn blue."

She nodded, starting to feel numb, and let Craig take over. He spirited her into the house, wrapped her in towels and then blankets. He fixed them each a snifter of brandy, which filled her with a seductive, sensuous warmth. Huddled in his arms in the bedroom upstairs, soothed by his attentions and the heat of brandy and blanket, she let herself be babied. It was easy to be taken care of, to blot out thought, and sleep beckoned, a blessed relief.

"Suzannah," he murmured in the darkness, his hands gently stroking the bangs of hair around her ears as she cuddled against him in the bed. "Don't worry . . . about us. You might be surprised at how things turn out."

Sleepily she bit her lip, moving restlessly in the cradle of his arms. "Oh?" she murmured. "What do you mean?"

"Those things you said before . . . about how you knew I was capable of making dreams come true . . . You may be right, you know."

She said nothing, only kissed the tip of his finger as it grazed her lips.

"If you have faith in me," he went on softly. "And you seem to, then don't be so concerned about my future. I may be better equipped to handle it than you even know."

His words were comforting in her woozy state, even though she suspected they were idle hopes he was alluding to. Sighing, she shook her head. "I'm sure you are," she murmured. "It's okay . . . don't talk . . ."

"Dreams *can* come true, Princess," he murmured. "You wait and see."

Her heart throbbed with an aching pang at his hopeful words. Was he that naively innocent, after all? She knew better than to count on dreams. Even slipping into sleep, the painful irony of it struck her deeply—he thought he was soothing her fears, but his unrealistic, dreamer's words were only confirming what she dreaded. Craig was living in fantasy. And she couldn't live there with him.

She shut her eyes tighter, willing back the returning tears. In the morning they would talk. She'd have to tell him, explain that their being together was impossible . . . Now, she wanted to savor the last minutes of this blissful, warm, and secure feeling. Kissing the soft skin of his shoulder, she settled even closer to him, drifting into troubled sleep.

CHAPTER TEN

THE TRAY on the little table next to the bed was perfect: fresh-brewed coffee, nicely browned toast, pink grapefruit, a little bouquet of daisies, and even the morning paper neatly folded. The sun was shining brilliantly. Birds sang in the wind-rustled tree branches outside. But for Suzannah, seated on the edge of her bed, staring morosely at the coffee cup in her hand, it might as well have been the dankest, darkest December morn. There was a black cloud hanging over her head, and it had been there since her eyes flew open at the shrill ringing of the telephone an hour earlier.

She caught sight of herself in the window. Her hair was a mess, and although there was a bloom in her cheeks something more than a good night's rest had put there, she felt pale and wan inside. As she gazed at the window, her eye was caught by something in the grass outside the gazebo. With quickened pulse, as she stood to get a better look, she recognized the glint of a metal clasp on her sandals, and the bright blue of her cotton skirt in a crumpled heap by the edge of the salias. In a rush, the ecstatic pleasure she'd enjoyed there came back to her in all its vivid glory. She turned away from the window, feeling a flush fill her cheeks.

She'd have to pick the clothes up before Mr. Ross arrived with the lady interested in the house. That had been the first phone call, which had awakened her from a rosy, serene dream. No sooner had she been fully awake, then the black cloud had settled into place, formed of equal parts guilt, regret, fear and self-recriminations. Alone—Craig was gone, having left the tray by her bed and disappeared before she woke—Suzannah had stalked the carpeted halls of the great house, chewing fingernails and muttering dark oaths at the various curious cats who followed her in her restless pacing.

Maybe if Craig had been there, it would have been different. Maybe he would've been able to soothe away all her anxieties. But left to her own devices, Suzannah had tried and convicted herself in record time. She'd done The Wrong Thing, and it was no one's fault but hers. In the clear cold light of day, she realized that her late-night thoughts had been melodramatically skewed. *He* wasn't the one who was going to be hurt—*she* was. He, the uncommitted, devil-may-care drifter, who would be leaving any day, any moment now (was he already gone for good?) would probably feel just fine about their . . . fling. But she was full of remorse already. She knew she was already half a head and a heel, at least, in love with Craig Jordan.

Sighing, Suzannah bit into her toast, though she didn't have much of an appetite. Why couldn't she be like Lila? Love them, leave them, stay wonderfully uninvolved . . . She was resolved, at least, to heed Lila's advice, though. It *was* self-destructive to get in any deeper with Craig; even if he didn't run out on her, it would be footloose Charlie all over again. No, she was supposed to land, or catch, as Lila put it, a bigger fish. The actress spoke of courtship as if it were a sport or a business proposition. Suzannah doubted she could ever be quite that cynical, but wanting to be pragmatic had led to the second Wrong Thing she'd done, compounding the felony: She'd agreed to go out with Jack Baxter, when he'd phoned, shortly after Mr. Ross.

Jack had been suave and insistent, and Suzannah, befuddled and vulnerable. Thinking she'd best plan for a future without Craig, she'd accepted Jack's invitation of wining and dining—for that very night. The young tycoon was going to New York to clinch some picture deal, and it was his one free night. Suzannah, figuring if she put the man off she'd ultimately back out altogether, had impulsively agreed. Now she felt even worse. She didn't want to see Jack Baxter.

She didn't want to see Craig, for that matter. She looked forward to his reappearance with dread. But when he did show up, she planned to have a talk. She wanted to make it clear that last night had been a once-in-a-lifetime rendezvous, not to be repeated. They'd be . . . friends, for the duration of his stay. That was the best thing, she was sure.

Sure, she was sure. Suzannah downed her coffee with a grimace, and geared into action. Mr. Ross and client were due within the hour.

"Gorgeous," said Mrs. Tyler. "Your Aunt has an artist's soul, I can see it everywhere."

Mr. Ross coughed quietly into his palm behind her. Suzannah nodded at the portly matron, who was wearing what appeared to be the contents of a vault on her overripe and overdressed figure. Rings, earrings, bracelets, necklaces, and pins glittered in the air and jingled as she moved through the living room, oohing and ahhing at every detail.

Until meeting Mrs. Tyler, Suzannah had only glimpsed creatures of her sort in the society pages of newspapers. This latter day dowager was wearing garishly opulent clothes and accessories that were meant for the ballroom. Suzannah found her perversely fascinating; she was not really a snobbish woman, she surmised, just existing on some other plane.

"Well, I don't know what Mr. Tyler will think," she sniffed, turning to Mr. Ross. "But I simply love everything about the place. It's so . . . quaint, and full of character!"

Suzannah swallowed. That took the cake, referring to a five-bedroom mansion with pool and ten acres as "quaint." Suddenly she felt a stab of regret, followed by a prick of anger. Why, they were discussing *her* house in the cavalier, possessive way. *Not* her house, she corrected with a sigh. Had she grown too used to living in Lucille's world? Soon the dream would be over . . .

Mr. Ross moved in then, smooth and practiced on his own turf, talking figures, options, possibilities, tax shelters.

Released from her troublesome musings, Suzannah stepped back and let him take over, glancing at Lucille's antique clock over the sofa. It was nearly two, and Craig still hadn't returned.

"And what's this?"

Mrs. Tyler had snatched something up from the table in the foyer and was bending over it, squinting through thick glasses. Suzannah walked over to see. The prospective buyer had Craig's sketch of Suzannah in her tanned and wrinkled hands.

"Oh, it's a drawing that a . . . local artist gave me," Suzannah said, surprised at the woman's interest.

"Lovely!" Mrs. Tyler breathed. "Why, it's . . . simply masterful!"

Suzannah looked at Mr. Ross, a little perplexed. "Mrs. Tyler is a collector," he told her. "She owns a gallery in Santa Monica."

"I must have this," Mrs. Tyler said, peering over her glasses at Suzannah. "Is it, by any chance, for sale?"

"Well, not really," Suzannah began. "That is, I hadn't really thought about . . ."

"But I'm in love!" Mrs. Tyler exclaimed, as if this fact ruled out any possibility of argument.

Suzannah stared at her, a new thought suddenly formulating. Much as she liked the little sketch, if the wealthy woman was that interested, maybe it could be worth some money—money Craig obviously needed. In another day or two he'd be unemployed again. And after all, he'd disowned the drawing as a trifle. Surely he wouldn't mind if she was able to do him a good turn by selling it . . .

"Well, if you're serious, Mrs. Tyler, perhaps . . ."

The woman was already fumbling at the catch to her bejeweled handbag. "I've got my checkbook here," she muttered. "What would you be willing to sell for?"

Suzannah tried to think straight. She hadn't the slightest idea of what to ask. She turned to Mr. Ross, but he merely gave a little shrug, smiling. "Well, it's really a favorite of mine," she began uncertainly.

"Who is the artist?" Mrs. Tyler asked. "Has he been exhibited before?"

"His name is Craig Jordan," Suzannah said. "He's not—"

"Never heard of him!" Mrs. Tyler exclaimed. "That's all the better. I love discovering fresh talent! Now, what are you asking?"

Suzannah cleared her throat nervously. "I guess . . ." At least a few hundred, she figured. Two, or . . . "I'd sell it for around three . . ." She paused. Three fifty? Was that too much?

"Fine," Mrs. Tyler said abruptly. "Three thousand is quite reasonable, I'd say. It's a treasure of a drawing, really . . . its simplicity has a Japanese quality! Especially the way the girl's body tapers down into only the merest sug*ges*tion of feet . . . exquisite."

Suzannah opened her mouth, shut it, and then stood by, heart pounding, as Mrs. Tyler wrote out a check for ten times the amount she'd thought she should ask for. Mrs. Tyler seemed about as set back by the purchase as most people would in buying a dollar lottery ticket.

Suzannah took a last look at the little sketch as Mrs. Tyler left, and promised her she would send this "simply sparkling talent" down to her gallery with some more of his work. Mr. Ross said he'd be back in touch with her about Mrs. Tyler's decision on the house, and other prospective buyers' visits. And then Suzannah was alone with the cats, to contemplate the check and the arrival of Craig.

She was standing at the picture window that looked out on the patio, lost in thought, a copy of the latest *Woman's Wear Daily* clutched in her hand, when two arms slid around her waist, and she jumped, startled. She hadn't heard him come in, but she barely had a moment to comprehend what was happening as he pulled her to him, pressing her back against the length of his body, his lips nuzzling her earlobe.

"Wait . . ." she murmured, trying to pull away. But he was replacing his lips with a searching, deliciously teasing tongue tip, causing chills to run from her ear to her spine. The paper fluttered from her hands to the polished wooden floor. His hands rose from her waist to claim her breasts beneath the sheer rose shirt she wore, and the skin tingled to vibrant life at his commanding caress.

"Don't . . ." she whispered, uselessly, and then she turned to him, unable to stop herself, the hands that she'd intended to push away his shoulders settling, instead, upon them, as she lifted her face to be kissed.

He claimed her mouth with a sureness spurred on by the responsive moan that came from deep in her throat. She moved against him, helpless in his powerful embrace, her lips parting beneath the insistent, silkily provocative thrust of his tongue.

She found herself returning the kiss with a passionate intensity, sensuous longings reawakened inside of her like so many budding flowers at his skillful touch. It took a great deal of willpower to come to her senses, but she managed it, only when their lips broke breathlessly apart. She stepped back, guiltily covering her mouth with her hand as he gave her a quizzical look.

"Lips hurt?" he suggested, eyes twinkling.

"No," she said worriedly. This was starting off completely wrong, this encounter. She'd wanted to be cool, calm, and collected, maintaining her distance and certainly not letting things get . . . physical. So much for plans, but nonetheless she forged ahead with the rest of her scenario. "Where have you been?" she asked, stepping back as he made another attempt to embrace her. A strangled yowl behind her and a whizzing exit of a ball of fur indicated she'd stepped on someone's tail.

"I did a few errands in West Hollywood," Craig said. "And I had to pick up a few things at the beach house. Sleep well?"

It was an innocent question, but it put her in mind of the warmth of his embrace and the wonderful feeling of cuddling against him between the cool sheets . . . She shook her head. "No," she said. "I mean, sure. Thank you for the breakfast tray. It was very thoughtful."

Craig shrugged. "This butler stuff can be habit-forming. Along with some other things . . ."

He was stepping forward to reach her again. Suzannah abruptly moved away. "Don't, Craig . . . please."

He cocked his head, eyes narrowing. "What's got into you?" When she didn't immediately answer, he folded his arms, looking her over from head to foot. "Ah," he said quietly. "It's the morning after . . . or the day . . . and you're feeling that fear and trembling."

"I guess," she said. He wasn't far wrong. "Listen, can

we . . . talk, about some things? I think we should talk."

Craig's face brightened. "By all means. Actually, I have some things I'd like to talk to you about."

"Oh," she said uncertainly. "Well. I was thinking maybe we'd go out."

His eyes widened. "Just what I was thinking."

"You know, to a restaurant, or a bar, or something. Some place nice."

Craig looked at her, a faintly ironical smile on his face. "You mean, in public? You and me? The lady of the house and her caretaker? Sounds a little risky."

"Don't start with that stuff," she warned him. "You know I don't care."

"I guess you don't," he said easily. "I'm happy to hear it."

"Good," she said. This was already feeling as difficult as she'd dreaded it would. "Why don't we go . . . now?"

"Fine," he said. "I'll bring the car around front."

When she walked out the front door a few minutes later, having put on some shoes and a man-tailored jacket she liked to wear for occasions in between dressy and casual, Craig was standing by the back door of the Rolls, indicating she should take a seat. Suzannah shook her head.

"I'm not playing," she said firmly. "I sit up front with you."

"That's good," he grinned, and he went around to the other side to open the front seat door for her.

As they rode into town she tried to keep the conversation casual. The check from Mrs. Tyler was burning a hole in her pocket. She tried to concentrate on it, because she was hoping that her good news would somehow balance out what he might construe as bad—mainly, her decision that they shouldn't continue to see each other, at least, not as more than friends.

Craig seemed as subdued as she was. She wondered what it was that he planned to talk to her about. He seemed in good spirits. It was hard to sit so casually by his side, feeling him so close, his scent and presence stirring her blood as they shared the seat. The tension she felt only reinforced her resolution, though. If even being near him was so overpowering, she was truly in trouble, and she had to extricate herself fast. It was a good thing he was leaving soon. She had to keep repeating that, however, because it was hard to believe.

A valet in front of the restaurant on Melrose took the car from Craig, and they went ahead in. It was a fern-and-brick-wall establishment with old-fashioned Casablanca-like fans above, and little partitioned tables in recessed areas, a perfect place for quiet and intimate conversation, true to the description Lila had given her some days ago. The headwaiter showed them to a table that overlooked a little outdoor garden area in back.

It was late afternoon, and the restaurant wasn't crowded. Suzannah settled into her booth seat, flinching as Craig took her hand on the table and gave it a gentle squeeze. She looked at him, so handsome with the orange sunlight slashing across his tanned face, dark against the white collar of the button down he wore. How was a woman supposed to be only friends with a man who looked like he did? Come to think of it, how *had* she resisted him as long as she had? But that was an unproductive train of thought.

The waiter hovered nearby. "Something from the bar?"

Craig looked up. "Let's be decadent and celebratory," he said to Suzannah. "Champagne?"

Suzannah stared at him, startled. How could he afford it? But then, he was certainly about to be able to. Ironically, champagne was just the right choice. "All right," she smiled.

Craig quizzed the waiter on the brands they carried, then made a selection. When they were alone again, he reached for her hand once more. "So, tell me," he said. "What do you want to talk about?"

Stalling anymore was useless. Suzannah took a deep breath. "Us," she said, and gently but firmly removed her hand from his grasp. "Craig, I've been doing a lot of thinking."

"Probably too much," he said, sitting back, his dark eyes studying her face.

"Just enough," she said, and she looked down, nervously toying with the place setting. "Look, I don't know how to do this with any . . . eloquence, but I want to tell you a couple of things." She stole a glance at him. He was waiting, his expression open, unjudgmental. "First of all," she went on softly, "I want you to know that the time we spent together last night was . . . wonderful, Craig. I . . ." She shook her head helplessly. "I loved being with you . . . but . . ."

"But?" he prompted quietly.

"But we can't be . . . together, like that, again. We can't go on like this, Craig."

She looked up to meet his eyes. To her surprise, he seemed almost amused. "That sounds like a line from an old movie, Suzannah," he said, in a tone that was kindly chiding. "But, tell me, why?"

Suzannah bit her bottom lip. "Because . . ." She sighed. "Because there's no future in the two of us being together," she blurted out. "For so many reasons."

"Name them," he said simply.

"First of all, I don't live here. I'll be leaving as soon as the house is sold. I have a whole other life up the coast, and you . . . well, you're here."

"Go on."

"And, more importantly," she hurried on, hoping the momentum itself would carry her through. "I'm not . . . I don't want to be involved in a relationship," she said, looking down again. It was too hard looking him in the eye. "I told you before, and I meant it. I'm single now and happier . . . being free."

"Oh?" His voice wasn't mocking, but merely curious. "You are?"

"Yes," she lied. "I have a career to take care of, and being independent makes it easier."

"I see."

At least he seemed sympathetic. "And the thing is," she continued, steeling herself for this particularly awkward hurtle. "I'm starting to . . . care about you, Craig. I mean, really . . . care. And that's no good," she said, looking up at him again. "I wish I was the kind of woman who could do what I did . . . that is, have the kind of experience I had with you last night . . . and be, oh, I don't know, be unmoved or unaffected . . . But I'm not," she finished abruptly, feeling completely self-conscious beneath his silent, watchful gaze. "I'm an old-fashioned girl, I guess," she said, with an awkward attempt at a self-deprecating smile. "I get attached, I get involved, I start to want . . . things," she sighed. "Security, for example. Commitment. A home with someone . . . you know, the whole bit. And I don't want to ask you for the kind of things . . ." Her voice trailed off.

"That I can't give you?" he finished for her.

She looked at him, feeling miserable. "I guess," she said softly.

Craig cleared his throat, turning to watch the waiter approach with the champagne. The time it took for him to uncork it and serve them each a glass seemed like an eternity to Suzannah. When he'd left at last, Craig raised his glass to her in a silent toast. Suzannah did the same, and took a gulp of the bittersweet, sparkling liquid, its bubbles dancing in the glass suddenly absurdly incongruous to her.

"Suzannah," Craig said quietly. "If I'm understanding you correctly, you're trying to tell me that you feel about me the way I feel about you."

"Well, I . . ." She stared at him, feeling the beginnings of a blush fill her cheeks.

"I'm in love with you, Suzannah," he said. "I'm not afraid to say it, and you shouldn't be afraid to either."

"But," she started, with a hopeless sigh. "I can't—"

"And from what you're telling me," he went on, ignoring her, "the only problem is, you think I'm incapable of loving you . . . in the way you need to be loved. Isn't that it?"

"Well . . . You said yourself that you were only taking things day by day . . . that you liked your solitude, that you'd be moving on . . ."

Craig smiled. "I said that when I barely knew you." He reached for her hand again. "But things have changed. I'm not too interested in solitude anymore."

"That's . . . sweet, Craig, but . . . there are other things you can't change—"

"I know," he said impatiently. "You think I'm a drifter. A man without a future, that was what you said, right?" He grinned. "But what if I had a future. What if things weren't merely what they seemed?"

"What if," she repeated, shaking her head.

"Look," he went on, holding her hand tighter. "I don't blame you for not trusting me. I know I've given you a lot of heat for wanting the finer things in life, wanting some comfort and status, but I can understand that. I can understand your wanting some support from a man after you've been through some struggles on your own." The glimmering light in his dark eyes seemed to burn brighter as his gaze held hers. The intensity and excitement in his voice confused her. "But Suzannah, the thing that means the most to me is that you've cared . . . you care . . . for me, a man you think has nothing to offer you, hasn't got a name, or fame and fortune . . ." He smiled. "I love you for that, Suzannah. You're a one in a million. I can't tell you that enough." His fingers caressed hers as his eyes appeared to caress her face. "And now," he went on, "Things will be different—"

"Craig, you've got a lot to offer a woman," she interrupted, heatedly. "You shouldn't say these things. You're talented, really, and you should have faith in that. In fact . . ." She was clutching the check in her pocket now, remembering her other reason for bringing him here. "I've got a great surprise for you."

"Really?" He grinned quizzically. "That's what I was going to say."

"You were?" She looked at him uncertainly. But the check was already in her hand, and she held it out. "Here," she said, triumphantly. "This is for you."

He stared at the check in her hand, then took it from her, eyes narrowing. Looking up from the scribbled figures, he gazed at her, confused. "What's this? I don't get it."

"Mrs. Tyler is a woman who came to see the house today. She happened to see that sketch you drew of me at the beach and she fell in love with it, literally," she told him, smiling.

"That little sketch? You . . . you sold it to her?"

Suzannah's smile faded. Craig didn't look pleased. She had a distinct, foreboding feeling that she might have made a terrible mistake. "Well, yes," she said uneasily. "I mean, I liked the sketch myself, and of course I wanted to keep it, but she was so enthusiastic—"

"She offered you this kind of money?" He sounded both incredulous and outraged.

"Well, not exactly," Suzannah said. "I started to ask for three hundred and she misunderstood me, and . . ." She shrugged. "She was ridiculously wealthy, Craig. She had pearls and diamonds practically coming out of her ears—"

"You sold her that sketch," he repeated slowly, as if still unable to believe it.

"Well, you said yourself that you didn't care for it much,"

she said defensively. "And I . . . well, of course I wanted to keep it, but I thought you could use the . . . I mean, I thought you'd be pleased . . ." she bumbled on. "You know, that your work was valued . . ."

There was a look on his face that she'd never seen before, and it was nearly frightening. "You know what this is?" he asked, in a murderously quiet voice, holding up the check. "This is charity. It's a patronizing payoff, that's what it is."

"Wait a second," she protested. "Who's patronizing or paying off? And how can it be charity—it's your work! You should feel proud!"

"Proud?" He grimaced. "I'm appalled!" He slammed the check down on the table, giving it a look as if it were some loathsome beast. Then he turned the full intensity of his blazing eyes on her. "First of all, that sketch isn't worth much more than the paper it was penciled on. It might have had sentimental value . . ." He spat the word *sentimental* out as if it were an unsavory morsel of food. "But when it's purchased by some rich lunkhead with money to burn and no eyeballs in her head, it's only a silly whim!"

"Just because you can't see how good your own drawing is," she began, indignant, "doesn't mean you have to get all—"

"Second of all," he thundered, cutting her off, "I'd rather get paid for the hard work I do, and when I do, I know exactly what it's worth and why. Third of all, this whole setup stinks!"

"What do you mean, setup?" she cried.

"You bring me here and launch into a verbal Dear John letter," he fumed. "You tell me you care about me but you can't care and all this malarky, and what you're really leading up to is a kiss-off! You add insult to injury by giving me this!"

"No," she wailed. "You've got it all wrong. I wasn't—"

"You think you're helping me out? Hey, buddy, it's been grand, but it's time to move on, here's a few thou to tide you over? That's obscene!"

"Craig," she said, feeling more wretched by the second. "I guess I can see why it looks that way to you, but honestly—"

"I don't need this kind of money!" He smiled, but it was

a grimace devoid of humor. "My God, if you only knew how funny this is . . . or how pathetic . . . !" He slapped his head. "It's unbelievable!"

"You and your pride," she fumed. "What's wrong with having some money for a genuinely creative act? You're taking this all wrong!"

"I'm supposed to be grateful?" He shook his head.

"I'm not asking for thanks!" she cried. "I was doing it because I cared!"

He narrowed his eyes. "Because you felt guilty," he said grimly.

"No!" she protested, but there was enough of a grain of truth in what he said to make her voice falter.

Craig stared at her, his face dark, eyes piercing. Then he lifted his champagne glass and downed the contents in a single gulp. Slamming the glass down, he rose from his seat. As she watched, horrified, he lifted the check and tore it neatly in two, right before her face. He tore it again, and the pieces fluttered to the table top.

"Have Mrs. Tyler make another one out to you," he said coldly. "She can pick up the tab for the champagne."

As she stared up at him, frozen in shock, he turned on his heel and stalked down the aisle, not looking back as he left the restaurant. The door closed behind him with a muffled crack that cut through the soft music piped into the room.

Suzannah sat, immobile, feeling as if she were what had just been ripped in pieces and dropped upon the table. Numb, she blinked back the tears that stung the edges of her eyes, and lifted the champagne glass to her lips with trembling fingers.

Flat.

CHAPTER ELEVEN

"ANOTHER DRINK?"

Suzannah had been gazing, lost in thought, at the vast arrangement of birds-of-paradise, orchids, heliconia, and other flowers spilling from hanging clay pots and shooting up from the carefully manicured, glass-enclosed artificially lit garden. She turned back to look blankly at Jack Baxter.

"More wine?" he suggested. "A brandy?"

"No, thanks," she smiled. "The coffee's fine."

Jack smiled back, and turned to the waiter who was lingering in the pastel shadows next to an elaborately carved dark wood mirror. "A Remy for me," he said. "And more coffee for the lady."

As the blond-haired, black-tied waiter nodded and departed, Suzannah stared at the mirror. In the reflection, half of the vast room could be seen. Michel's was filled to capacity with urbane, beautifully dressed men and women, dining on what was considered the best food in Los Angeles, amidst splendidly designed opulence that bordered on overkill. The distant bar was of solid pink marble, the walls that were not pastel tile trimmed with lights were taken up with twenty-five-foot-high mauve drapery. The service was perfect, friendly, efficient, immaculate model-type men moved quietly and swiftly about the room. Laughter was subdued, conversation a continual pleasant murmur. Deep tans were everywhere.

It was, in short, the quintessence of style and status for the higher priced spread in Hollywood. Suzannah, who not so long ago might have been awed to see the inside of such an establishment, let alone dine there, was filled with a sudden perverse urge to take a can of spray paint and deface the molded walls with a big black *X*. Then the little jolt of anger faded as quickly as it had risen, and she realized that Jack Baxter was looking at her expectantly again, as he had throughout their meal.

"Well," he said, resting his chin in his hands and fixing her with a look that indicated he was endlessly patient. "If you don't stop talking now I'll never be able to get a word in edgewise."

Suzannah smiled wanly. "I'm sorry," she said. "I realize I've been kind of preoccupied."

"Kind of?" He raised an eyebrow. "If you don't mind my saying so, I was starting to wonder if you were really here."

"I'm here," she said. "And I've really enjoyed the meal." She had enjoyed what she'd eaten of her delicious filet mignon seasoned with fresh ginger and garlic, and the taste of Jack's grilled jumbo shrimp, flown in, he'd informed her, fresh every day from New Orleans. With half a heart she'd enjoyed the vintage wine, and the little thrill of being seated immediately as the maitre d' greeted Jack like an old friend, whisking them past a buzzing crowd of people in front to a prime table by the glass garden wall in back. Even in her deep blue funk, she'd been impressed by the number of famous faces who had greeted her escort, by the exorbitant menu prices he'd summarily ignored, by the bicoastal, transcontinental jet setting Jack described as a typical week's work.

But none of it penetrated, ultimately, her invisible veil of depression. Or, she realized, not so invisible. Jack had finally given up trying to coax her into higher spirits. He shook his head now, as she sipped her coffee, and for once, didn't attempt a smile.

"I'm glad you enjoyed the meal," he said. "I'm only sorry you haven't enjoyed my company."

"It's not that, Jack," she said quickly, sorry to see her doggedly debonair companion showing some strain. "It's just been a . . . rough day, that's all. And it's a shame . . . I really had been looking forward to this."

It wasn't fair. She *had* been looking forward to being wined and dined in such style. Here she was, having everything money and fame could buy . . . and that big lunkhead Craig Jordan was spoiling it all? No matter how hard she tried, she couldn't keep his angry words from ringing through her mind, couldn't keep from seeing his face superimposed over that of every handsome man in the place. She'd pick up a piece of the elegant silver and see it through his eyes, hear his disdain for all this frou-frou and indulgence, whispering in her ear. It was maddening.

"Maybe you'd like to talk about it," Jack was saying. "Your rough day?"

Suzannah sighed. She wasn't about to go into her fight with Craig. Jack might have been the understanding type, but he was, after all, trying to . . . court her. She'd been rude enough as it was. "No, I don't think so," she said, managing what she hoped was a convincing smile. "Next to the kinds of heavy deals and major crises you've been talking about, my idea of a rough day would probably strike you as absurd."

Jack shrugged. "Deals and crises are one kind of headache. Yours seems more personal, and those take a heavier toll, don't they?"

Jack Baxter hadn't gotten where he was by being unperceptive. Suzannah nodded. "I guess so," she said quietly. "But talking about it won't really help, I'm afraid."

Jack nodded sympathetically. "Well, why don't I drive you home? I'd been planning on asking you back to my hotel for a drink, but I can see tonight's not the night."

"No," she agreed, though not wanting to appear ungrateful for his attentions. "Can I take a rain check?" she added, hoping to seem like less of a wet blanket. "Maybe when you're back in town."

"Sure thing," he said expansively, that ever sunny smile back on his handsome face once more.

On the drive home she did manage to be more superficially cheery, forcing herself to keep up an amiable chatter. From what she figured, the man had just spent what amounted to a couple of months' rent on her San Francisco apartment in a few hours, and she felt guilty being the unresponsive recipient of it all. She let herself be kissed goodnight in Hollywood style, and agreed politely that they should get together again. Though most probably she'd be back in her hometown by the time he returned.

It was just as well. She knew it made no sense to see Jack again whether he was sincere in wanting to see her, she didn't know, but she wouldn't be surprised. His type always saw cool disinterest as a challenge . . . But for all his wealth, status, and style, he didn't do a thing for her. When the door shut with an echoing clunk behind her, Suzannah walked slowly to the foot of the winding staircase and sank to the bottom step, her head in her hands. She couldn't remember the last time she'd felt so desolate.

A few fat felines yowled and meowed around her as she sat, staring morosely into the darkness, feeling too tired and forlorn to even turn on a light. Vaguely, she registered the fact that there had been no lights on over the garage. *He* wasn't here. She didn't doubt it. She had no idea where he'd gone, on foot, after storming out of the little café on Melrose. When she'd driven the Rolls home there'd been no sign of Craig, and he still hadn't returned when Jack came by to pick her up a few hours later.

Listlessly, Suzannah rose and walked, zombielike, into the kitchen, where she methodically fed the beasts she'd neglected before leaving. She was halfway through the process when she realized, peering more closely at the dishes, that someone had already taken care of the cats' dinner. So he had come back, after all.

For a moment her resentment and anger welled up inside her like a fist. Where was he? She'd give him a piece of her mind! How could he be so pigheaded and insensitive, so puffed up with pride and arrogance? How dare he accuse her of patronizing him when she'd only wanted to help him out? Who did he think he was, anyway?

The momentum of self-righteous picque carried her as far as the picture window in the den, but then she halted, staring out at the yard, arms folded, lips set tight. Why go talk to him at all? Why should she be the one to talk, when she'd only be inviting more of his misplaced accusations?

She frowned, looking toward the garage. Something told her he wouldn't be coming to talk to her, and the idea made her suddenly uneasy. Doubts and self-recriminations began seeping back into her thoughts, as they'd been doing all evening. After all, she had hurt his feelings . . . and even if he'd taken her gesture the wrong way, she could see how it had happened . . .

Suzannah sighed. Face it, she told herself ruefully, you just can't stand the idea of leaving things up in the air, of not trying to work it out with him . . . you care about him too much. That was where the whole damn problem had started, hadn't it? With her caring?

She opened the glass door at the other end of the den and stepped out onto the patio. Maybe there were ways to apologize without compromising. Maybe there was a way she could let him know she understood, but that she felt he'd wronged her as well. Formulating a speech that would encompass all these complex issues, Suzannah headed for the stairs to the garage.

At the foot of the staircase she stopped, some wrong element in the picture registering. His motorbike was missing. Had he gone out again, then? Her heart beginning to beat faster, she stalked quickly up the steps. After a perfunctory knock on the door, she opened it, and froze.

Empty. Even in the dim light she could sense the room's vacancy. And when she turned on the light switch, her fears were confirmed. There wasn't a sign of Craig's habitation. His suit bag was gone, and only a few empty wire hangers still dangling from the wooden rafters indicated anyone had been up there at all. Easel, sketch pad, canvas bag, even the pillows, blankets, and linen were gone, the last items, she surmised, with a feeling of growing panic, probably back in the house, from which they'd come.

For a long moment she stood in the doorway, not wanting to believe he'd really left for good. Why wasn't there a note, at least, some sort of a good-bye? With her heart thumping more painfully in her chest, she turned, fumbling for the light, and then walked quickly down the stairs. At the bottom she paused, her mind whirling. What now?

It was only then, as the panic mounted within her, that Suzannah realized she'd never expected him to leave. She'd thought about his leaving abstractly, amicably, parting when the gardening job was done, a friend to keep in touch with, or some such . . . nonsense, she told herself now, with a dull thud of aching disappointment in the pit of her stomach. Secretly she'd never pictured him leaving at all, she realized. And certainly not like this.

Too overwrought to stand still, she stalked the path back to the patio. She'd been a fool to take him for granted. She *was* a fool, thinking she'd been the only one with vulnerable feelings, thinking that he'd be there waiting for her if she flew off to seek all the things she'd thought she wanted . . . when it was him, she thought, the obviousness of it hitting home like a slap in the face. She knew she loved him, she'd been fighting off the truth of it for days, but she *knew*, now, with a horrible intensity, that she'd thrown away the only thing that really mattered to her.

The next move was instinctive. Her body acted of its own accord as her mind scattered in all directions, her heart pounding painfully. As if on some remote control, she retrieved the keys to the Rolls from inside the kitchen, moved swiftly back to the garage, started up the motor, and was driving out into the darkness of Canyon Drive in a matter of minutes.

Thankfully, traffic was light. She jumped red lights, tires squealing on curves taken too sharply. Her knuckles were white as she gripped the wheel, and she peered at the road ahead as if she could see her destination from miles away. He had to be there. Where else would he have gone? Even if his friend was still occupying the beach house, surely he'd put Craig up for a night.

After what seemed like interminable stretches of winding road, she was finally on the Coast highway. Finally the little unmarked turnoff was in her headlight beams. Suzannah steered more carefully down the zigzagging driveway, knowing too well that it was tricky to navigate, and not knowing if a vehicle would be parked in her path when she reached the end.

But there wasn't another car, and there wasn't, she saw

with a leap of anxiety, a motorbike. She cut the motor of the Rolls, flipped off the headlights and quickly alighted from the car. The ocean's steady pounding on the beach was the only sound as she made her way up the little path to the beach house door. There weren't any lights from within.

She knocked impatiently on the weather-beaten door, her apprehensions increasing when nobody answered. Growing desperate, knowing it was futile, she pounded the door with a surge of frustration—and stepped back, startled, as it swung open before her.

But it was only the force of her fist that had opened the loosely closed and obviously unlocked door. When she stepped inside, there was no one to greet her, not the angry Craig she'd been picturing all the way over, or the phantom friend that was supposedly the cottage's current resident. No, the little shack was as empty as the rooms over the garage had been.

Distraught, thrown off-balance, she lurched into the squalid room. From what she could see, no one had been in there since Craig had. There were no signs of another inhabitant, no bags, no personal articles, nothing. Bewildered, she stalked the place from end to end, half-expecting Craig to pop out of some dark corner like a ghost. Outside in the dim moonlight, the hammock swayed in the wind. The waves, indifferent to her plight, crashed ceaselessly on the beach.

When she turned from the windowed doors, her foot struck a bottle, which startled her as it rolled to one side. Bending to pick it up, Suzannah looked at the label. Odd, but she could swear it was the very wine bottle she'd shared with Craig that night. If someone else had moved in afterward, why hadn't they disposed of it?

But this was just a minor mystery in the midst of her major catastrophe. She'd lost Craig. He'd left no phone number, no forwarding address. She hadn't the slightest idea of where to begin looking for him. Should she wait where she was?

She waited by the windows, watching the ocean in nervous anticipation for a quarter of an hour before the realization that he wouldn't be coming sank in with some instinctual certainty. Something told her that if he didn't want to be found, he wouldn't be, not by her.

She took a last look at the desolate stretch of beach, and then left the little shack, shutting the door firmly behind her. She walked listlessly to the car, opened its door, and sat in the front seat, staring into the darkness until her eyes clouded over with tears, and, huddling over the steering wheel, she wept.

She cried hot tears in what seemed like an endless torrent, her shoulders shaking with sobs, until finally, the wave of hopelessness and sorrow ebbed. Sniffling, she sat up, fumbling for tissues from her bag. This was where it had all began, less than two weeks ago, sitting at the wheel of the Rolls in this little cul-de-sac. It somehow only made sense that it would end there, too. Suzannah blew her nose, and turned on the ignition. There was nothing to do but begin the long drive home.

There was nothing worse, Suzannah decided, sitting with her legs dangling in the pool in the midst of a bright sunny afternoon a few days later, than getting what you think you wanted.

She'd wanted her affair with Craig to end before it went any further. So it had. Was she happy? She was miserable. She'd wanted to sell her clothes to the rich and famous denizens of Beverly Hills. Just that morning, she'd made a sale to the owner of a boutique on Robertson Boulevard, a store that catered to the sleek and the chic. Was she ecstatic? She was only faintly pleased.

She'd wanted to enjoy the life of luxury that she had never had. Here she was in her pool, with her grounds and her mansion and her car and her everything. Did it make her feel wonderful? Not even close. Suzannah had never believed the old clichés about money not being everything, about rich people having everything but not being happy. For the first time in her life, the clichés made sense.

The only thing that could have made her happy, she mused, watching the swirling ripples in the water as she listlessly kicked her feet back and forth, was having the only thing she'd told herself repeatedly she didn't want: Craig.

He hadn't called, of course. He'd disappeared as if he'd never existed. She was left alone in her luxurious, empty environs to consider the unkindness of fate, alternately hating the man and yearning for him with a force that made her chest ache. Again and again she considered the bitter irony of that last day. Just when she'd come round to understanding that all those simple pleasures were indeed the priceless things he'd said they were, that whether or not Craig was poor, he was the man she wanted to be with, come what may . . . poof! All was lost in a puff of smoke.

The phone was ringing inside the house. Suzannah jumped up, hurrying out of the walled area, knowing even as she ran that it wouldn't be Craig. Most probably it was Mr. Ross with another client. A steady trickle of people had come to see the place, and Ross had assured her that Aunt Lucille's property would be sold within the next week or so. That worked out perfectly. She could return to San Francisco with her missions accomplished, a little richer, if she sold more clothes, a lot wiser, and infinitely sadder.

She trotted into the den, still dripping, and grabbed the phone.

"Hey, love, how goes it?" Lila asked cheerily.

"It goes," Suzannah said. "How are you?"

"Well, certainly a lot more chipper than some," Lila said. "How long do you intend to be in mourning?"

"I don't know," she replied, feeling a twinge of resentment. Lila had taken the news of Craig's abrupt evacuation as a turn for the better, as well as an inevitability. Though she'd sympathized with Suzannah initially, she'd taken to calling frequently now, trying to set up blind dates for her with industry notables. "If you're calling to set me up with another hot prospect, Lila," she said dryly. "I still don't know if I'm ready . . . or if I ever will be."

"Oh, buggernuts," Lila scoffed. "You can't shut yourself up in that big old joint and mope forever. Besides, you're better off, remember? Auntie Lila knows best. Now listen, sweetcakes, I have just the thing to chase away your blues."

"I can't imagine what." Suzannah sighed.

"A party!" Lila crowed. "And it's a good one, too, plus it's not 'til the end of the week, darling, so you'll have plenty of time to dry your wee tears and coax a smile onto your gorgeous little mug! Won't you?"

"It's a possibility," Suzannah allowed.

"This is a can't miss," her friend went on. "A bunch of us've got an invite to a house in the hills that used to be owned by the Barrymores or someone, for dinner, dancing, and drinks. The man who owns the place now runs a record company or two, isn't that nice? But he'd really like to direct a movie, they all do. At any rate, half of Hollywood, that is, the good half, is bound to show so you simply must come, there's no excuse. All right?"

Trying to wriggle out of it seemed like more of an effort than agreeing to go. And she was starting to feel too isolated. So, with a minimum of fuss, Suzannah gave in, hoping that in the four days until the party she might regain some of her equilibrium.

The next day helped. She got a phone call from another boutique, unsolicited, from a man who'd seen the dress she'd sold Deidre Mills. Could she bring some things over to his shop on Wilshire? She did. And he bought three.

Two days later, Mr. Ross brought a couple over who were serious and impatient buyers. Aunt Lucille was cabled in Europe and the wheels began turning with sudden velocity. The closing was set. It looked as if the house was going, and in a matter of days, she would be, too, heading back to San Francisco with some money in her pocket, a lot less clothes, and one broken—but hopefully, not irreparable—heart.

"Not too shabby, I'd say," Lila murmured in her ear, as Suzannah walked with her past the smiling woman in silver lamé who was taking coats and wraps from guests in the front hall of a house that appeared large as an airplane hanger. Obviously an architectural homage to an older generation's sense of grandeur, this mansion looked to her like something from an old MGM movie, which made perfect sense, when she thought about it.

Their heels clicked on shining black and white parquet marble floors as they followed little clusters of guests, some dressed to the nines, some in more studied casual attire, through the arches of the hallway to a gargantuan living room already filled with a haze of smoke and the continual clink of glasses and jewelry, and the rising buzz of conversation.

Suzannah was content to let Lila lead her around. Her friend seemed a lot less intimidated by such environs than she was. She was introduced to a number of people whose names she promptly forgot, dazed as she was by the parade of people with faces either striking, vaguely famous looking, or easily recognizable as belonging to stars of screen, radio, and fashion.

She let one charmingly inebriated man in a pin-striped suit and a small silver hoop earring induce her to try his perfect martini. A few sips into the drink, she agreed it was as perfect as she'd ever tasted, complimented him on his earring, and moved on, becoming emboldened by what seemed like a very loose and convivial atmosphere.

She lost Lila to a pair of French filmmakers with thick accents and cigaret holders who were scouting for American talent. She caught up with her again sometime later as she stood by the grand piano, listening to a rock star try to pick out the chords of an old Cole Porter song.

"Listen," Lila whispered excitedly at her ear. "You've got the chance of a lifetime tonight! C.J. Young is here!"

"Here?" She looked at Lila, surprised. "But he never goes to these sorts of things, from what I've heard. He's a regular recluse."

"I know, I know, but he's just opened his first store in Los Angeles—yesterday—and someone got him to come. Why don't you go introduce yourself?"

Suzannah nodded, remembering having passed the new store, that day when Craig had taken her to Annabella's. Then she realized what Lila had just said. "What do you mean, introduce myself?" she said.

"Babycakes, will you never learn? Seize the moment! You're an attractive woman, he's an attractive man, you've got something significant in common..."

Suzannah shrugged. "He probably hates being approached by people in the industry," she said. "Though I guess it wouldn't hurt..."

"I've never met the fellow, but I understand he's gorgeous," Lila said. "So even if you don't land a job with him or something perhaps other things"—She wiggled her eyebrows in mock suggestiveness. —"might come of it."

Suzannah sighed. "Oh, stop," she said. "I'm not interested."

"Then look at it as business," Lila said. "All the contacts get made at parties like these. So go to it, girl."

Lila guided her through the crowd to another more dimly lit room, which opened out upon a magnificent view and a swimming pool that was lit from below.

"Elliot pointed him out to me, though I didn't get a good look. A dark haired man in a worsted tweed suit," Lila told her. "He was last sighted going outside for a breath of air. So why don't you?"

Suzannah smoothed her hair. "Why not?" she murmured, and downed the rest of her second martini. That was the right thing to do, for in the few moments it took to step outside into the warm night air, the alcohol entered her system, and any vestiges of self-consciousness fell away from her. Lila was right. She had nothing to lose by introducing herself to a legendary self-made millionaire. She should be making as many acquaintances in the world of fashion as she could.

Suzannah paused just past the open doorway. The dark-haired man in a tweed suit was the only one out there, presently. He was standing a few yards away with his back to her, looking out over the glowing turquoise pool at the panoramic sparkle of city lights in the valley below. He looked, even from behind, like an attractive and urbane fellow. The cut of his suit was perfect, of course. The pose he'd struck was casual, and the understated elegance of his attire gave him an aura of graceful, athletic poise.

Suzannah approached him slowly, feeling a little buzz of excited expectation. She cleared her throat. "Mr. Young?" she asked softly, when she was right behind him.

C.J. Young turned around. And the empty martini glass Suzannah had been holding fell to the ground, cracking on the cement with a little tinkle.

"You?" she gasped.

"Suzannah!" Craig Jordan exclaimed, his eyes widening at the sight of her.

She stared at him, disbelieving, her mouth agape. He'd shaved. His hair was neater. And he was wearing clothes that cost thousands of dollars—but he hadn't paid. No, because he'd designed the whole ensemble himself, the—

"Snake!" she whispered, her throat suddenly dry. "You . . ." Words were failing her.

"Wait a second," he frowned. "Before you go off calling me names—"

"Are you . . . really . . ." Each word was an incredulous hiss. "C . . . J . . ."

"Yes, I'm he," he said impatiently. "Which is what I was finally about to tell you, when you tried to shove that check—"

"Finally?" she croaked. "And what in God's name took you that long?"

"I was waiting for the right time," he began, indignant. "I hadn't planned on holding out so long, but—"

"But you were having too good a time, is that it?" she cried, infuriated. Things were starting to make a crazy sense inside her whirling brain: his mysterious past, the miraculous appearance of that red dress in Lucille's closet, his odd behavior at Annabella's boutique . . .

"Things didn't exactly go the way I'd planned," he said. "It started out as a harmless put-on—"

"Harmless?" Her voice rose. "Playing with me? Leading me on, letting me think you were some poor and homeless nobody—"

"You jumped to your own conclusions!" he retorted. "That first night at the beach I let you think whatever you wanted. After all, I didn't think I'd ever see you again—"

"Then why did you?" she asked, with menacing evenness.

"Why did I see you? I wanted to," he exclaimed. "Besides, you blew my cover."

"Your cover? What do you mean?"

"Nobody in the world knew where I was, which was the whole idea. And then, because you flattened my wheel, I had to come out of hiding," he went on, thrusting his thumbs into the belt loops of his elegant trousers. "It just so happened that a friend of mine who edits a gossip rag came into that gas station after you left. He's got a house in Malibu and he immediately wanted to know what I was doing there and would I come over for dinner"—Craig grimaced, pointing with his chin toward the house full of partygoers. —"which is exactly what I was trying to avoid in the first place. I just wanted some peace and quiet seclusion."

So that was the pretext for Craig's story about a friend who wanted his beach house back. "Then there wasn't any man kicking you out of the cottage on the beach," she said. "You made that up! What for?"

"I was only planning to stay over for one night," he said sheepishly. "At your place I mean, until I could find another place to go."

"So?" she cried. "Why couldn't you tell me who you were?"

"After you told me who *you* were?" he shot back. "Do you know how many women and men crawl all over me as soon as they know who I am, trying to get jobs, sell me patterns, make me see their collections? Suzannah, I didn't know if you were any good, and I didn't know you well enough to trust you. You might have tried to use me, and you might have turned out to be indiscreet!"

"So instead you made me the butt of an extended joke!" she fumed. "Very funny, Mr. Young!"

"It wasn't a joke," he said stiffly. "There's nothing funny about the way I began to feel about you. The funny thing was you giving me the boot when you decided I wasn't good enough for you!"

"That's not the way it was," she retorted, feeling her cheeks reddening. "But I couldn't see us going on together, if you . . ."

"If I weren't anybody worth knowing?" he finished for her wryly.

Suzannah glared at him, her mind still reeling. So all that time, when she'd tried to offer him suggestions on getting work, when she'd let him chauffeur her around, when she'd let him make love to her—he'd known! He'd watched her make a fool of herself, and said nothing! The humiliation she felt burned like a molten knife twisting within her.

"How could you?" she cried.

"How could *you?*" he muttered darkly. "I was prepared to tell you who I was, and why I had to leave. My store was opening. I was going to tell you, but that payoff you tried to give me stopped me cold!"

"So I was wrong!" she blurted. "I know what it must've seemed like, but that check represented nothing but good intentions! I thought I was doing the right thing, and I only realized later . . ." She stopped. Tears of frustration and mortification were welling up inside of her. She struggled to force them back.

Craig frowned. He seemed to be struggling with his own emotions. "You mean you're sorry? You know why I was so angry?"

"I'm sorry I ever met you," she muttered, looking away. She wished she could sink through the ground.

"Then . . ." His eyes searched hers. "Then it was just . . . bad timing . . ."

"Bad timing?" She stared at him, incredulous, the tears filling her eyes. "What about yours? How could you just . . . desert me like that, Craig? Just when . . . I was realizing how much you meant to me!" she blurted out, before she could stop herself. "You never gave me a chance to realize I might have been making a mistake . . . that I was scared . . ." She couldn't go on. Biting her lip, she turned away, blinking back the tears.

"Suzannah." His voice was softer now, almost plaintive. She stiffened as she felt his hand touch her shoulder. "Maybe I *was* too hasty. But in my anger at your selling that sketch, I started to believe what you'd told me . . . that you couldn't love me, that you weren't willing to have faith in a future with me. I began to think I didn't really know you like I thought I did."

"And I thought I knew *you,*" she muttered bitterly. "You must have thought I was a prize chump!"

"No," he said, turning her to face him again. "I was in love with you," he said quietly. "The you that resisted acting rich, and thinking rich, and trying to get rich quick. The beautifully innocent you that stubbornly held onto romantic dreams . . ." His eyes held hers, no longer angry, but full of a searching, longing intensity that kept her imprisoned in his grasp, though she wanted to break away. "Don't you understand? I thought I was losing the you that I loved. I thought you were turning into someone more cynical, hardened, like so many others I've known . . ."

"I'm sorry I disappointed you," she retorted, trying desperately to break his seductive hold on her. Her anger at being tricked and betrayed was still raging within her, deafening her to his apologetic tone.

"Then . . . I *was* wrong," he said softly, his eyes urgently questioning.

"You were wrong to play with me like that!" she snapped, pulling away.

"Suzannah . . ." His hands caught her shoulders again.

"Let me go!" she cried, twisting in his grasp.

"I shouldn't have left," he said, in a tone of growing wonder. "You *do* love me . . ."

"Wrong again," she muttered defiantly, still struggling to get away. "I might have loved Craig Jordan, but I don't want anything to do with *you!*"

"But, Princess," he began, a smile hovering on his lips, and a strange light glowing in his eyes as he tried to pull her closer. "We're one and the same . . ."

"I'm no princess!" she cried. "And you're not a prince . . . you're a"—She pushed him back with all her might —"toad!"

She'd gotten free. And he'd lost his balance. With a look of desperation, Craig flailed his arms in the air—and fell backward into the pool.

There was a mighty crack as he hit the surface, sending a wave of water into the air. Suzannah stumbled back, her dress soaked by the spray. Not waiting to see if he'd sink or swim, she ran for the open doorway. A gaggle of astonished guests, eyes bulging, rushed toward and past her as the sounds of Craig's sputtering gasps and splashing filled the air.

"Party's over!" Suzannah called, grabbing hold of Lila.

"What the—?" her friend began.

"We played charades, and I guess I was a sore loser," Suzannah told her grimly, as they pushed their way against the current of curious onlookers. "Let's get out of here."

"Suzannah," Lila murmured worriedly. "How many martinis—?"

"I'm ready for a double," she said wryly. "Lila, I just landed a millionaire—and I threw him back."

CHAPTER TWELVE

"WHERE DO YOU want these, Suzannah?"

Suzannah looked up from the calculator on Veronique's cluttered desk in the back of the store, where she was trying to make sense of the bills and receipts that had accrued in her three weeks' absence. Kristin, the younger salesgirl, peeked out at her from behind a huge bouquet of pink and yellow gladiolas.

"Oh, no," Suzannah sighed. "More?"

"It's starting to look like a morgue out there," Kristin said, setting the flowers down in the umbrella stand by the desk. "I'll get some water."

"We've run out of vases?"

Kristin's reply was a little laugh. The long-legged blonde moved past Suzannah to the little washroom behind her. Suzannah leaned over to inspect the glads, and reached between the moist green stalks to extract the card she knew she'd find there.

"What's he say this time?" Kristin called, over the running water.

"The usual," Suzannah muttered, shoving the card in her

pocket. "Do you want to take this bunch home with you?"

Kristin re-emerged with a full pitcher, which she unceremoniously dumped into the umbrella stand, a ceramic pot that most probably had been a vase in a former life. "I took the lilacs," she said, straightening up. "Yesterday's shipment. Maybe Veronique would like these."

"I'll ask her when she gets back," Suzannah said. There was a musical tinkle of bells from out in front that indicated the arrival of a customer. "Can you stay up front for a bit? I'm still up to my ears in figures."

"Sure," said Kristin. "Say, does your friend have a friend? I kind of like his style."

"We're not on speaking terms," Suzannah said. "Otherwise I'd be happy to ask."

Kristin shot her a puzzled look, and went through the billowing lace curtain in the doorway to the main room of the boutique. Suzannah turned back to her calculator. But before adding any more figures, she took out the little card and stole another look at the message scrawled on it.

> How much silence can a man take?
> Oh, Suzannah . . .
> How much stubbornness can a woman have?
> Missing you . . .
> Love, Craig

She frowned, fingers gripping the edges of the card, flexing to rip it in half. But instead, she put it back in the pocket of her smock, knowing full well she'd put it with the growing collection of cards, telegrams, and express letters that was gathering in the top drawer of the bureau in her apartment. Again, she thanked the fates for having let her inherit a phone number listed in the name of her apartment's former tenant, an old school friend, and not her own. Otherwise, she had a feeling it would be ringing off its hook. Craig was certainly a persistent man.

In the ten days since she'd been back, his attempts to get in touch with her, or rather, get her to contact him, had doubled. Her ignoring the bouquets that arrived daily, and the written communications, only seemed to inspire a more dogged pursuit on his part. C.J. Young was apparently not a man who took no for an answer.

Suzannah glanced at the clock. She tried to concentrate on the last row of figures. As soon as Veronique returned, she could leave; Kristin would close up. But the elegant gladiolas kept distracting her as she tapped in numbers on the buzzing calculator, and she had to add the column twice. By the time another tinkle of bells announced the arrival of her boss, she'd had to start all over again.

Veronique took the gladiolas. "But I don't understand," she said, as Suzannah put on her coat. "Why is it you continue to . . . resist this man, who has such . . . romantic style?"

"He played a mean trick on me," Suzannah told the older woman. "I don't want to see him again."

"I think you do," Veronique purred, fluttering her lashes at Suzannah in her most knowing, continental manner. "But even so, where is the joy in this? You want to get him back? Then, instead—"

"I don't want to get him back," Suzannah insisted.

"No, no," Veronique waved her hand impatiently. *"C'est que ce* . . . get back . . . *at* him, I mean: *revanche!* Revenge, *oui?* You must play a trick, yourself."

Suzannah shrugged. "I can't imagine how," she said, and purposely changed the subject. "Kristin sold that jump-suit we had in petite. Should we order another?"

Veronique nodded absently, fingering the gladiolas. "You should do *some*thing," she murmured. "Since you're back, you are too sad." She shook her head. "Even with the flowers, it gets depressing . . . we'll lose business!" she cried.

Suzannah smiled, waving good-bye. She was used to Veronique's teasing. She hurried through the shop into the late afternoon sun, glad to be walking in the crisp, windy San Francisco air. The fog would be rolling in within the hour, but this time of day was perfection, her favorite; the sky was that shimmering blue-blue, the color she'd thought of when Craig had said, on the beach . . .

There he was again. Suzannah frowned, squaring her shoulders more defiantly against the wind as she walked up the hill of Potomac Street. Was she ever going to get that man out of her mind? Maybe it *was* a useless battle. She did miss him, there was no denying that. Most of her initial anger had been replaced by messy, conflicted feelings of remorse, embarrassment, resentment and longing—a confusing tumult of emotions that only added up to a big inner question mark.

As she picked up some vegetables for a dinner salad at the open natural produce stand on the corner of her block, she tried to reason everything out methodically again. *He* wasn't angry anymore, obviously, his dip in the pool notwithstanding. His cards spoke only of reconciliation. But she still felt used and abused. What right had he to fool with her emotions like that? Obviously, he'd thought she needed to learn some lesson about values. Well, she'd learned it, painfully, when she thought she'd lost him. She'd suffered when she realized that a "poor" man's love was worth more than any riches she could attain. But it still maddened her to know she'd been manipulated. Maybe Veronique was right. If there were some way to even up the score . . .

Her phone was ringing when she unlocked her apartment door. Suzannah rushed in, depositing her bag of groceries on the wood-block table, and grabbed the receiver. "Hello?"

"Aha," said a husky male voice. "Success at last."

Suzannah stiffened, her pulse pounding faster. How had he gotten hold of her number? "What do you want?" she said, trying to keep her voice devoid of any telltale emotion. "And how did you find me?"

"You know what I want," Craig said. "And I won't reveal my sources on getting your number. Now tell me . . . don't you like flowers?"

"I like them fine," she said carefully. "It's you I'm not so sure about."

He chuckled. The low resonances of his voice were tickling her ear, making it difficult for her to keep a clear head. She could visualize him, on the other end, and an image of his face and figure made her heart pound even more forcefully. "Suzannah," he said softly. "Don't you think it's time we let bygones be bygones?"

She thought a moment. "I'll say bye, and you be gone," she said, smiling in spite of herself. "How's that?"

"Not bad," he said, and she could hear the answering smile in his voice. "But seriously . . . why haven't you called? I've given you every conceivable number where I can be reached."

"What's the point?" she asked. "What's there to say?"

"You could say you forgive me," he suggested. "For being too quick to judge you, for having left the way I did."

"What about for making a complete ass of me?" she answered. "That might put me over my forgiveness quota."

Craig sighed. "I've already said I'm sorry in as many ways as I can think of," he said quietly. "I want to see you, Suzannah."

"I . . ." She stiffened her reserve. "I don't think that's a good idea."

"It's all I can think of," he said earnestly. "It's all I do think about. Why not give us a chance, Suzannah?"

"Look, aren't you a busy man?" she said. "Don't you have a mini-empire to preside over? I'm a working girl, myself, and I'm not about to drop everything to rendezvous with you."

"You don't get it, do you?" he said. "All right, then . . . I'll come up there and see you."

"Here?" Her heartbeat increased. "But . . . No, Craig, that's—"

"Try and stop me," he said breezily. "I may be busy, but I'll make the time, believe me."

"Well, I . . ." She paused, panicking. What would she do if he suddenly showed up in San Francisco? Fall into his arms without much protest, most probably, she mused ruefully. It didn't seem fair. She'd lost enough dignity as it was. "I'm surprised at you, Mr. Young," she said, as coolly as she was able. "Now that I know what an important man you are, how can you trust me? I might just try to take advantage of your name and your power. I'd stay where I was, if I were you."

"I'll take my chances," he said. "I'm in this for the long run, sweetheart. There's something very important I want to speak to you about, and I'd much rather do it in person."

"Oh?" she said nervously.

"Yes," he said. "What are you doing tomorrow night?"

"I'm busy," she said promptly.

"I had a feeling you'd say that," he answered dryly. "But, Suzannah, listen to me. I understand why it was hard for you to think about a future for us, when we were together—"

"Big of you," she muttered.

"But the obstacles you were so worried about really don't exist," he hurried on. "I *can* take care of you. I *am* a responsible kind of guy. You don't have to worry about going bankrupt, or getting ploughed under by somebody's idle dreams and schemes, if you're with me. I'm not like Charlie at all, really. You know that, now."

"That's right, you're a regular prince," she said sarcastically. "And I'm supposed to be so awed, I swoon right at your—"

"No, that's not what I mean," he began.

"—feet, and that makes everything okay, is that it? I should be ready to ride right off into the sunset with you because you're the answer to every woman's dreams, right?"

"Suzannah," he sighed. "I'm not saying that."

"You're thinking that, I'll bet," she said grimly. "How could I pass you up? When you're rich, and you're famous, and—"

"I love you," he said.

It effectively halted her tirade. "Oh, yeah?" she said, after a pause. It was all she could think of to come back with.

"Yeah," he said, and she heard that smile in his voice again. "I love you, you stubborn lady, and that's the only thing that matters. Surely you can't hold the rest of it against me."

"I'm thinking about it," she said moodily.

"What are you doing the night after tomorrow night, then?"

"I . . ." She improvised feverishly. "I'm having dinner with my folks." Her folks didn't even live in San Francisco. But it seemed like a good excuse.

"Really?" he said. "Well, I wouldn't mind meeting them."

"Oh, no," she said quickly. "They'd mind, I'm sure . . . meeting you."

"They would?" he asked, puzzled. "Why's that?"

"Well, they're . . . they're very . . . ah, very . . ." She cleared her throat.

"Very very?"

"Yes," she answered, nodding vehemently.

"Unsociable?" he suggested.

"That's right," she said. "And very, you know . . . particular. About who they have dinner with."

"I see," he said. "Well, perhaps we could meet for a drink, after your dinner with them."

Suzannah sighed. "You're making this difficult."

"No, Suzannah," he said gently. "You are. And I can tell you, family dinners or whatever you've got lined up, I'm coming up there within the next forty-eight hours."

Suzannah looked helplessly at the ceiling. Her resistance was wavering. But as she thought about it, a peculiar idea, borne of their peculiar conversation, began forming in her mind. Maybe there *was* a way to turn the tables on him, and play a little prank of her own . . . "All right," she said. "Friday night."

"Great!" he said. "But, isn't that your night with the folks?"

"We'll work something out," she said. "Why don't you give me your phone number in L.A.?"

As soon as she was off the phone with Craig, she sat down at the kitchen table deep in thought. It might take some doing, but it could be managed, with a little help. And she knew just where to turn for the help she needed. Smiling, Suzannah picked up the phone again, and dialed Los Angeles. With any luck, Lila would be in . . .

"Suzannah," said Lila. "Meet your father: Edward Carleton Raines."

He looked, Suzannah noted happily, absolutely perfect for the part. In his late fifties, with thinning silver hair, large, distinguished, with nose glasses and a stuffy, conservative banker's style of dress—black dress coat and gray striped trousers—the actor Lila had come up with appeared quintessentially old money.

"A pleasure to meet you," he said stiffly, in a gruff voice, and then he winked, an uncharacteristic smile softening the hard set of his jaw, as he took Suzannah's hand.

"Suzannah will tell you anything you need to know," Lila said. "As prep, of course. We've got some time before the victim arrives."

"Good show," her "father" said, then turned to Lila. "Oh, I'm sorry, Lil, I'm American tonight, aren't I?"

"That's right," she said. "And this," she went on, indicating the exceedingly well-dressed, middle-aged woman to her right, "is your mother, Victoria Raines."

"Charmed," the woman said, with a brittle smile.

Suzannah stared at her, a little awed. Her "mom" looked every bit a Vanderbilt dressed and coiffed in a way that unmistakably spelled snob. "Are those real?" she couldn't help asking, pointing to the plethora of pearls around the actress's neck.

"Paste," the older woman answered.

"I'm your brother," the dark-haired young man behind her interjected, putting out his hand.

"Hi," Suzannah said, unable to suppress a smile. He looked like the ultimate preppie, in expensive Ivy League apparel, right down to the Bass Weejun loafers and the Princeton tie.

"Now, the idea here, as I understand it," Lila said. "Is to show no mercy. C.J. Young has put this poor woman through the wringer because she supposedly thought he wasn't good enough for her. Now he apparently expects to sail in here and sweep her—and her properly awed family—off their feet, because he is, in fact, a millionaire, and no woman in her right mind would think of spurning him. So it's your job, tonight"—she turned to the group of servants also hired for the occasion, to include them in her speech—"to make Mr. Young feel that in spite of his impressive status"—she drew herself up, archly putting her nose in the air—"he's still not good enough at all!"

An hour and a half later, Suzannah paced nervously back and forth in the entrance hall of the house she'd connived to borrow, from some friends of Veronique's, for the evening. Located in the heart of the Nob Hill area, its architecture and furnishings denoted Victorian luxury and high status in the extreme. Its owners would be returning toward midnight, and they expected every chair in place and no antique artifact disturbed. Cleanup after dinner would take some time. So if Craig happened to be late . . .

The doorbell chimed. Suzannah scurried down the hall to the dining room doorway. "All set?" she whispered. Receiving an affirmative reply, she quickly walked back to the curtained entrance alcove.

When she opened the outer door, Suzannah realized that all of her elaborate schemes hadn't prepared her for seeing Craig again. The visceral shock that went through her as they came face to face took the wind out of her for a moment. Looking into his dark velvet eyes as he stood before her, his hair gleaming softly in the amber porch light, his handsome features tanned and rugged, each line of his face so oddly familiar, gave her heart a tug and moistened her lips, her heartbeat rising as he took her by the hand and drew her toward him.

"Wait—" she tried to say, but it was too late. His mouth claimed hers with a tender urgency that rendered resistance impossible. The pressure against her lips and the very tip of her tongue was slight, yet it shook her from head to toe. With slow, firm guidance, he brought her closer to him, sliding his hands over her shoulders, tracing the line of her spine with his fingertips, his hand finally slipping down to intimately cup the curve of her hips. Head swimming, she felt her insides funnel into a whirlpool of longing. Her tongue returned his urgent strokes with a hungry eagerness, as he molded every inch of her body to his own.

She savored the experience of tasting his moist and open mouth for a suspended, breathless moment of flaring arousal, before consciousness finally flickered to life behind her half-closed eyes. Wrong! blinked a red neon sign in her mind. Cancel! Pull Out!

The inner wrestling match was even more formidable than the outer movement of gently but firmly pushing him away, but she did it, coming up for air and backing up a step. "Please, Craig!" she whispered, in a voice that was husky with desire. "Not here . . . not now!"

His smile was positively devilish, as he ran his still moist tongue over his lips. "Where then?" he whispered back, his eyes flickering with undisguised desire over her body, lingering briefly as if in a phantom caress over the hollow of her neck and the rising curves of her breasts. "And when?"

Suzannah shook her head, motioning him inside. "Mother would have a heart attack," she murmured.

"Oh," Craig nodded, and followed her inside, looking about him with some curiosity. Suzannah couldn't help noticing that he cut quite a perfect figure in a suit of his own design, his slightly tousled dark hair adding a sexy contrast to the elegantly neat lines of the well-tailored jacket and pants. She also noticed, to her secret delight, that he seemed a trifle bewildered by the environment, his eyes flickering over the brass and old wood appointments of the ornate hall. "Say," he murmured. "I didn't realize your folks were so . . ." His words trailed off as he looked up to the entranceway behind her, where, Suzannah realized, turning, the formidable Mrs. Raines was descending the staircase.

"Oh, there you are, darling," the woman said, with a tone at once familiar and formal.

"Mother, this is Mr. Young," Suzannah said.

Mother moved forward, and with the slightest flare of her nostrils and a certain cast in her eye, subtly but surely indicated she was in some way displeased with the appearance of Suzannah's guest. "How nice to meet you," she said, nasal and a touch frosty, putting out her bejeweled and limp-wristed hand for him to take.

"Good to meet you," Craig said cordially. Suzannah could tell he was already off-balance.

"Mr. Raines will be down shortly," Mrs. Raines sniffed, her smile glitteringly artificial. "Would you care for a cocktail?" She gestured grandly toward the living room to their left.

As they followed the woman, whose bearing was intimidatingly regal, into the room, Craig slowed Suzannah with a touch on her arm. "Maybe I should have come in black tie," he whispered. "You didn't tell me things were so formal."

"Oh, don't worry," she whispered back. "Just be yourself."

"Right," he said, but his expression, she was happy to note, was far from confident.

"So, Mr. Young, where did you make our daughter's acquaintance?"

Craig looked up from his soup. The ornate dining room had been silent except for the subdued clink of soup spoons for a moment. The dark wood table was uncomfortably long and wide. Suzannah was opposite Craig, with her "brother" to her right, and a "parent" at either end. A butler stood quietly in a corner of the room, observing. Suzannah noticed that when the elderly man wasn't serving, he stood with his eyes fixed on Craig, suggesting that he felt the young man might pocket the silverware if he was left unobserved.

Craig cleared his throat, addressing Mr. Raines. The older man's conversation up to that point had been distant and superficial, concerned with San Francisco weather versus that back East. "Well, we . . . ran into each other at the beach," Craig said, shifting uncomfortably in his seat. He glanced at Suzannah as if for assistance. She merely gave him an encouraging smile.

"The beach?" Brother Chip exclaimed. "I was just down at Big Sur. A real bohemian scene. Those surfers were going for it in a major way. Do you surf?"

Craig stared at the younger man. "No," he said, clearly taken aback. "Do you?"

Chip's eyes widened. "Hardly," he muttered, and returned to his soup.

"You have a house there, then?" Mrs. Raines suggested pleasantly. "Some friends of ours own property in Laguna."

"No, I was visiting," Craig said. "I live in New York."

"Oh, that's right," huffed Mr. Raines. "Victoria and I used to have many friends there. The Whites . . . the Philip Whites . . . possibly you know them?"

"No," Craig said. "Don't believe I do."

"Then there's Arthur Fuller's family . . ."

"I'm afraid not," said Craig.

"And let me see . . . Senator Evans? You know of the Evanses?"

Craig shook his head.

"I went to Cornell with Bob Evans—the Senator's son," Chip chimed in. "Say, where did you go to school, Craig?"

"F.I.T.," Craig said. Chip looked at him in undisguised shock. Both parents exchanged a look, and Suzannah could have sworn the very temperature in the room had just dropped a few degrees.

"Rilly," said Chip. "That's . . . something."

"I understand you're in the, ah, fashion industry," Mrs. Raines said. She might have been speaking about working in the mines. Craig looked at Suzannah uncertainly, waited for the butler to clear his plate, then cleared his throat again.

"Yes, I'm a designer," he said. "Perhaps you've heard of the C.J. Young line?"

Both parents raised their heads slightly, as if trying to catch the timbre of some foreign dialect. "Line?" said Mr. Raines, playing with his mustache. "Oh, yes . . . I think so," he said vaguely.

"It's that, you know, casual stuff, Dad," Chip said. He turned to Craig. "He's a Brooks Brothers man," he explained. "Me—" he held his palms up. "I prefer L.L. Bean."

"Is it . . . blue jeans?" Mrs. Raines queried. "Like Gloria Vanderbilt's done?"

Craig stroked his cheek. "Well, not quite," he began.

"Craig's clothes are special," Suzannah said. "I wouldn't compare them to another designer's, really. What he's got on, for example . . ."

Mr. Raines leaned forward slightly, fixing Craig's suit with a myopic stare. "I suppose you do well with that sort of thing," he allowed.

Suzannah noticed a little vein in the side of Craig's temple throbbing slightly. "I do all right," he said, and glanced at Suzannah. She gave him another reassuring smile.

"Well, now, F . . . I . . . T . . ." Mr. Raines obviously found this distinctly nonivied school a most peculiar choice. "How did you, ah, enjoy it, there?"

"Well, it was great, really," Craig began uncertainly. "I got in on a scholarship—"

"You don't happen to know the Robinsons?" Mr. Raines broke in, as if desperately trying to place Craig in some strata he could relate to.

"No, sorry," Craig said, and sighed.

"Pity," Mrs. Raines said. "Although, really, I don't see how you would have run into them, in your business . . . You remember Mr. Robinson, don't you, dear?" she said to Suzannah. "He runs the Chase Bank back East?"

"Oh, yes," Suzannah said, and she shot Craig a look, as if to say: "Pay no attention to this stuff."

"So, you . . . design," Mr. Raines said, biting down on the word with his teeth, as if testing a quarter for resilience. "All kinds of clothing? I don't suppose you . . . That is, it's, ah, menswear you're involved in?"

Mrs. Raines tittered. "Really, Edward, you don't think

there's anything objectionable about designing dresses!"

Craig opened his mouth, and then shut it, and looking nervously behind him, met the suspicious gaze of the butler, who promptly looked away.

"Well, well," Mr. Raines said, with false heartiness. "To each his own, I always say. I'm a banker, and I was raised to be one—never thought of anything else. My father was a banker, and his father before that . . ." He gave Suzannah a fatherly smile. "You of the younger generation have a great deal more freedom in deciding what you wish to do with your lives." He looked back at Craig and his smile faded. "Though I must say, choosing to spend one's time with a thimble and sewing needle . . ."

"I don't actually do the sewing," Craig said, his voice tight. "I design the clothes."

"How . . . creative," Mrs. Raines offered.

Craig cleared his throat. "I had no idea Suzannah came from a family of"—he paused, then chose the word more carefully than Suzannah suspected he would have under less forcedly polite circumstances—"bankers."

"Oh, she's always been so independent," Mrs. Raines said. "You'd think she was ashamed of us." She laughed at the preposterous idea, and Craig shot Suzannah a look. She mimed an "I can't help it, they're my folks" expression at him.

"What did *your* father do?" Chip asked, leaning forward.

"He was a grocer," Craig said abruptly. "He had a small store in Little Italy, and he did very well with it. My mother worked there, too, and I even did, when I was a kid. Worked hard," he added darkly. There was a moment of silence.

"How . . . colorful," said Mrs. Raines.

"I love Italian food," said Chip, enthusiastically.

Suzannah coughed, and gripped her napkin tightly, holding it in front of her face, as Craig's color changed perceptibly. She decided she'd better come to his aid. "You should really see some of Craig's work," she told her father. "He's one of the best there is. If you pick up any copy of *Vogue* or *Harper's*, you'll see his designs."

Chip snorted derisively. "I'd like to see that," he said, and grinned at Craig. "It's *Forbes* and the *Wall Street Journal*, all the way."

"Grew up in the city, did you?" Mr. Raines said, eyeing Craig now as if it were Borneo or Calcutta he was speaking of.

"Yes, on the East Side," Craig said.

"Sutton Place is charming," Mrs. Raines said. "Don't you think?"

Craig squirmed in his seat. "Actually, I grew up a bit farther downtown," he said. "But, yes, it's nice by the river, up past the bridge."

"Bridge," Mr. Raines murmured. "That's the fellow I knew from New York University . . . Arnold Talbot, a championship bridge player. I don't suppose . . ."

"I'm a poker man, myself," Craig said apologetically, and silence reigned around the table once again.

The cool night air was a balmy refreshment after the stilted, stuffy atmosphere of the town house. Suzannah walked down the steps with Craig, who was loosening his collar, slowly shaking his head, and taking great gulps of air. "I don't know, I don't know," he muttered.

"What don't you know?" she asked him innocently, falling into step beside him on the sidewalk.

"You don't mind walking a bit? Because I really do have to talk to you," he said.

"It's fine," Suzannah said. "I know you were dying to get out of there. I don't blame you. Mother and Father were being awfully severe . . ."

"Severe?" He turned to stare at her. "Who do they usually have over for dinner? John Paul Getty? Good Lord!"

"I'm sorry," she said. "But I tried to warn you—"

"Suzannah," he said, and he took hold of her shoulders. "I don't know how you've done it, but I'm truly impressed."

"What do you mean?" she asked apprehensively.

"I don't know how you've managed to emerge from a family like that with your head on straight," he said wonderingly. "But you have, and I'm amazed. I never would have guessed it."

"Well, like I told you, I left the brood pretty early on," Suzannah said. "I've never taken anything from them, and I still don't intend to. I've never really adopted my father's values—"

"Thank goodness," Craig scowled. "Now, I know this might offend you, but I have to tell you the truth, Suzannah. Your father is exactly the kind of person I've grown up hating my entire life!"

"I won't defend him." Suzannah sighed.

"Every step of the way, when I was working my way up, I had to deal with that kind of snobbery, from all those blue blood haute couture mavens, and it nearly drove me nuts!" he fumed, jamming his hands into his jacket pockets. "I'm sorry, I just have to speak my mind."

"I understand," she said. "I was watching you in there, and I know it was difficult for you. You showed remarkable restraint." She'd actually begun to feel sorry for him, in the home stretch of dinner. The group of actors had been very effective. They managed to insinuate that every conceivable aspect of Craig's background and upbringing was beneath contempt. She'd seen Craig struggling to control himself through all the snide remarks, and had been moved, in spite of herself, to realize he was remaining civil and polite himself, for her sake.

"If that man weren't your father!" Craig said, and then shook his head. "Sorry. It's just a shame, though."

"Why's that?" she asked.

"Well, in terms of you and me," he said slowly.

Here it comes, Suzannah thought, pulse quickening. She'd wondered how deeply the dinner would affect Craig's attitude toward her . . .

"What about you and me?" she prompted, as he paused, gazing thoughtfully at her face.

"Well, it's going to make things difficult," he mused.

"Oh," she said quietly.

"They're not going to be happy," he said moodily.

"They're not?" she asked, confused.

"About our marriage," he said. "They'll be upset, to say the least."

"They'll . . . our . . . what?" she choked, staring at him.

"I want you to marry me," he said simply. "That's what I came up here to talk to you about. And I hadn't counted on your folks being so . . ."

"Wait a second," she said, her heart thumping furiously. "You want me to marry you?"

"That's what I said," he nodded, a faint smile on his lips. "Do you want me to get down on one knee? I will, if you want me to."

"That's okay," she said dumbly, unable to stop staring into his eyes.

"So what do you think?"

"Think?" She could barely think. She could only look and look at his beautiful face, and feel very light inside, as if she were starting to float an inch above the ground.

"Want to?" he asked softly, and he reached out to cup her chin in his hand. "I think I could make you happy."

Suzannah swallowed. "Maybe you could," she murmured. "Are you serious?"

"Suzannah," he said, and with his other hand, he tenderly moved a curl of hair from her eye, as the wind rose. "I don't care if you come from a family of snobs. I don't care what your name is, or what you do, or . . . anything. I just care about you, period. I love you. That's all I've been trying to tell you . . . and I know that you love me, no matter how you deny it. I've known it since that night we were together, on the lawn . . ."

Suzannah felt a shiver pass from his touch right down to the tips of her toes. "It's true," she whispered.

"I was trying to explain, when we were at the café," he went on. "How much it meant to me that you loved me as a stranger, not knowing a thing about me. Well, how could I love you any less, whether you were born on Nob Hill or in . . . a slum? What difference does any of it make?"

"None," she murmured, feeling tears begin to moisten her eyes.

"Then marry me," he said softly. "We'll make up our own way of living, whatever way we like it . . . we can live in a castle or a hut . . . or both," he grinned. "Whatever's comfortable. As long as we have each other, that's all that counts . . . What do you say?"

"I . . . I don't know what to say," she told him. An extraordinary mixture of emotions were welling up inside of her. "Are you sure it's such a good idea?"

"I'm sure," he said, his eyes smoldering with warm desire, as he reached out to take her hand.

Suzannah cleared her throat. Did he still think she was

a pushover? She wasn't about to make it quite as easy for him as he seemed to expect. "But I live here," she said, trying not to let the ticklish, provocatively delicious feeling of his hand enclosing hers sway her. "I suppose you expect me to uproot—just like that?"

"We'll work it out," he said. "I'm very flexible. I've been thinking of getting a place out here anyway."

"And what about my work?" she persisted. "Aren't you afraid I'll try to use you . . . to further my career?"

"Use me," he said urgently, holding her hand tighter, his voice a husky growl of sensual invitation. "Use me all you want."

"You're sure you're just not trying to steal *my* design ideas?" she suggested coyly, narrowing her eyes.

"I wouldn't dream of it," he murmured. "But we could collaborate . . ."

He lifted her hand to his lips. The soft, exquisitely tremble-provoking feel of his moist skin against hers indicated just what sort of collaboration he really had in mind. She was running out of ideas to hold the man at bay. "But I hardly know you," she murmured, shivering as he kissed the soft skin of her wrist. "Maybe our being together . . . was a fluke. Maybe we'll disappoint each other."

"Impossible," he breathed, bringing his tongue and teeth into play, nibbling the base of her thumb, his eyes still holding hers.

She believed him. "Maybe . . ." His tongue flicked at the softness of her palm. She closed her eyes involuntarily, and sighed. "Oh, Craig . . . maybe it *is* a good idea . . ."

"Say yes," he murmured.

Suzannah opened her eyes again. How could she say no to this completely beautiful man? Suzannah Young, she found herself mentally experimenting. Suzannah Raines Young? Hey, but wait—"I don't even know your real name," she protested. "Is it really Craig?"

"Carlo, originally," he said. "My father's name. And our last name was Juliano. But he christened me Young instead of junior, because he wanted me firmly Americanized." He smiled. "My friends call me C.J. or—yes—Craig."

"I like . . . Carlo," she said, savoring the sound.

"Then say, 'Yes, Carlo,'" he suggested. "Please," he whispered, and the husky urgency in his voice made her tremble with arousal.

"Yes . . ." she began, and then his lips covered hers. She reveled in the delicious warmth of his soft skin, losing herself in the shelter of his enveloping embrace. His lips moved on hers slowly, tenderly, slipping away only to whisper words of love into her ear.

"Oh, Suzannah," he murmured, as she clung to him. "Now we don't have to play any more games. We can just be together, the way I've wanted us to be . . ."

His words suddenly reminded her of the evening's charade, and a game that needed to be ended. "Oh, Craig," she said softly. "There is one thing that you should know, before . . . we go any further."

"Yes, love?" he whispered.

"You won't have any trouble with my parents, when they hear about this. I'm sure they'll be pleased."

"Pleased?" he said, incredulously. "After the way they raked me over the coals?"

"Oh, them," Suzannah smiled. "Those are only friends of Lila's . . . actors. My parents live in Chicago."

"What?" He lifted his head, eyes narrowing. "What do you mean?"

"I hired them." She sighed. "It was a trick, a prank—the whole dinner. I just wanted to even the score, after what you did to me."

"You mean . . ." He stared at her. "They're not your parents? You hired actors, just to . . ." he choked. "That's a pretty elaborate trick! How the hell did you—"

"You paid for it," she told him, unable to suppress a smile.

"I did?" His voice was rising in bewilderment and outrage.

"That check you ripped up—well, I had Mrs. Tyler make out another one, to me, just as you suggested. It covered the expenses of flying the bunch of them up from Hollywood, and paying them for a night's work. Believe me, it was worth it."

"It was, was it?" he growled.

"To see you get a taste of your own medicine, Mister

. . . Carlo Juliano Young," she added, her smile broadening as she watched the flush deepen in his cheeks.

"I see," he muttered, between clenched teeth. "Of all the dishonest . . . watching them put the screws to me like that . . ."

"You're right," she nodded. "It was a terrible thing to do. I started to feel bad, and I wanted to tell you. But I was waiting for the right moment, you know?"

"I see," he said, with a little groan.

"And when I found out, just now, that you could love me anyway, even knowing the sort of woman I was—"

"I know," he nodded ruefully. "You were terribly moved."

"I was," she said. "But really."

"Suzannah," he said evenly. "Have you ever been spanked?"

"That sounds interesting," she teased, stepping away from him. "But, Craig, don't tell me there's a hidden, kinky side to you . . ."

"Apparently," he said, trying to get hold of her. "There's more to both of us than meets the eye . . ."

"Well, I guess that's what honeymoons are for," Suzannah suggested. "Where are we going, anyway?"

Laughing, she tried to get away from him, but Craig caught hold of her, pulling her close beneath a street lamp on the corner. "To the moon," he murmured, smiling. "That's where I should send you."

And then she was scooped up in his strong arms, and his dark eyes sparkled before her face and he bent to claim her mouth, filling her up, taking her with a kiss that was half a warning, half a promise, and all ravishing passion. Fingers gliding through her hair, he teased, taunted, and tasted her in long, melting strokes that gave tantalizing glimmers of the pleasures to come.

"Umm," she sighed. "I'm already seeing stars . . ."

A Memo From C.J. Young

Walt:

You know, you were right. I should *leave the office more often. The building didn't fall down without me, and I became the luckiest man alive! So I'm sure you'll be happy to find me gone again. And you'll be even happier to find your raise has gone into effect.*

I don't know how long we're honeymooning. For all I know it won't ever end. But to come out of the clouds for a brief moment, let me estimate a return in about three weeks. I'll call, or wire, or send a carrier flamingo with a message in a pineapple. Excuse me, Walt, it's a little hard to be serious when you've hit nirvana. Just carry on as you did before!

Oh, and don't worry about those guys tearing the wall down in the suite upstairs. I'm expanding that office to make room for a new designer we're hiring as soon as I get back. You're going to love her, Walt. I know I do. Get the name right for the plate on the door—Suzannah Raines Young—and put some flowers in there when the dust settles, will you? Put flowers everywhere, while you're at it! The office is going to be a lot more colorful from now on . . .

Best,
C.J.

COMING NEXT MONTH IN THE SECOND CHANCE AT LOVE SERIES

EYE OF THE BEHOLDER #262 by Kay Robbins
First he proposes, *then* he courts her...with picnics and poetry, mischief and magic. Artist Tory Michaels is totally undone by whimsical wife-hunter Devon York!

GENTLEMAN AT HEART #263 by Elissa Curry
For Alexis Celestine, convincing notorious ex-pitcher Jake Shepard to make a beer commercial proves almost as tough as fielding his incredibly sexy plays for her.

BY LOVE POSSESSED #264 by Linda Barlow
Like a man possessed, darkly powerful Francis O'Brien stalks flamboyant Diana Adams across the Mexican countryside, torn between his duty to protect her...and his long-smoldering desire for revenge!

WILDFIRE #265 by Kelly Adams
Pressed intimately against the earth, with flames leaping up all around, ranger Molly Carter struggles to tame her wildfire passion for the sensitive yet dangerously daring woodsman Sean Feyer.

PASSION'S DANCE #266 by Lauren Fox
Though she, too, is a veteran of a physically punishing career, dancer Amelia Jorgenson swears she has nothing in common with a "jock" like Randy Williams... except, perhaps, desire...

VENETIAN SUNRISE #267 by Kate Nevins
Antiques dealer Rita Stewart steps into Venice and enters a dream filled with vibrantly handsome, endearingly roguish Frank Giordano. But is his glittering sensuality blinding her to his darker side?

QUESTIONNAIRE

1. How do you rate ______________________________
(please print TITLE)
- ☐ excellent ☐ good
- ☐ very good ☐ fair ☐ poor

2. How likely are you to purchase another book in this series?
- ☐ definitely would purchase
- ☐ probably would purchase
- ☐ probably would not purchase
- ☐ definitely would not purchase

3. How likely are you to purchase another book by this author?
- ☐ definitely would purchase
- ☐ probably would purchase
- ☐ probably would not purchase
- ☐ definitely would not purchase

4. How does this book compare to books in other contemporary romance lines?
- ☐ much better
- ☐ better
- ☐ about the same
- ☐ not as good
- ☐ definitely not as good

5. Why did you buy this book? (Check as many as apply)
- ☐ I have read other SECOND CHANCE AT LOVE romances
- ☐ friend's recommendation
- ☐ bookseller's recommendation
- ☐ art on the front cover
- ☐ description of the plot on the back cover
- ☐ book review I read
- ☐ other ______________________________

____

____

(Continued...)

6. Please list your three favorite contemporary romance lines.

____

____

7. Please list your favorite authors of contemporary romance lines.

____

____

____

____

____

____

8. How many SECOND CHANCE AT LOVE romances have you read? _______________

9. How many series romances like SECOND CHANCE AT LOVE do you read each month? _______________

10. How many series romances like SECOND CHANCE AT LOVE do you buy each month? _______________

11. Mind telling your age?

☐ under 18
☐ 18 to 30
☐ 31 to 45
☐ over 45

☐ Please check if you'd like to receive our free SECOND CHANCE AT LOVE Newsletter.

We hope you'll share your other ideas about romances with us on an additional sheet and attach it securely to this questionnaire.

• •

Fill in your name and address below:

Name _______________

Street Address _______________

City _______________ State _______________ Zip _______________

Please return this questionnaire to:

SECOND CHANCE AT LOVE
The Berkley Publishing Group
200 Madison Avenue, New York, New York 10016